SPECIAL MESSAGE TO READERS

THE ULVERSCROFT FOUNDATION
(registered UK charity number 264873)
was established in 1972 to provide funds for
research, diagnosis and treatment of eye diseases.
Examples of major projects funded by
the Ulverscroft Foundation are:-

- The Children's Eye Unit at Moorfields Eye Hospital, London
- The Ulverscroft Children's Eye Unit at Great Ormond Street Hospital for Sick Children
- Funding research into eye diseases and treatment at the Department of Ophthalmology, University of Leicester
- The Ulverscroft Vision Research Group, Institute of Child Health
- Twin operating theatres at the Western Ophthalmic Hospital, London
- The Chair of Ophthalmology at the Royal Australian College of Ophthalmologists

You can help further the work of the Foundation
by making a donation or leaving a legacy.
Every contribution is gratefully received. If you
would like to help support the Foundation or
require further information, please contact:

THE ULVERSCROFT FOUNDATION
The Green, Bradgate Road, Anstey
Leicester LE7 7FU, England
Tel: (0116) 236 4︎︎︎

website: www.u...oft.com

Wendy Soliman was brought up on the Isle of Wight in southern England but now divides her time between Andorra and western Florida. She lives with her husband Andre and a rescued dog of indeterminate pedigree named Jake Bentley after the hunky hero in one of her books. When not writing she enjoys reading other people's books, walking miles with her dog whilst plotting her next scene, dining out and generally making the most out of life.

WITH THE DUKE'S APPROVAL

Four years since Napoleon was finally vanquished at Waterloo, Europe remains in political upheaval. Lord Clarence Vaughan, Earl of Romsey, is at the heart of the diplomatic negotiations to ensure peace prevails. When Lady Annalise Sheridan, sister to the Duke of Winchester, is abducted from a society ball whilst in Clarence's care, he suspects forces opposed to the government's peace plan are responsible. For the first time in his life, Clarence is prepared to put his personal feelings ahead of his duty, in order to protect the lady who has captured his heart. But will he succeed?

WENDY SOLIMAN

WITH THE DUKE'S APPROVAL

Complete and Unabridged

ULVERSCROFT
Leicester

First published in Great Britain in 2014

First Large Print Edition
published 2016

A catalogue record for this book is available
from the British Library.

ISBN 978–1–4448–2725–5

Published by
F. A. Thorpe (Publishing)
Anstey, Leicestershire

Set by Words & Graphics Ltd.
Anstey, Leicestershire
Printed and bound in Great Britain by
T. J. International Ltd., Padstow, Cornwall

This book is printed on acid-free paper

1

London 1819

'Do people take pleasure from this frivolity?' Portia looked dubiously around the over-crowded yet sumptuously appointed ballroom and wrinkled her nose.

Annalise smothered a smile. Anyone who mattered was in attendance at the Duchess of Bexley's ball, one of *the* major social occasions of the season. Those who did not matter went to extraordinary lengths to inveigle invitations. Only Portia could describe the event as frivolous.

'Certainly they enjoy it,' she replied. 'It's important to be seen in the right places.'

Portia remained unimpressed. 'How ridiculous.'

'People go to considerable trouble to cultivate the expressions of boredom you have mistaken for . . . well, boredom.'

Portia rolled her eyes. 'I hesitate to ask why.'

Annalise released the smile she had valiantly been holding in check. 'Those of us in danger of being left on the shelf pretend not to mind for fear of appearing desperate, hence our contrived indolence. It is extremely hard work.'

'You? Desperate?' Portia scoffed. 'You are always mobbed by gentlemen keen to win your approval, or whatever it is gentlemen wish to win. And now I come to think of it . . . ' Portia glanced around. 'Where are they all?'

Annalise slipped further behind the concealing pillar she and Portia were standing beside. 'You, on the other hand,' she said, ignoring her sister's question, 'ought to pretend enthusiasm. It is your first season. You are supposed to swoon from an excess of pleasure.'

Portia made an unladylike scoffing sound at the back of her throat. 'Have you ever known me to swoon?'

'Perhaps not, but there is nothing preventing you from pretending. Goodness knows, most people in this room are putting on an act of some sort. It wouldn't do for the Duke of Winchester's younger sister to gain a reputation for being aloof.'

'I'm not in the least aloof. I just don't see the point of balls. Besides, I hate crowds.' Portia hid her face behind her fan and sneezed. 'I never know what to say to people, and even if I could think of something amusing, it's so noisy my witticisms would go unappreciated.' A wry smile graced her features. 'A bit like me, I suppose.'

Anna patted her sister's hand. 'Don't falter now. The worst is behind you. You got the ordeal of presentation out of the way and are officially launched.'

Portia harrumphed. 'You make me sound like a ship.'

'Well, don't sail off into the sunset quite yet. You promised Mr. Duffield the next dance.'

'Oh Lord, I'd quite forgotten he asked me.'

'Portia, pay attention!' Anna bit her lip, endlessly amused by her sister's genuine disregard for society's rules. 'He is one of *the* catches of the season.'

'Then why is he bothering with me?'

Anna wanted to shake Portia. She was such a goose, always analysing every situation, suspicious of every kind word or gesture. 'Why should he not? You look very pretty, and I should be quite out of charity with him if he did not notice you.'

'Hmm.' Portia didn't sound convinced. 'What of you? Don't tell me you are without a partner. Goodness, I think I might swoon after all.'

'I'm saving myself,' Anna replied loftily. 'I have had quite enough of having my toes trampled upon for one night. I intend to

3

waltz with Lord Romsey. I'm perfectly sure my toes won't suffer from *that* experience.'

'Ah, now I understand why you keep peeping around that pillar.' Portia grinned. 'You're lying in wait for Lord Romsey.'

'You understand nothing. Lord Romsey is our brother's friend and a close neighbour. It would be unpardonably rude if he didn't dance with us both.'

'He hasn't asked me, which rather proves my point.'

'He hasn't asked me either, but I'm sure he intends to. All of our brothers are still angry with him, so he would be sensible to recover his position by behaving agreeably towards us.'

Amos, Annalise and Portia's second brother, the duke's named heir, was the first of the six siblings to marry. That auspicious event had taken place the previous autumn at Winchester Cathedral, followed by a magnificent reception at the ducal seat of Winchester Park. Amos had delighted the family by introducing Miss Cristobel Brooke to its ranks. She and Amos had met under peculiar circumstances involving a plot against the government. It was Lord Romsey's task to unravel that plot, but in so doing he inadvertently left Crista exposed to danger, earning ducal disapproval.

Annalise came out a year ahead of Portia and had been inundated with attention. The duke, her brother Zachary, had entertained several advantageous offers for her hand, all of which she declined. None of her suitors had stirred her passions. Having seen the deep and abiding love that had bound her parents' marriage, she was determined only to marry when she found a gentleman who moved her heart in a similar fashion.

The moment she laid eyes on the glamorous earl at Winchester Park the previous summer, she knew she had found such a man: Portia had got that part exactly right. But, annoyingly, Romsey hadn't shown her any particular attention. He always appeared to be occupied by some crisis or other pertaining to his position as a member of His Majesty's Diplomatic Service. That was all well and good, but Anna wasn't prepared to sit back like some shrinking violet and wait for him to notice her. Some other lady might catch his attention in the meantime, which couldn't be permitted to happen. It was time to take matters into her own hands.

'Oh look. There's Frankie.'

Portia waved, Lady St. John acknowledged the gesture and joined the girls.

'What a crush,' she said by way of greeting.

'I was just saying as much to Anna,' Portia replied.

'You look as fresh as a daisy, so it cannot be so very crowded,' Anna told their neighbour. 'That gown is a sensation.'

'Oh, this old thing.' Frankie laughed. 'Don't look like that, Anna. It really is old. I had it made when I was still in France, two years ago now.'

'It's positively ancient then,' Portia agreed, grinning.

'Besides, both of you look adorable. And, as to remaining cool, be advised by me and take advantage of the terrace and all that lovely fresh air.'

'But it's freezing out there!' Portia cried. 'There's frost on the ground, and it wouldn't surprise me if it snowed.'

'I have a very thick shawl,' Frankie told them in a theatrical whisper. 'Hidden behind the red leather chair in the library. Feel free to make use of it. You can't miss it. It's rather extravagantly coloured.' She shrugged. 'I do so like to make a statement. Anyway, it's exceedingly warm, which is all that really matters.'

'How clever to think of that,' Anna replied. 'How . . . ah, but of course, you are residing here with the duchess, which allows you the freedom to scatter your possessions about the place.'

'I don't plan to stay in town for long so it seems pointless renting a house, especially since my friend was happy to accommodate me.'

The crowd appeared to swell, and the noise and heat levels increased.

'My sister finds this pointless,' Anna said.

Frankie smiled. 'Jaded already, Portia?'

Portia bit her lip. 'There must be something wrong with me.'

'Actually,' Frankie said, 'I agree with you, but one is expected to be seen.'

'So Anna tells me.' Portia blinked, looking rather startled. 'Mrs. Anderson is holding you in a death glare from across the room, Anna.'

'Oh no, not again.'

'What have you done to displease her?' Frankie asked.

'Miss Anderson has a handsome dowry and has set her heart on Lord Roker.' A giggle slipped past Anna's guard. 'Unfortunately that gentleman seems besotted with me. I don't give him the least encouragement but Mrs. Anderson still holds me responsible for his defection.'

'Oh dear.' Frankie looked amused.

'Who is that, making such a grand entrance?' Anna asked.

The three ladies looked towards the archway leading into the ballroom. 'Ah, that's

Count von Hessel,' Frankie said.

'He's very good-looking,' Anna said, 'and well he knows it.'

'Oh, he does,' Frankie replied, wrinkling her nose.

'Do you know him?' Portia asked.

'We met a few times after the war.'

'Von Hessel is Prussian?' Anna asked. 'I recall he distinguished himself at Waterloo.'

'Once the Prussians decided whose side they were on,' Frankie said. 'That's Miriam Outwood on his arm, looking fit to burst with pride.'

'Ah, we came out together,' Anna said. 'I heard the count had offered for her.'

'They made their announcement at Lady Trumper's ball last week.'

'Presumably Miss Outwood has a sizeable dowry,' Portia mused. 'Without wishing to be unkind, what else would attract such a vain man to such a plain young lady?'

'We ought to be shocked by such pragmatic observations falling from the lips of one so young,' Frankie said with an engaging smile. 'But we can hardly scold you for telling the truth. Still, if Miss Outwood is content with the situation, who are we to judge?'

The ladies watched the count as he looked around, nodding haughtily to acquaintances. When he appeared satisfied enough attention was focused on him, he swaggered into the ballroom and finally remembered to pay his respects to his hostess.

'I don't envy Miss Outwood,' Anna said. 'I think she will live to regret her decision.'

'Very likely,' Frankie replied.

The count walked in their direction, noticed Frankie, scowled, and then inclined his head with the minimum of civility. Frankie didn't acknowledge him at all, but Anna saw anger flit through her eyes and wondered why the two disliked one another quite so intensely.

'I wonder what has become of Mama,' Anna said.

'I saw her just now in deep conversation with Lady Markham,' Frankie replied.

'Oh dear, poor Vince.' Anna clapped a hand over her mouth. 'Now Mama finally has the satisfaction of seeing one of her sons married, she is quite determined the other three will follow his example. Vince made the mistake of dancing twice with Miss Markham last week and now . . . well, I think Mama and Lady Markham must be making wedding plans.'

'What of the duke?' Frankie asked, suspiciously casually. 'Who does the duchess have in mind for him?'

'I don't think even Mama would dare to

make any suggestions to Zach,' Anne said, sharing a glance with Portia. 'Zach will only do what Zach wishes to do.'

'How very sensible.'

Frankie sounded as though she was speaking from bitter experience. And yet, when she spoke of her late husband, also a member of the diplomatic service and, like Lord Romsey, prominently involved in the peace negotiations following Napoleon's defeat, she never said anything to his detriment. Frankie was a beautiful, complex and mysterious woman, far cleverer than she allowed people to know and, in Anna's biased opinion, absolutely perfect for Zach.

'Ah, the quadrille,' Anna said. 'And here comes Mr. Duffield to claim you, Portia.'

Portia grinned. 'And Lord Roker is hard on his heels.'

'Oh Lord, walk with me, Frankie.' Anna linked her arm through Frankie's, pausing only to see her sister safely delivered to Mr. Duffield's care before turning away from the rapidly approaching Lord Roker. 'He simply will not leave me alone.'

Frankie raised a brow in evident amusement. 'He is a nice-looking young man, from a good family. You could do worse.'

'Frankie!' Anna stopped walking and fixed her friend with an accusatory glower. 'Fie, shame on you! You claim it's commendable for Zach to please himself, yet I may not do the same thing?'

Frankie seemed perfectly unperturbed by Anna's rebuke. 'I was simply pointing out that Lord Roker is one of the catches of the season. Half the girls in this room sigh if he so much as passes their position, and yet he neglects them all in favour of you. I wasn't suggesting you should encourage him. Merely feel the compliment so you can relate the details to your grandchildren years from now.'

Anna grinned, her fit of pique forgotten. 'Very well then, I shall consider myself duly complimented, but if we could turn in this direction,' she said, swerving to the left, 'we shall avoid encountering Lord Roker.'

'I am entirely at your disposal.'

'When do you return to Winchester?'

'I shall stay in town for another few weeks, then return to the country . . . Ah, here are the duke and Clarence.'

Anna looked up and saw Zach and Lord Romsey approaching them. Zach was deep in conversation with Lord Romsey, the man Anna firmly intended to waltz with. Her heart did a strange little flip as she observed thick, dark blond hair falling in sleek waves across deep blue eyes that gleamed with unsettling intelligence. His graceful movements caused more than one female eye to be drawn towards him, Anna noticed, feeling an irrational stab of jealousy. It was tempered when it occurred to her those female eyes could just as easily have been drawn to Zach. He looked every part the suave, eligible duke, all the more desirable because of the air of detached politeness he had cultivated, discouraging all but the most determined from approaching him. Their attention probably *was* for her brother, Anna decided, since he was a man of greater consequence in terms of both status and wealth.

Lord Romsey was something of an enigma — a very fascinating enigma. He had spent all his adult years as a diplomat. Frankie and her husband had frequently encountered Lord Romsey in France and Belgium during and after the wars, which is why they were on such intimate terms. He had only returned to England fairly recently, following the death of his father, to assume the earldom and take control of his estate close to Southampton. But he was still kept fully occupied with his duties as a diplomat. She wondered if he ever put his own interests first and took the time to enjoy himself. He was here, at a ball, but she doubted if his intention was to dance. Everyone knew all manner of important matters of state were settled at social occasions.

'It must be very lonely for Lord Romsey,' she said speculatively, watching as the gentlemen's approach was delayed for the third time by yet another determined matron. 'Zach tells me he has no siblings, and now both of his parents are dead. He must rattle around in Romsey House and wonder what to do with himself.'

Frankie laughed. 'Clarence always knows precisely what to do with himself.'

'I am sure he never wants for occupation, but that is not what I meant to imply. As one of six children, and part of such a close and loving family, I can't imagine ever being truly alone.'

'You are very fortunate, Anna. Most large families of my acquaintance fight all the time and cannot abide the sight of one another, but — ' Frankie's face came alight with comprehension. 'Ah, I see. Your interest is not speculative.'

'I was merely making an observation. Besides, judging by the way people are reacting to Lord Romsey in this ballroom, he need not be alone if he would prefer not to be.'

'Clarence probably hates London society as much as your sister claims to. He's just better at hiding his boredom.'

'Well, he is a diplomat, so he ought to be.

But as to Portia, I think she may not dislike society as much as she pretends.'

Both ladies smiled as they watched Portia laugh at something Mr. Duffield said to her.

'Portia is very attractive . . . when not being compared to you.'

'Frankie!'

'Don't sound so shocked, my dear. You know it's true. Besides, as a widow no longer bound by the dictates of diplomacy, I have earned the right to speak as I find.'

'You,' Anna replied, fighting a grin as she squeezed Frankie's arm, 'are quite beyond redemption. I think that's why I enjoy your society so much.'

They laughed, but before Frankie could voice another of her irreverent comments, Zach and Lord Romsey were before them. Pleasantries were exchanged.

'Mama is colluding with Lady Markham,' Anna told Zach with a mischievous grin. 'Poor Vince! You really ought to do something.'

'Vince is perfectly capable of looking out for himself,' Zach replied with a negligent and very elegant flip of one wrist. 'He would not thank me for interfering.'

'Frankie was just now telling me she plans to return to Winchester soon for the hunting,' Anna said. 'Do you hunt, Lord Romsey?'

'Unfortunately, I seldom get the time or opportunity.'

'Surely your duties cannot be so very arduous that you cannot enjoy a day's sport?'

'I was unaware you planned to return to the country so soon, Lady St. John,' Zach said at the same time.

'There is no earthly reason why you should have been privy to that information, Your Grace.'

Anna bit her lip to prevent a smile from escaping. The interest Zach had just taken in Frankie's affairs was, by his standards, extreme. It could definitely be construed as encouragement, and yet Frankie treated it almost dismissively. She was either being very clever, or she really did have no amatory interest in Zach.

'Ah, Lady Annalise, there you are.'

Damnation, Lord Roker had found her. Anna pretended not to hear him, especially since the musicians had just struck up a waltz. Anna slid a desperate sideways glance at Lord Roker, and a supplicating one at Lord Romsey.

'May I have the pleasure of this dance, Lady Annalise?' Lord Romsey asked, living up to his diplomatic reputation by immediately understanding her difficulty.

'By all means.'

She placed her hand on his proffered sleeve, and he led her past the glowering Lord Roker. Anna was pleased to notice Zach leading Frankie into the dance as well. Smiling to herself, she wondered what her mother would make of that.

2

'Thank you,' Lady Annalise said, as Clarence took her in his arms and they fell into step.

Clarence arched a brow. 'Did I do something?'

His lovely partner smiled up at him, all sparkling eyes, dimples, and suppressed mischief. 'I can understand why you excel at your profession.'

Clarence returned her smile. 'I had every intention of asking you to dance, even before I saw Roker hovering. The only surprise was that you were not already engaged. Well, that and your disinclination to dance with Roker.'

'That's two things.'

Clarence's lips twitched. 'So it is. I can see I shall have to watch myself in your company, Lady Annalise.'

'Because I can count?'

'Because you find the attentions of one of the season's favourites not to your liking.'

'Lord Roker is charming, and . . . er — '

'Rich, titled and handsome?'

'Actually, I was going to say, rather stupid.'

Clarence chuckled. 'Surely, his other attributes make amends.'

'Not for me.'

'Because you do not need his money, don't care about his title, and . . . ' Clarence took pleasure from the sight of lovely eyes, housed in a lovelier face, brimming with mirth. 'Help me out, Lady Annalise. What possible objection could you have to his good looks?'

'Oh, I am perfectly prepared to admit he's handsome but unfortunately he's taken to writing odes . . . dedicated to me.'

Clarence permitted his surprise to show. 'I thought young ladies enjoyed that sort of thing.'

'They would be better if he could think of a word that rhymes with *blue.*'

Clarence choked on a laugh. 'Oh dear.'

'Quite. He compared my *eyes of blue* to radiant sunshine.'

'They are not blue,' Clarence said softly.

'I beg your pardon?'

'Your eyes are silver, with blue flecks.' He held her gaze for a protracted moment, mesmerised by the eyes in question. 'If the oaf can't discern that much, then he doesn't deserve you.'

She laughed. 'I might like Lord Roker better if he stopped following me around.'

'He is not the only gentleman to be captivated by you.'

She arched a brow. 'You have been

watching me, Lord Romsey?'

'I am a diplomat. I notice things. It's what I am trained to do and can't seem to help myself.'

'Then I shall forgive you.'

Clarence led her into a turn and resisted the urge to hold her a little closer. He was already on shaky ground with Winchester following the unfortunate business with Miss Brooke, now Lady Amos Sheridan, for which Winchester rightly held him responsible. He also had good reason to know Winchester was obsessively possessive of his sisters, as were all of their brothers. Annalise was a diamond of the first water: beautiful, lively, witty, and intelligent. If Clarence had been in the market for a wife, her name would have featured high on his list of possibilities. But he was not. He couldn't spare the time for courtship. He and the duke needed to work closely in an effort to restore law and order to their adjoining districts. With the political unrest that had swept the country following the wars, fuelled by the Prince Regent's ostentatious extravagance at a time when half the returning heroes were unable to find gainful employment, there was a growing need for the upper classes to pull together and lead by example.

'What a generous nature you possess.'

'Hardly generous, Lord Romsey. It is very easy to be generous when it costs one little.'

'I cannot imagine you being anything other than kind and thoughtful. I saw how you were with Miss Brooke when she was first brought to your notice. You treated her quite as an equal, which she very evidently was not.'

'Oh bah, I deserve no credit for that. Crista is a delight. Besides, it didn't take a genius to observe that Amos was madly in love with her.'

'Perhaps I should recruit you for the diplomatic service. It seems I am not the only one with a keen sense of observation.'

'Certainly you should.' She sent him a playful smile. 'If women ruled the world, there would be no occasion for wars. We are far too sensible to resort to violence.'

Clarence laughed as he carefully negotiated them past a crowded part of the floor. The suggestive rustle of her silk skirts as they brushed against his legs sent his mind on an inappropriate detour. Perdition, this would not do but, the devil take it, he was only human and Lady Annalise was temptation incarnate.

'In the spirit of neighbourly harmony,' he said, when they had left the clustered part of the floor in their wake, 'I shall refrain from mentioning Queen Boudica or Lucrezia Borgia.'

'So I should hope.' She tilted her chin and sent him an adorably mischievous smile. 'There are exceptions to every rule. Please don't ask me to name all the men who have created wars for their own selfish reasons, Lord Romsey, because it would take me the rest of the evening.'

'Indeed, I would not dare.'

Count von Hessel sailed past them with Miss Outwood in his arms. Miss Outwood looked radiantly happy. The count looked bored. He inclined his head towards Clarence but his eyes lingered speculatively upon Lady Annalise.

'Miss Outwood seems very pleased with the count,' Lady Annalise remarked. 'But I cannot bring myself to envy her.'

'You have something against the count?'

'I don't know him and have no particular wish to. I fancy the count spends longer over his toilette than Miss Outwood does hers. He seems to like himself very much indeed. It's difficult to imagine him cutting a dashing figure at Waterloo or fearlessly leading his troops against Napoleon. What if he were to get blood on his uniform?'

Clarence laughed aloud, attracting curious glances from other dancers. 'What a delightful imagination you have.'

'I happen to be a very good judge of

human nature,' she replied loftily.

And in this instance, she most likely was. There was something about von Hessel that didn't sit comfortably with Clarence. The hand holding Lady Annalise's waist tightened without his permission. Damnation, a man would need to be a monk not to respond to the enticing minx's lively wit.

'If Miss Outwood were to hear you, she would probably think you were jealous.'

Lady Annalise tossed her head, setting her curls dancing. 'Miss Outwood is not blessed with the ability to think deeply about anything. If she were, she would not have accepted the count.'

'Hmm, perhaps not the diplomatic service for you, after all.'

'If diplomats spoke the truth instead of playing clever word games, then we would all know where we stood.'

Clarence couldn't recall a time when he had enjoyed a conversation more. 'Ah, but who decides what is and is not true? It is perfectly true the walls of this room are painted blue. No one can dispute that.' She nodded. 'But what shade of blue, Lady Annalise? I wager every person you ask would give you a different answer, absolutely convinced they spoke the truth, since they would have no reason to distort the truth.'

'Whereas, were you to ask each gentleman where he spent the previous night — '

'Lady Annalise!' Clarence choked on a laugh. 'I shall pretend you didn't say that.'

'Don't look so scandalised. I have four brothers, so am qualified to make such remarks.'

'They discuss their . . . er, exploits with you?'

'Of course not. But if Portia and I are to learn anything worth knowing, we must piece together what scraps they accidentally let slip and assemble the evidence for ourselves. They think they are being discreet, but there is little we don't actually know about their activities.'

Clarence doubted that but thought it better not to take issue with his engaging partner.

'So you contest my assertion that Miss Outwood lacks sense?' Lady Annalise asked after a brief pause.

'Even if I were to be so bold, I believe you are about to convince me otherwise.'

'We came out together last year. I recall an especially tedious occasion upon which a lady from the royal household spent an inordinate amount of time impressing upon us all just how fortunate we were. The cream of the crop is the way she described us, rather as though we were prize-winning vegetables.'

Clarence laughed. 'No one could describe

you as a vegetable, Lady Annalise. That is one truth upon which I think we can safely agree.'

'I am so glad you don't look at me and visualise a turnip, Lord Romsey.'

His laughter intensified. 'Hardly that.'

'The royal emissary asked each of us what we planned to do for the disadvantaged when we had households of our own and were in a position to be charitable. We all talked about visiting our tenants, the usual things. I spoke of enforcing the Act of Parliament that already exists to help climbing boys, but which is quite shockingly ignored.' Clarence flexed a brow, surprised a lady as well protected as the minx in his arms knew anything about the plight of chimney boys. More surprised still that she knew the law protecting them was regularly flouted. 'Miss Outwood, on the other hand . . . well, she said she didn't think she would like to set foot inside any of her papa's tenants' cottages because they were dirty and she feared catching a disease.' She sent him a triumphant smile. 'There, I rest my case.'

'Miss Outwood ought not to have said such a thing,' Clarence replied. 'But just think for a moment about how that notion came into her head? Who made the rest of you think you ought to care for your tenants?' He lowered his voice to a seductive purr. 'Who made you think about the chimney boys?'

'Ah, I see what you mean. We learn from our mothers.'

'Precisely. And Mrs. Outwood is obsessed with ill-health because several members of her family have died from fevers.'

'How can you possibly . . . ' She looked up at him and laughed. 'You don't know any such thing. You just said that to make me feel ashamed.'

'The point I'm trying to make, rather ineptly it seems, is that Miss Outwood wasn't being selfish. She said what she honestly believed to be *the truth.*'

Lady Annalise wrinkled her pert little nose. 'Being a diplomat is not as easy as it appears.'

'It is not a career I would recommend to a free-thinker such as yourself.'

'Then what am I to do with myself?'

Clarence's chuckle rumbled in his throat. 'What indeed?'

'What of you, Lord Romsey? What did you learn at your father's knee?' She shook her head. 'No, don't tell me. He taught you to be diplomatic.'

'Yes, I suppose he did. I can't remember ever imagining I would do anything else.'

'And you have spent your life living up to his expectations, at the expense of your own pleasures.'

'Good heavens, what a very peculiar thing to say.'

'Forgive me for being indiscreet.' She lifted one slender shoulder. 'It's a family failing.'

Clarence laughed. 'Hardly that.'

'No, I suppose Zach isn't indiscreet, but the rest of us have always been encouraged to speak our minds. In my case, I sometimes forget myself when I am with a person who makes me feel I can be myself.'

'I am very glad you feel that way with me,' Clarence replied, smiling into her eyes.

'Do you ever put the pursuit of your own pleasures ahead of your duty, Lord Romsey?'

'I beg your pardon?'

'Oh dear, there I go again. What I meant to say was you appear to spend all your time fixing things. Your diplomatic career, starting the Southampton Police Office, maintaining your estate.' She shook her curls. 'It can't leave you with much time to enjoy yourself.'

'I am enjoying dancing with you, Lady Annalise.' *Far too much.*

'Well then, I am glad to have been of service.'

Clarence choked on a laugh, wondering if the chit had any idea what her words implied. Beautiful, lively, well-dowered, the sister to a duke, with all the advantages the connection to such a prominent family would bestow upon her husband, he was astonished she had not married during her first season. He was sure she would do so before the end of this one, and the sharp pang of regret that realisation caused Clarence took him by surprise. He must be more tired than he thought.

'I was pleased to observe that you and Zach are on congenial terms again,' Lady Annalise said after a short pause.

'We have business interests in common which kept us engaged in conversation before — '

'Before you came to my rescue. Do you and Zach plan to police the entire south coast?'

Clarence raised a brow. 'Why do you ask?'

'I shall never recover from the shame if this gets out, but I do read the newspapers.'

Clarence laughed, something he seemed to be doing a very great deal of while in Lady Annalise's company. 'Your secret is safe with me.'

'Thank you. And so, you see, I know just how troubled the times are. I blame the prince. He has no business spending so lavishly and conducting his war with his wife quite so publicly. What sort of example does that set? He is not the first man to make a bad marriage and he ought to have the good manners to suffer the consequences behind closed doors.'

'Quite,' Clarence replied, enjoying himself enormously.

'And as for all those poor men who fought valiantly for their country only to come home to no jobs and no prospects . . . ' She shook her head. 'It's truly shocking, and I can quite understand why General Ludd has become so popular. Although, of course, I also understand why you and Zach must find a way to maintain order.'

No question about Lady Annalise's cognitive powers, Clarence thought. 'You really are a most unusual young lady,' he said. 'And definitely a deep thinker.'

'Oh no, you mistake me for Portia. Now *she* really does study world affairs and shakes her head at the way things are.'

The dance came to an end, and Lady Annalise dipped a graceful curtsy.

'Thank you so much.' Clarence placed her hand on his sleeve and forged a path to the edge of the room. 'That was vastly entertaining.'

She shot him a shrewd sideways look. 'I hope you are not laughing at me.'

'Indeed, my lady, I would not dare.'

'Heavens, it is crowded, and very hot,' Lady Annalise said. 'Portia was right about that.'

'Would you care for a turn on the terrace?'

Clarence glanced down at her flimsy ball gown, a deep shimmering pink, and shook his head. 'Perhaps that would not be advisable. It's freezing outside. I should hate for you to catch one of Miss Outwood's fevers.'

'Ah, but I have an answer to that.'

Clarence refrained from rolling his eyes. He was a diplomat and ought to be able to manage one lively young lady without assistance. Selfishly, he wanted Lady Annalise to himself for a little while longer. The comment she had made about making time for his own pleasures had lodged in his brain and seemed in no hurry to quit it again.

'And that answer is?'

'Come with me.'

Lady Annalise turned towards the stairs leading up from the ballroom situated on the lower ground floor. Clarence escorted her through the crowd and up the winding stairs.

'Just a moment.'

She slipped through the open door to the library and returned almost immediately with a thick, brightly coloured shawl draped around her shoulders.

'Frankie's,' she said by way of explanation. 'Shall we?'

3

Lord Romsey opened the door to the terrace and stepped back so Anna could walk through it ahead of him. Her overheated body was hit by a blast of Siberian air, causing her to shiver and pull Frankie's shawl more closely about her.

'We can go back inside if it's too cold for you, Lady Annalise,' Lord Romsey said. 'In fact, that would probably be wise.'

'I won't hear of it.'

She tucked the fingers of the hand resting on his arm into the crook of his elbow. Her gloves were so thin as to be inconsequential, and she wanted to prevent her fingers from freezing to death.

'There is frost underfoot. Take great care. It will seep through your slippers in no time and you will incur — '

'One of Miss Outwood's fevers,' she finished for him, smiling.

'Quite.' She could hear a reciprocal smile in Lord Romsey's voice as he tilted his head upwards and examined the sky. 'We shall have snow before morning.'

'Oh good, I like snow.'

'You are a romantic at heart, Lady Annalise, in spite of your determination to disappoint half the *ton* by rejecting their proposals.'

She turned to look at him. 'What makes you imagine I have received any proposals?'

Rich laughter vibrated through his body. 'As you yourself pointed out, many of the young bucks turned loose on the *ton* are not the brightest sparks in the tinder box. But even Roker has fallen for your charms.' He patted the hand resting on his arm. 'I rest my case.'

'Why ... why does my — ' Anna swallowed and took a moment to find her voice. The feel of Lord Romsey's fingers had a most disconcerting effect upon her, making her forget what she had been about to say. Oh yes, inappropriate proposals. 'I am not ready for matrimony.'

'How very sensible of you.'

'You have something against marriage, Lord Romsey?'

'Not in the least, but I do think people tend to rush into it without proper thought.'

'Allowing their hearts to rule their heads, you mean?' She quirked a brow. 'I cannot imagine you ever allowing your feelings to overcome common sense.'

'I have resisted temptation, thus far.'

'Hmm.' Anna wasn't sure what he meant by that and changed the subject. 'Why does my liking winter weather make me a romantic, in your opinion?'

'Snow is devilishly inconvenient. It's pretty enough when it falls, I'll grant you, but once on the ground, it's a very different story. Horses can't get about, accidents occur and life generally grinds to a halt.'

'I have never thought of it in that light. How very spoiled you must think me.'

He didn't deny it. 'We are just about the only people foolish enough to venture out of doors,' he said instead.

'I happen to think we are very sensible.' Anne treated him to a sparkling smile that he probably couldn't see in the dim lighting on the terrace. 'Besides, you are a diplomat, and everyone knows diplomats must be very clever.'

'You appear determined to pay me compliments I don't deserve.'

Anna felt the muscles in the arm upon which she rested her fingers flex and contract. She glanced up at his handsome face and would give a very great deal to know what was going on in that clever brain of his. He cut such a dashing figure, with his broad shoulders displayed to fine advantage in a superbly cut coat of the finest blue wool, and a silk waistcoat embroidered with gold thread. A sapphire winked from the folds of his neckcloth. His breeches were finest buckskin, fitted tight, and his elegant legs were displayed in white patterned stockings. Anna felt pride in his companionship but compassion for the man he had become. Lord Romsey's elegant manners covered a very troubled, slightly lost soul. She didn't know how she was aware of it, but somehow she simply knew it was true.

They had not reached the end of the terrace before she came to a decision. Her soft heart recoiled at the thought of this complex gentleman spending all his waking hours doing his duty, putting others before himself. All the time his father had been alive, his son lived up to his expectations, and continued to do so after his death.

It simply would not do.

When she mentioned snow, his first thought was for the danger and inconvenience it caused. Hers was of boisterous snowball fights on the lawns of the Park — all of her siblings participating, no quarter asked for or given. Lord Romsey had probably never done that. Well, of course he had not. He had no siblings to compete against. Nor could he have ridden bareback, racing hell for leather across fields in direct competition with four brothers. He had missed so very much.

When she mentioned Miss Outwood's lack of intelligence, his immediate reaction was to seek a reason for it, simply because that was the way he had been encouraged from the cradle to apply his mind. Spontaneity did not form a part of Lord Romsey's character and Anna thought that was a great pity. She decided then and there to make him her charity project. She would teach this intelligent, complex and very handsome aristocrat how to relax and enjoy himself, or die in the attempt.

Waltzing with him had been a very agreeable experience. He danced superbly. He would be required to dance with all manner of ladies at various diplomatic soirees, she imagined, but that didn't explain why she had felt so capriciously abandoned in the circle of his arms, or the firestorm of emotional turmoil that had gripped her.

She was prepared to admit Lord Romsey was the only gentleman she had met since her come-out who could make her heart flutter. Perhaps that was because he was quite a few years older than she was and he had seen and done so much to make him fascinating in her eyes. But he was also a slave to duty, and there was no place in his life for a wife.

Good heavens! Anna almost stumbled when the nature of her thoughts registered. A strong arm shot out to steady her.

'Did you slip?'

'Oh no, I beg your pardon. I was not paying attention.'

'What were you thinking about?'

'Fie, Lord Romsey, you cannot ask such a question.' She shook a finger at him in mock annoyance. 'If I were to answer you honestly, you would be disappointed by the pedestrian nature of my reflections. Besides, if you possessed that knowledge it would strip me of all mystique.'

His rich, throaty laugh sent a shockwave of thrills cascading through her body. 'You, my dear, will always be a charming mystery to me, and I shall never tire of trawling your lively imagination.'

'Gallantly said.'

'Does that mean my inappropriate question is forgiven?'

'Question?' Anna sent him a teasing smile. 'Did you ask me something?'

Lord Romsey chuckled, after which they continued their chilly perambulation in companionable silence. Anna breathed deeply of the frigid air and returned to her cogitations. Without being vain, she was aware she could take her pick of a husband from amongst the many young men who pursued her with single-minded determination. None had excited her interest. Lord Romsey, on the other hand, had done so without appearing to try. Unfortunately, he was not of a mind to marry. He had told her so in not so many words. Perhaps he sensed her interest in him and was kindly setting her on her guard. She was not about to beg. Besides, she could not marry a man who did not return her love and who wasn't prepared to give her at least a portion of his attention. Lord Romsey's time was completely taken up with his myriad responsibilities, and he had none to spare for domestic felicity.

Anna squared her shoulders, squelching her disappointment. Be that as it may, there was one thing she could do for him. She could introduce him to an aspect of his character he probably didn't know existed by teaching him to behave spontaneously. Everyone deserved to let their guard down occasionally; even important diplomats like Lord Romsey who was altogether too serious.

They still had the terrace to themselves. Much as Anna enjoyed being with Lord Romsey, she was now frozen to the bone and couldn't prevent herself from shivering.

'You're cold,' he said. 'We ought to return to the ballroom.'

'In a minute. I don't mind the cold. It provides a welcome respite.'

'From your admirers. How do you manage? Being pursued all the time must be exhausting.'

'It doesn't help that I could be the ugliest, most boring woman on God's earth, but because of who I am, I would be pursued just as vigorously.'

'You don't know whether the coves admire you for yourself or for your fortune and connections?' Lord Romsey stroked his chin. 'It had not occurred to me to consider your situation in that light.'

'And you have no diplomatic advice to offer me?' she asked, glancing up at him with a capricious smile.

'I'm not sure there is anything in the diplomatic handbook to cover such a situation.'

'An unfortunate oversight.'

'Quite. I shall make the powers that be aware of the omission at the first opportunity. But in the meantime, I must rely upon my wits to save face.' He sent her a teasing smile. 'My suggestion, for what it's worth, is to listen to your heart and allow it to guide you. You would not be happy united to a man you did not love or respect. You will know when you find the right gentleman.'

'Yes,' she said, the laughter dying on her lips. 'But what if he does not desire me?'

'Now, you're being foolish.' He fixed her with a smouldering expression that caused her breath to hitch in her throat and welcome heat to invade her frozen limbs. 'There is not a gentleman alive who could resist your charms.'

Except you. Anna was saved from the trouble of formulating a response when the door was thrown open and a gentleman headed towards Lord Romsey, waving a piece of paper in his direction.

'What is it, Pierce?' he asked irritably.

'Pardon the intrusion, my lord. An urgent communiqué from the Foreign Office.'

Lord Romsey turned to Anna with an exasperated air. 'Allow me to escort you back — '

'Always on duty, my lord,' she said softly. 'No, don't trouble yourself on my account. I shall remain here a moment longer. Read your note, by all means.'

Lord Romsey appeared torn. 'I really ought to take you back inside first.'

'Nothing can happen to me here.'

Anna moved away from the light being shed through the windows, allowing Lord Romsey to stand there and read his note in private. She strolled a little further away from him, dimly aware of him speaking in a lowered voice to Pierce, who was presumably his secretary. She gazed out across the inky blackness of the gardens one floor below them, illuminated by the light spilling from the ballroom. She heard faint strains of music, louder overtones of hundreds of voices, feeling part of it all yet strangely detached.

There was something wrong with her, she thought. She ought to revel in being young, rich, and fêted, but already high society was losing its appeal. She moved further down the terrace. Lord Romsey appeared very agitated by whatever the communiqué said and she didn't wish to give the impression that she was eavesdropping. She imagined he would leave since he was obviously needed elsewhere. The ball would be a very dull affair without him and she would prefer to go home. But it was only just past midnight and her mother would expect to remain for at least another hour or two.

Anna lifted her face and felt fat snowflakes fall onto it. She trailed her gloved hand along the frosty balustrade, crying out in surprise when she saw movement in the periphery of her vision and felt something lock onto her wrist. She wondered if Lord Romsey had crept up on her, but she glanced his way and saw he was still in deep conversation with

Pierce. Besides, he would never clasp her wrist in such a vulgar manner. Panic consumed her. Lord Romsey hadn't heard her exclaim above the noise coming from the ball, and she tried to convince herself that the touch to her wrist was a product of her imagination. Except it hurt like the devil, so how could it be?

Before Anna could decide, she felt a sharp tug on her arm, her feet left the floor, and her body tipped over the edge of the balustrade. Again she cried out, louder this time, but was unaware if she was heard. She was falling fast onto the frozen ground beneath her and could do nothing to help herself. Lord above, she would break her bones, if not her neck. Either that or she would freeze to death before she was found.

Except, she didn't hit the ground but was caught by a strong pair of arms. The side of her face came into sharp contact with a rough jerkin that smelled disgusting. Then a sack was pulled over her head and her entire world went black.

★ ★ ★

'Right, Pierce, you know what to do.'

'I apologise if — '

'On second thoughts I'd best come with

40

you and put the Foreign Secretary's mind at rest.'

'It might be for the best, my lord. He is in rather a state.'

Clarence rolled his eyes, unable to recall a time when he had not been. 'Give me a moment to return Lady Annalise to her mother and I shall be with you.' Clarence turned, but the lady who had entrusted herself to his care was nowhere in sight. 'What the devil? Did Lady Annalise pass us and go back into the ballroom?' he asked sharply.

'I did not see her, my lord.'

'She must have done.'

Clarence felt a strange premonition as he strode the length of the terrace, calling her name, becoming more agitated by the second. There seemed to be more people than ever in the ballroom when he re-entered it, and more still spilling out of the adjoining card and supper rooms. It was a terrible crush, but Lady Annalise was taller than average and he ought to be able to see her head.

He could not.

With each room he searched, finding no trace of her or any members of her family, he became increasingly concerned. Common sense told him she could not have been spirited away from the duchess's terrace on the first floor of her mansion. But she didn't seem to have returned to the house either. There had to be a simple explanation, he told himself repeatedly. Clarence had been engrossed in conversation with his secretary, it was true, but he would still have noticed her passing their position. There were two other doorways leading to the terrace but due to the inclement weather they were locked from the inside. Only Clarence and Lady Annalise had been foolish enough to brave the elements. That was highly unusual. Terraces were usually thronged at balls with couples keen to snatch a few illicit minutes away from the eagle eyes of their chaperones.

After several minutes of frantic searching, he had still failed to find any trace of her. Damnation, he should have insisted upon escorting her back inside! He looked up and encountered Winchester and Frankie walking his way, laughing about something. They both turned to look at him, their laughter abruptly fading, presumably in response to his grave expression.

'Where's Anna?' Winchester asked. 'I thought she was with you.'

'She was.'

Succinctly, Clarence explained what had happened. 'I am so very sorry. I tried to make her come back inside but she insisted upon remaining outside.'

'So you blame Anna for your neglect?' Winchester's frown was condemning. 'Damn it, Romsey, do you make a habit of losing members of my family?'

'She can't have gone far,' Frankie said, easing the tension with her calm voice of reason. 'She must have passed you while you were speaking with your secretary, Clarence, and you were too engrossed to notice her. There is no other explanation. There's no need to look so concerned, Your Grace,' she added, turning to Winchester. 'She will appear at any moment and wonder what all the fuss is about.'

'We must conduct a co-ordinated search.' Agitation took the place of Winchester's habitual calm as he motioned to his brothers, Vincent and Nathanial.

'What's wrong?' Nate asked.

Winchester's explanation earned Clarence scowls of disapproval.

'Lady St. John. Have the goodness to check the withdrawing rooms for any signs of my sister,' Winchester said.

'I am residing here with the duchess. Would you like me to have a quiet word with her also? She can set her servants to search.'

'Yes, please do that. Nate, find our mother.

See if she has seen Anna. Try not to alarm her. We don't want Anna's temporary disappearance to become public knowledge.'

Clarence nodded his approval, aware Winchester would be thinking of his sister's reputation. He was responsible for this farrago, damn it! Lady Annalise had been in his care, but once again duty had interfered with a rare attempt to enjoy himself. He deserved the murderous looks being sent his way by all three Sheridans. They could not possibly make him feel any worse than he already did.

'Vince, take the supper rooms. Romsey, the card rooms, although I can't imagine why she would have ventured in there. I shall scour the ballroom. Meet back in this position everyone when you have completed your searches.'

The gathering dispersed, reassembling less than half an hour later with the disquieting confirmation that Lady Annalise was nowhere to be found.

'Nate,' Winchester said. 'Take our mother and Portia home and stay there with them. If Annalise should happen to appear at Sheridan House, send word at once. The rest of us will remain here and continue the search.'

'Search where?' Clarence asked. 'There is

nowhere left to look.'

'There must be,' Winchester replied. 'Anna is somewhere. We just haven't found her yet. Could she have fallen over the balustrade into the gardens below?'

'Unlikely, but we have explored all the most likely possibilities.'

'Come along. No, not you, Lady St. John. Remain here. We shall return directly.'

Winchester took the lead as he, Vince, and Clarence headed for the terrace.

'She'll freeze to death if we don't find her soon,' Vince said, an urgent edge to his voice.

'She was wearing a thick shawl,' Clarence replied as the three men found the door to the grounds hidden at the end of a corridor behind the ballroom. 'It belonged to Frankie.'

'Well, that's something I suppose,' Winchester replied tersely.

Winchester grabbed a lantern from a table beside the door and held it aloft as they searched the ground beneath the terrace. Snow was falling, dusting the ground like sugar. This was all his fault, Clarence accepted. One of his many enemies had seen them dancing together, then strolling on the terrace. Lady Annalise had been taken by an opportunist to get back at him. He just knew it. In these uncertain times, he had as many enemies amongst the upper classes as he did elsewhere. A lot of them were present tonight. Count von Hessel sprang to mind. He recalled now how he had looked so closely at Lady Annalise when they passed one another on the dance floor. Clarence hadn't thought much of it at the time. Any man with eyes in his head couldn't fail to admire what he saw. Damnation, he had let his guard down and now Lady Annalise was paying a heavy price for his momentary lapse!

'Here!'

Vince's voice drew the three men's attention to a patch of ground where footprints indented the snow. Immediately beyond them, caught on the spikes of a bush, was a torn piece of brightly coloured shawl.

'Someone has taken her,' Winchester said, turning to hold Clarence in a glare frostier than the conditions.

4

Annalise was thrown into a carriage, still with the vile-smelling sack over her head. Some-one bound her hands and feet so tightly she thought it might cut off her blood supply. She felt lightheaded, frightened, and angry at the same time, as well as completely helpless. She was given a push and fell full-length onto a tatty seat.

'Stay down and don't move,' a gruff voice commanded.

Then the door slammed and the carriage moved off. At first Annalise remained where she was, waiting for her head to stop spinning and her heart to cease pounding so violently. Then she realised what she had been told to do — or rather, not to do. Don't move, indeed! She had never been good at taking orders and had no intention of starting now.

Annalise eased her aching body into a sitting position, unable to dislodge the sack since her hands were bound behind her. Even so, sitting up, that small act of defiance, gave her some satisfaction and helped overcome her terror. She had never admitted it to anyone but she was afraid of the dark. Not being able to see, as well as not knowing where she was going and what fate awaited her, caused that fear to intensify.

Breathing deeply, even though that action brought the vile sacking closer to her mouth and forced her to suck its fumes into her lungs, she endeavoured to calm down and reason the matter through. She was still alive and presumably that situation would endure, otherwise why the carriage and the sack to prevent her seeing her captors and where they were taking her?

She thought back to the terrace, and Lord Romsey. Was that only a few minutes ago? It seemed like another age. She had been momentarily too shocked to react when she felt herself falling but it quickly became apparent to her that her unfortunate *accident* was actually a carefully contrived kidnap. Had she been specifically chosen or did these ne'er-do-wells simply assume any young lady in attendance at such an auspicious ball would have a well-placed family prepared to pay handsomely for her safe release? If that was the case, they were sadly misinformed about the pecuniary situation of many of the country's leading families. It occurred to her that Lord Romsey and Zach were right to be concerned about the state of law and order in England if rogue gangs had become desperate

48

enough to infiltrate a major society occasion.

All of those thoughts had spun through her head while she tumbled through the air in an ungainly ten-foot fall. Never one to embrace passivity, she fought like the devil against the rogue who caught her. Her actions appeared to take him by surprise. He had probably expected her to swoon, not fight like a tigress. But Portia wasn't the only female member of her family not given to swooning. Anna struggled so violently she almost managed to scramble out of the man's abhorrent grasp, but he recovered quickly and easily subdued her.

'Unhand me, you oaf!'

'Shut up and keep still, or it'll be the worse for you,' a rough voice replied.

Nothing could be worse than this. If this . . . this reprobate thought she would calmly permit him to abduct her, he clearly didn't know she had grown up with four brothers who permitted her to join in their rough and tumbles without making any allowance for her supposedly weaker state. But it had been some years since she had behaved thus, and she was clearly out of practice. The man became tired of her trying to gouge his eyes, restricting her hands by pressing one against his horrible body and painfully grasping her other wrist.

Fine, but her feet were still free. Annalise was petrified, but fear and anger lent her superhuman strength. She aimed her heel in the area of the man's groin, pleased when she heard him emit a low hiss of pain. Unfortunately, her blow wasn't debilitating since she was wearing flimsy satin slippers. Oh, what she would have given to have her sturdy half-boots on her feet at that moment! The man slapped her face so hard that her neck snapped backwards. She cried out, feeling her lip split and the tangy taste of blood fill her mouth.

'She's a live one,' said another voice, chuckling. 'Reckon you won't be much use to Meg for a few nights now.'

'Shut up, you fool! No names.'

Ye gods, there were at least two of them! Annalise went limp in the man's arms, aware she wouldn't be able to get away from them both. Better to let them take her wherever they planned to, wait for them to let their guard down and then assess her situation.

She felt herself being lifted up into the arms of another man. They must be taking her over the garden wall. Of course. That would be how they had got in. They could have simply headed for the mews at the back of the mansion but carriages belonging to guests would be clustered there, along with their drivers. They would be bound to notice a woman with a sack over her head being carried out. But how the devil did they intend to get her over the wall and down the other side? She had no intention of co-operating.

No co-operation was needed, damn it. They had thought this out well. Kidnappers with brains. Just her luck. The original man pulled himself over the eight-foot wall, stood on something they had left on the other side and his partner-in-crime handed Anna down to him.

'Let him take you and don't make a fuss,' the man passing her down said. 'Make a noise and it'll be all over for you.'

Anna believed him and abandoned all thoughts of struggling. If she fell with her head still covered, she could do untold damage to herself, always supposing her abductors didn't kill her first. Besides, her head was still ringing from the heavy blow the first man had delivered to her face and she was in no fit state to run for her life.

She heard her captors grunt as they negotiated her over the wall. And now, here she was, trussed up like a chicken in a carriage that was being driven slowly through the falling snow. Anna thought of Lord Romsey's warning about the dangers to vehicles in snowy conditions and half-wished that this one was being driven a little faster. If they had an accident, then surely she would be rescued? Except, if they were taking her to a poor part of town, her situation might actually go from bad to worse. Not that she could imagine anything worse than this, but still . . .

Anna tried to pay attention to the sounds and smells along the route they took, as well as the direction in which they were headed, but there were so many twists and turns she became hopelessly muddled. She was fairly sure they had left the better part of town, but that didn't help her much. Any noise from other vehicles was drowned out by the snow. Because she couldn't see, and because she was so uncomfortable with her hands and feet bound so tightly, she found it hard to focus on their route. She was near freezing to death in her flimsy ball gown and had lost Frankie's lovely shawl. She would have to apologise for that, she thought inconsequentially.

Anna counted down the seconds inside her head, by that means trying to work out how far they travelled. The horse was moving at walking pace and, by her calculation, they had been on the road for about thirty minutes when the carriage finally came to a halt. As soon as the door was thrown open, she smelt dank river air, which was definitely not good. They could hide her in the docks for months with its labyrinth of warehouses, alleyways and slums and no one would discover her whereabouts.

A blanket was thrown over her body. She was lifted by the same vile-smelling man, and someone else wrapped the blanket around her. Presumably, they didn't want a lady in a silk ball gown to be seen in the district. Not that anyone would be about at this hour but she had already decided these rogues were a cut above the average criminal and they were taking no chances.

She heard a door being dragged open. It sounded heavy and the man cursed about the effort it took him. The second man carried her inside a building and up some stairs. He too complained since the stairs were clearly steep. With great good fortune, he might put his back out. Unfortunately, he did not, and they reached the top of the wooden stairs without mishap. Anna heard a key turn in a lock and she was carried into a room.

'There's a chair behind you,' the man said. 'Sit.'

Anna wanted to tell him she was not a dog. Instead, she sat, but only because her legs were too weak and too tightly bound for her to be able to stand. She wanted to tell the man that but decided to save her breath. In fact, she decided not to speak to them at all.

'Now, I'm going to remove the bindings on your hands and wrists. When you hear the door lock behind me, you can remove the sack. If you take it off before I leave and get a look at me, it's the last thing you'll ever see, m'lady. Do you understand?'

'Yes.'

Anna saw no point in arguing. She could tell from his steely tone he meant what he said. Besides, she wanted the use of her hands and feet to be restored to her.

'You can't escape from here, so just be a good girl and make yourself comfortable. Someone will be along to speak to you later.'

Anna showed no reaction when the man knelt to cut the bindings on her ankles, audaciously running a hand up one calf as he did so.

'Very nice,' he muttered. 'Such a shame we have orders not to touch you.'

Orders? Orders from whom?

Her hands sprang free when he cut the rope binding them. Anna circled her shoulders, tingles running down her arms as the blood flowed freely again and feeling came back to her limbs. Her wrists were sore, probably chafed, from where she had tried to free her hands. She could hear the man standing over her, breathing heavily, and she willed him to leave so she could remove the sack and assess her situation.

Eventually, she heard his footsteps, heavy on the boarded floor. The door opened then closed behind him and a heavy key turned in the lock. Anna reached for the sack, pulled it from her head and threw it aside. She blinked, waiting for her eyes to adjust to . . . to nothing. The room was in complete darkness. They hadn't even left her a candle, and that was almost more frightening for Anna than her actual situation.

★　★　★

Their hostess, having been told by Frankie what had happened, was distressed but also wise to the need for discretion.

'I wish I knew what happened,' she said. 'How it happened, for that matter. I mean, how did people get into my grounds undetected and pluck a lady from the terrace?'

'I have had people examine the garden,' Clarence replied. 'We think they came over the side wall.'

'They couldn't risk taking her through the mews,' Winchester replied curtly. 'The question is, where have they taken her, and why?'

'I questioned some of the carriage drivers,' Vince said, joining the group. 'One of them strolled round the side of the house just after midnight to answer a call of nature. He saw a small closed carriage there, which he thought was odd. Before he could investigate, it drove off.'

'Does he know which direction it took?' Clarence asked.

'Only one way he could go from there.' Winchester rubbed his chin, his expression thunderous. 'He would have to join Grosvenor Street, and from there he could go anywhere.'

'What do we do now?' Vince asked. 'Presumably there will be a demand for cash in return for . . . for, damn it, for Anna.'

'There's nothing more we can do from here,' Winchester said. 'I had half-hoped one of your servants might have colluded with the rogues, Your Grace, by giving them access to the grounds. We could have questioned him and found out more that way. But if they came over the wall, that cannot be the case.'

'We had best get back to Sheridan House,' Nate said from the edge of the group. 'Any communication will be sent there.'

'At least we know they won't harm Anna,' Frankie said. 'Not if their purpose is financial gain. And what other reason could there be for taking such a huge risk?'

Clarence knew Frankie was trying to keep everyone's spirits up, especially his. She must have seen the frequent hostile glances being sent his way by three very angry, very worried, male Sheridans. Clarence couldn't blame them for blaming him because this *was* all his fault. He should have taken better care of Lady Annalise. Frankie had a soft heart and was attempting to remind everyone that Anna wouldn't be despoiled, provided they paid handsomely for her release. If they wanted a virginal young woman for reasons Clarence refused to think about, they would not have gone to the considerable trouble of abducting one from a society ball.

Reassured, at least on that front, Clarence reapplied his mind to the question of Lady Annalise's release. He would insist upon paying whatever they asked from his own pocket. It was a small means of making amends for his neglect. Once he had paid, and Lady Annalise was safely restored to her family, he would seek retribution.

His blood ran cold at the thought of his delightful dance partner being manhandled by her abductors. She still must be terrified. Clarence was scarcely less so because there was nothing he could do for her now, except wait. As a diplomat, waiting was something he was accustomed to doing and he was remarkably good at it. But in this case, he already knew every minute Lady Annalise remained missing would be a torturous reminder of his inability to keep her safe.

She had delighted him with her irreverent ways, and the thought of doing nothing, of the endless waiting until they received word, filled him with impotent rage. Of course he would send people out to scour London, have every one of his large network of contacts, asking questions everywhere. But this was a well-executed plot, and he doubted whether he would learn anything worthwhile before the ransom demand came.

'I shall put arrangements in hand to have questions asked,' Clarence told Winchester, giving voice to his thoughts, 'and then join you at Sheridan House. I know you probably don't want me there,' he added, when he sensed all three brothers were about to object, 'but you need me. Frankie's right. Your sister won't be physically harmed but the sooner we can find her and get her to safety the quicker we can get to the bottom of why she was targeted.'

'You think she was taken because she was seen with you?' Winchester asked.

'I don't know what to think yet.' Clarence ground his jaw. He almost never allowed his temper to get the better of him. Anger deprived one of the ability to think rationally and seldom worked to one's advantage. On this occasion, he allowed it to swirl through him unchecked, welcoming the swell of thunderous rage, feeling ready to throttle the bastards with his bare hands just as soon as he discovered their identities.

Which he most assuredly would.

Someone had grossly underestimated Clarence by carrying out such an audacious crime — a crime that could not be permitted to go unavenged. Quite apart from his personal interest in the matter, it threatened the entire fabric of society as Clarence knew it, and that was totally unacceptable. A line had been crossed and the perpetrators needed to be taught a swift, brutal lesson in order to deter others.

Winchester nodded, first to his brothers, then to Clarence. 'Very well. We shall see you in Berkeley Square.'

Clarence took his leave of the duchess and Frankie, then strode across to Pierce, who was hovering in the doorway to the small salon in which this conversation had taken place.

'Have everyone ask discreet questions,' he said curtly. 'Call at every rookery, every den of thievery we know of, and make their

59

inhabitants aware they will not be left to continue with their criminal activities until we find the lady. Offer a reward for information but do not, under any circumstances, name the lady who has been abducted.'

'Leave it to me, my lord.'

'I shall be at Sheridan House. Keep me informed of developments, no matter how insignificant.'

Clarence lingered only long enough to see his orders carried out, then walked the short distance to Berkeley Square. He noticed several of the men under his command already patrolling the street, and those surrounding it. Not that Lady Annalise was likely to still be in this district but it paid to be thorough.

Clarence was admitted to the house and found the entire family congregated in the drawing room. He went straight to the duchess.

'I am most terribly sorry, Your Grace,' he said, bowing over her hand. 'But rest assured, we will not leave a stone unturned until we find Lady Annalise.'

The duchess was clearly distressed but managed to remain in control of herself. Lady Portia clutched one of her mother's hands, looked close to tears.

'We do not blame you, Lord Romsey,' the duchess said.

All three brothers were standing in a cluster in front of the fire. One of them made a derogatory sound but none of them spoke. Winchester's two wolfhounds, Phantom and Phineas, were stretched out full length on the hearth rug. They lifted their heads when Clarence walked in but quickly dropped them again and returned to their slumbers.

'Thank you, but I take full responsibility.'

'If a lady cannot stroll on a terrace during a ball in one of the safest mansions in London, then I don't know what the world is coming to. No wonder you and Zach are so concerned about the increase in criminal activity. This is beyond unimaginable.'

'That it is, Your Grace, but we shall get to the bottom of it.' Clarence's jaw clenched, square and unmoving. 'On that you have my solemn oath.'

'You think the people who took Anna will ask for a ransom, I understand,' Lady Portia said, wrinkling her brow. 'But how will they deliver their demand? They must know you will have the area around this house surrounded and will apprehend whoever approaches it.'

'They will send an urchin, one they recruit far away from where they are holding Anna,' Winchester said before Clarence could. 'He won't know the identity of the abductors, nor will we bother to ask him. We are not going to take any *more* chances with Anna's safety,' he added with a significant glance for Clarence. 'We will pay whatever they ask to get her back and then scour the country until we find her abductors.'

'God help them when we do,' Vince replied, scowling.

Winchester refilled his brothers' glasses, then his own. After a moment's hesitation, he filled another and passed it to Clarence.

'Thank you,' Clarence said, recognising the gesture for the olive branch that it was.

'And so we must wait,' the duchess said, showing signs of considerable strain, but not giving way to hysterics.

'That will be the hardest part,' Lady Portia said. 'Waiting, unable to do anything, feeling so useless.'

'Go to bed, Mother,' Winchester said with a kindly smile. 'You, too, Portia. We will wake you as soon as we hear anything but I doubt if it will be before daybreak.'

'I couldn't sleep,' the duchess replied.

Winchester took his mother's hand and gently pulled her to her feet. 'Try, for my sake,' he said softly. 'I can't worry about you and Portia as well as Anna. There is nothing you can do here. Leave things to us.'

'Zach's right, Mama,' Portia said. 'Let's go

upstairs. We can be of use when Anna is back. Have Mrs. Jessop send up hot libations for us both, please, Zach. They might help us to sleep.'

'I can summon Dr. Fisher, if you would like. He could give you something stronger.'

'No need,' the duchess replied with a tired smile. 'But he ought to be on hand for when Anna comes home. I am sure she will need him.'

'I have already sent word,' Winchester said, opening the door for his mother and sister, kissing each of them as they walked through it.

'Damnation, what a thing to have happen,' Nate said, grinding his jaw. He was the brother closest in age to Lady Annalise and probably felt her loss more keenly even than Winchester did.

'Right, Romsey,' Winchester said when the door closed behind the ladies. 'It's time for you to tell us who you think might have taken our sister.'

5

Annalise trembled, cold and truly afraid. The darkness and the ruthlessness of her captors had badly overset her. If only she could see. She felt her way cautiously around the room, dragging the blanket about her shoulders, no longer fastidiously turning her nose up at its odour. All she cared about was remaining as warm as she possibly could. Her legs still felt wobbly. Her feet were frozen, the frost on the terrace having, as Lord Romsey predicted, soaked through her slippers. Ignoring her physical discomfort, she continued to explore, using her hands to guide her. She deduced that she was in a storeroom of some sort. She could feel wooden crates all over the place and kept bumping into them, ripping her skirts and cutting her forearm on something sharp.

Something sharp? A weapon she could use. Her fingers eagerly explored. Damnation, it was just the corner of a heavy crate she couldn't even move, much less break apart and use as a club. She continued to feel her way beyond the chair she had been sitting in. There was a small window, the glass frigid to the touch. She didn't try to open it, knowing she was not on the ground floor. It would be suicide to try and clamber out of it, even if it did open. The snowstorm was raging harder than ever, a howling wind rattling against the walls of the building.

This had to be a warehouse on the wharf, she decided, feeling her way back to the battered old armchair in the corner of the room. She pulled her feet up beneath her bottom in a futile attempt to warm them and tucked the blanket around herself. It was thin, inadequate, but there was nothing else she could use. Whoever had taken her had chosen their hiding place well. No one would think to look for her here, she decided glumly, her teeth chattering, and there wasn't a hope of escape. Her situation was made ten times worse by the cold, even more so by her ungovernable terror of the dark. Fear tingled down Anna's spine. She had never felt so helpless in her entire life. Desperate, she thought briefly of pounding on the locked door and requesting a candle, but decided against it. If her captors had wanted her to see, they would have left her a light. She would just have to embrace that panic and somehow overcome it. Think about happier times, she told herself.

Her family must be frantic, wondering

what had happened to her. They would blame Lord Romsey, of course, which was most unfair. This was not his fault, was it? Anna was ashamed when it occurred to her that his being detained by his secretary when the two of them just happened to be alone on the terrace was rather convenient. She pushed the thought aside as being unworthy. What possible reason could Lord Romsey have to abduct her? Besides, she was the one who insisted upon walking outside. He had advised against it.

She thought about their lively discourse during their dance together and, joy of joys, heat invaded her insides, helping to counter the increasingly frozen state of her limbs. An odd, pleasurable sensation spread through her mid-section as she recalled Lord Romsey's shy, lopsided smile when he corrected her about the colour of her own eyes. No one had ever done that before. Of course, he was a diplomat and, as he had said himself, trained to notice small details. She should not read too much into his powers of observation.

Her brothers were all disgustingly handsome, self-assured hellions. Anna thought Lord Romsey to be just as handsome, but also self-contained, as though he had never learned how to have fun. Every word he spoke was measured, carefully thought through. Except when he danced with her. She was convinced he had enjoyed her society and allowed himself to relax.

But his fleeting pleasure would now be tempered by her brothers' anger and if Anna got out of this unharmed, Lord Romsey would not wish to know her. She had already caused him quite enough trouble, and nothing could be permitted to come between him and his blasted duty.

'We shall see about that,' she said aloud, more determined than ever to broaden his horizons.

Anna rubbed her hands together, then stood up and stamped her feet in a futile effort to restore some feeling into them. She waved her arms around and tried to get the blood flowing through her body, pausing when she heard voices on the other side of the door. She thought they belonged to the two men who had brought her here but she couldn't hear what they actually said. Perhaps that was not such a bad thing. Ignorance was sometimes bliss. She had obviously been abducted to order, otherwise why would someone be coming to talk to her? What possible information could she possess that required such dangerous, daring and drastic action?

Anna kicked off her damp slippers. They

were making her feet even colder. She felt about until she found the old sack they had used to cover her head. Using all her strength, she rent it in half, and then half again. She tied a piece around each foot as tightly as she could manage. Wiggling her toes, she felt a little, a very little, warmer. She managed a wry smile as she imagined what she must look like. A beautiful but torn ball gown, sacking on her feet, her hair falling all over the place, her lip cut and caked with dried blood and her entire body blue with cold.

But she was alive.

Never lose sight of that fact, she told herself repeatedly.

Anna was unsure how long she sat there, her arms cuddling her upraised knees beneath the ratty blanket, colder than she had been in her entire life. To her astonishment she must have dozed because something, some sound, woke her. No, not a sound, she realised, but lack of it. The storm had passed, the wind was gone, and it was now deathly quiet. She opened her eyes and gasped with relief. There was some light in the room. She could see the shape of the boxes stacked all around her quite clearly. It took her a moment to realise the light was coming from the window. The sky was now crystal clear, lit up by a near full moon.

She moved slowly and awkwardly on stiff limbs, shuffling across to the window. Yes, she was definitely close to the wharf. She could smell the rancid river and see other large warehouses looming nearby. What had actually woken her was the sound of a branch knocking against her window. It must have been drowned out before now by the storm. She looked more closely, astonished to see such a large tree flourishing between the warehouses. A large tree with strong branches. Just like the ones she and the boys delighted in climbing when they were younger. She shook her head. It was many years since she had climbed a tree. Besides, those trees had not been covered in frost and snow, nor had they been situated in an area with which she was unfamiliar. Even if she escaped, she was in a derelict part of town, wearing a ball gown and sacking slippers. She would be set upon in seconds, if only for the value of the silk gown.

She shook her head and returned to her chair, the brief hope that had flared quickly diminished. Escape was impossible.

Close to tears of despair, her head jerked up when she heard a new voice on the other side of the wall. A voice that exuded authority and to which the other two men deferred. This, presumably, was the person who had come to talk to her.

'Is she here?'

'Yes, sir. In there.'

'Let me see.'

Anna straightened her spine, expecting the door to open at any moment. Instead, a flap was pushed up in the wall beside the door and a light shone through it. It blinded Anna and she covered her eyes with her forearms. The light was abruptly withdrawn, the flap closed, and Anna's ears were assaulted by colourful swearing.

'You fools! You got the wrong woman.'

'But . . . but you said to get the one with the colourful shawl. You said she would be on the terrace at some point. She was the only one out there and she *was* wearing a colourful shawl.'

Dear God, it wasn't her they had wanted, Anna thought despairingly. It was Frankie. What would they do with her now?

'That is Lady Annalise Sheridan, the sister to a duke,' the newcomer said. 'Perdition, the duke will make the devil of a stink about this.'

Most certainly!

'How were we to know?' one of the men asked peevishly.

Anna heard a sharp slapping noise — a hand striking flesh — and someone cried out. She thought it was her original abductor. Anna hoped it hurt like the devil. She tried to still the frantic beating of her heart and think what this latest development signified. Nothing to her benefit, that much was immediately apparent. Her mind felt sluggish, affected by the biting cold, and thinking was almost too much effort. The newcomer knew who she was but Anna didn't recognise his voice. He sounded foreign, speaking English with a heavy accent. Thoughts of Count von Hessel, Miss Outwood's future husband, flooded her brain. She was unsure why. There had been a lot of foreign dignitaries at the ball that evening. She had been introduced to several of them, but not von Hessel. He and Frankie knew one another, but she knew a lot of the others, too. What possible reason would any of them have to abduct her?

One factor did manage to penetrate her addled brain. It was unlikely she would be offered an apology and returned home.

'You will have to get rid of her,' the newcomer said. Anna gasped, her worst fears realised. 'But leave it until I am well clear of the district.'

★ ★ ★

'Who do I think abducted Lady Annalise?' Clarence repeated Winchester's question in a measured tone. 'I would give a great deal to

71

know not only by whom but why. I am completely without firm intelligence to guide me. I had absolutely no idea anything like this was planned, which in itself is unusual. It's such an audacious crime that word really ought to have leaked out.'

'You both think this was no opportunistic abduction?' Vince asked, sharing a glance between Clarence and Winchester.

'Romsey's situation guarantees that he will have made enemies,' Winchester told his brother.

'Part and parcel of my role,' Clarence replied indifferently.

'There were a lot of foreigners at the duchess's ball,' Nate remarked.

'The Prince Regent enjoys entertaining our allies and takes personal credit for defeating Napoleon,' Clarence said, only years of training preventing him from showing the contempt he felt for the man's arrogance.

'I gather he has uniforms made, prances about in them, and re-enacts his part at Waterloo to his long-suffering guests,' Nate said.

Winchester nodded. 'Take it from one who knows. He does. He's actually convinced himself he was there and takes all the credit for the victory.'

'Remarkable,' Vince said, shaking his head.

'Did anyone stand out this evening, Romsey?' Winchester asked. 'Anyone with special reason to be annoyed with you?'

Clarence shrugged. 'I know things about a lot of the people in attendance tonight, most of it not to their credit. But it's not within England's interests to reveal that information and those men are astute enough to realise it.' Clarence scrubbed a hand down his face. 'Or, put another way, they are not desperate enough to kidnap a young lady to buy my silence. Tension still runs high throughout Europe but the prince actually helps by inviting the leading lights from Europe to feel at home here in England.'

'Even if they were desperate enough to resort to kidnapping, how would they know to target Anna?' Nate asked. 'To the best of my knowledge, you have not spent time in her company in public before tonight.'

'Whoever took Anna went to considerable trouble to get into the duchess's garden,' Winchester said. 'So they planned in advance, then lay in wait when the temperatures were freezing, on the off-chance Anna might appear.' He looked as dubious as Clarence felt. 'You really have upset someone, Romsey.'

The brothers shared a speaking look that excluded Clarence. 'It doesn't seem plausible,' Vince said. 'Unless the rogues planned

73

to sneak into the house, dressed . . . I don't know, in livery perhaps, passing themselves off as servants, or even as guests. It was so crowded, no one would have noticed. Once inside, they planned to capture someone that way. But then they saw Anna and made off with her.'

'It's possible,' Winchester agreed, fondling the ears of one of his dogs, 'but unlikely.'

'The temperature is a very good reason why you and Anna shouldn't have been out there in the first place,' Nate said, scowling.

'I did point that out to Lady Annalise but she laughed off my concerns.' Clarence inclined his head. 'Your sister was anxious to avoid Roker.'

Winchester nodded. 'Roker is an idiot.'

Clarence offered a wry smile. 'Your sister agrees with that assessment.'

'But still, taking her outside in sub-zero temperatures?' Vince shook his head.

'Have you ever tried to stop Anna when she has her heart set on a particular course?' Winchester asked his brothers.

'Hmm, you have a point.' The tension in Vince's shoulders eased and Clarence knew he had been vindicated to some degree. Forgiving himself would not be so easily achieved.

'Wherever she is,' Nate said, pacing the

room like a caged tiger, 'I hope she has some light. Our sister is afraid of the dark.'

'She accidentally locked herself in a dark cupboard on the nursery floor at the Park when she was little,' Winchester explained. 'It was some time before she was found and she never got over the experience.'

'Not that she would admit it,' Vince added, a fond smile playing briefly about his lips before he returned to his scowling. 'But it's nonetheless true.'

'Dear God.' Clarence ran a hand through his hair. 'We have to find her.'

'She will be so very cold,' Nate said. 'I can't bear to think of it.'

'No she . . . damnation, that's it!' Clarence thumped his thigh with his clenched fist. 'I'm a numbskull. I should have made the connection much sooner.'

'What?' asked three Sheridans in unison.

'She was wearing Frankie's shawl.' Clarence shared a glance between the brothers. 'It wasn't Anna who was the target, but Frankie.'

6

Hearing the man casually order his underlings to *get rid of her* caused Anna's inertia to be replaced by the urgent need for action. She was damned if she would meekly sit here waiting for her own execution. She briefly considered bashing on the door and offering the men a handsome reward if they returned her to Berkeley Square. In the end, she decided against it since she couldn't be sure they would agree.

She waited until she heard the newcomer's boots ringing on the stairs as he clattered down them. She waited a little longer, listening to the other two muttering curses, expecting them to grab her at any moment. If they had been given permission to kill her, there was no saying what they might do to her before that. Shuddering as she recalled the rancid breath of the first man, the feel of his hands on her leg as he untied her ankles, she decided she couldn't afford to wait any longer. No ransom demand would be sent. No one would come to her rescue.

She was on her own.

Anna walked across to the window,

convinced with the way her luck was running that it would not open. It was stiff but, to her considerable gratification, she was able to force it open. The freezing outside air blasted her face but she welcomed the feel of freedom, so close and yet tantalisingly just out of reach. The branches were close enough for her to be able to clamber from the window and grab the nearest one, except she would fall at the first hurdle if she attempted to do so with just her flimsy lace evening gloves covering her hands. She picked up the discarded parts of the sack and bound her palms with it, leaving her fingers free. Sighing, she ripped her skirts so she could tie them around her legs, using a ribbon from her petticoats to fasten the blanket around her shoulders.

As ready as she would ever be, Anna took a deep breath and pulled herself through the window onto the ledge. It was covered with ice and, even with the rough sacking to protect her feet, she almost slid to her doom. Gasping, she grabbed the window frame and just managed to save herself. Heart pumping, she took a moment to compose herself and thought about her predicament. The nearest branch was further away than it had appeared from inside. So too was the ground. Unaware how much more time was available to her,

Anna couldn't afford to linger. Her courage would fail her, or she would freeze to death, if she didn't move right away. She lurched forward, reaching for the branch with both hands, stupidly closing her eyes at the vital moment. She gasped as her frozen fingers, stiff and unwilling to bend, made awkward contact with the frosty branch. It felt as though they had been burned, although how it was possible to burn and freeze at the same time, Anna could not have said.

One hand slipped and she found herself clinging awkwardly with the other, the fingers already so cold she didn't think she could hold on. She glanced down — a long way down to the ground below her — as the muscles in her arms screamed for mercy. If she let go she would break her legs at the very least, and that she was fiercely determined not to do. Quite apart from anything else, she refused to do her captors' work for them.

It was the thought of Lord Romsey's eyes, alight with laughter, and of his lopsided smile when she said something that amused him that gave her the courage to struggle on. She swung her legs violently, making her body work like a metronome as she continued to cling one-handed to the branch that now flexed alarmingly beneath her weight. At the third attempt, she collided with considerable force against the frosty trunk of the tree, hitting her head on the branch above her and sending snow cascading into her hair, knocking the air from her lungs. She ignored the cold ice that trickled down her neck and hugged the trunk with both arms, struggling to regain her breath. She felt mildly euphoric to have got that far. Now all she had to do was climb down the branches until she reached solid ground.

Gulping, Anna lost no time in doing precisely that. She was awkward, chilled to the bone, and her feet slipped on every branch. Her shins were bashed and bruised, as were her hands, but she ignored the discomfort and concentrated on reaching the ground. Anything was better than being contained in that small room with no light, no heat, and no prospect of being released. If those brutes wanted to kill her, they would have to catch her first.

Her fingers were so cold that by the time she was six feet from the ground, she simply couldn't hold on anymore. She slithered, almost gracefully, to the ground, rolling into a ball to break her fall. She cried out when she jolted her shoulder and her cheek fell against a drift of icy snow. Winded, she slowly sat up and took stock of her situation. All of her limbs still appeared to be in working order.

Her shoulder hurt and pain ricocheted through her when she tried to move it. But apart from that, she appeared to be in one piece.

Anna scrabbled to her feet, aware that every second could be vital. Dampness seeped into her feet, which was when she realised she had gone from bad to worse. Unless she could find shelter quickly, she would freeze to death. It had to be the coldest night in living memory and she didn't even have any shoes. She pulled the threadbare blanket over her head and held it close around her body. Then she walked. She needed to head west, away from the river, towards the better part of town. The only difficulty was, she was unsure in which direction west actually was.

Leaving the river behind her, she moved forward with weary determination, trusting her instincts to guide her. Daylight was just beginning to break but the sky was no longer clear, a fresh bank of thick cloud having rolled in. More snow was on the way. The sun struggled to break through on the horizon. The sun rose in the east, implying that she was going the right way. Buoyed by this small achievement, she walked in the lee of the tall warehouses, taking advantage of the protection they provided from the biting wind. Her feet were already frozen, the rest of her barely less so. She felt light-headed, nauseous, and utterly exhausted. She thought of home, of roaring fires, hot toast, Lord Romsey's compelling eyes, and forced herself to keep moving.

Anna noticed shadows moving in doorways and realised that people were actually trying to sleep in these atrocious conditions. Dear God, and she thought things were bad for her. She wanted to talk to them, ask where she was and if they could help her. But she did not dare. They would never believe she was in a position to help them in return. She had worn a delicate seed pearl necklace to the ball. Astonishingly she still had it on and that alone would be enough to get her killed.

And so she kept moving, eyes downcast, startled by every unfamiliar sound, noise, and smell. Ignoring them as best she could, she hoped against hope she would be mistaken for a person who lived on the streets rather than one worth accosting. A claw-like hand reached out to grab her at one point. She shrieked and pulled herself free. Cackling laughter echoed in her wake as she rushed awkwardly down the street, distancing herself from her accoster.

It felt as though she had been walking forever, although it could not have been above ten minutes. Even so, she was terrified, frozen to the marrow, and completely exhausted. Her shoulder, where she had fallen on it, hurt every time she made an abrupt move, bringing tears to her eyes. Unless she could find shelter within the next few minutes, somewhere to wait out the fresh snow she could smell in the air, she would simply lie down where she fell. The misery of being so cold had drained all the determination out of her. Even images of Lord Romsey's handsome features, relaxed as he showed her a rare glimpse of the man he could be when he was not behaving like the consummate diplomat he was trained to be, failed to revive her.

She was in a sorry way indeed.

The air was so cold it hurt her lungs to breathe it in. She saw smoke winding up from a nearby chimney and fought the urge to head in that direction and huddle against the stack. Instead, she stared ahead, at first thinking she was hallucinating when she heard gruff voices and then a horse's whinny. A little energy returned to her body as she wiped fresh flakes of snow from her eyes, peering intently into the distance. Could she have happened upon an inn? She quelled the burst of elation that erupted within her breast, having learned over the past few hours to exercise caution. But the closer she got, the more sure she became. Yes, she could smell horses! The gods were finally smiling upon her. She could demand entry to the inn and have them send someone to Berkeley Square to summon Zach. She would be safe!

Hope faded when saw two men charge up to the inn from the opposite direction and rouse the night porter. It was her captors. If they had approached from the same street as her, they would have caught her. Encouraged by her narrow escape, Anna concealed herself behind some old ale casks stacked at the side of the inn. She couldn't see the men's faces, but she would recognise those voices anywhere. It was definitely them.

'What's with all the noise?' the night porter demanded gruffly.

'My sister's gone missing,' she heard one of the men reply. 'Maid to a fine lady, so she is, but something ain't quite right in her head when there's a full moon. She pinched her mistress's old ball gown and went out in the snow dressed in it, a blanket over her shoulders. Daft as a doorpost, but I'm that fond of her. Don't like to think of her wandering the streets in this weather.'

'Dicked in the nob, you say.' The porter shook his head. 'Ain't no one like that been here.'

'Well, if you see her — ' Anna heard coin changing hands. ' — send word to . . . '

Damnation, they moved away and Anna couldn't hear anything more. But the exchange made up her mind for her. She'd been missed already and couldn't risk asking the landlord for help. He would know she was a lady soon enough, just from her voice. That fact alone was enough to work against her in this part of town, given the level of resentment harboured towards her class.

She shivered in her hiding place, waiting for her captors to take themselves off and for things to settle down again. When she considered it was safe, Anna moved forward, paused at the entrance to the mews and actually smiled at the sight that greeted her. A horse had just been brought out from a stable, presumably because its owner wished to make an early start. It was tied to a post, wearing just a halter. The groom had left it there and taken himself off. She expected him to return at any moment with the horse's saddle, but he did not.

Aware she would never get a better opportunity, Anna didn't hesitate. She slid as stealthily as a wraith into the yard, looking to left and right through the rapidly falling snow. She heard voices coming from nearby; the grooms talking to one another, complaining about the cold. Before they remembered they had duties to attend to, Anna ran up to the horse, a solid, hopefully dependable, cob. She patted its neck, unfastened the halter rope and led it away, the sound of its hooves muffled by the straw put down to cover the snow and the fresh snow covering that straw.

'Come along, sweetheart,' she said. 'Do this for me and your future is assured. All the oats you can eat for the rest of your days, and lots and lots of lovely fresh grass. The very best of everything. I promise you.'

The horse rubbed its muzzle against her aching shoulder, causing Anna to wince, but went along happily enough, probably glad to be on the move. Thanks to her brother Amos, who had indulged her when she insisted upon copying the boys and riding bareback as a child, not having a saddle wouldn't be a problem. But getting on the horse's back would be. It was too tall for her to vault from the ground, even if she didn't have an injured shoulder, but there was an upturned ale cask near the back of the inn. Just what she needed. She stood on it, glad to have had the foresight to tie her gown around her legs, and slid onto the cob's broad back.

Slapping the halter rope against its neck, she dug her frozen heels into warm flanks and encouraged the mare forward. She went willingly and Anna actually smiled, triumph sweeping through her as she turned the most beautiful horse in the world in a westerly direction. No voices came after her from the mews, demanding to know what she thought she was doing. She gave up a prayer of thanks for lazy grooms.

At last, something had worked in her favour, even if she had turned into a horse thief in the process. Zach would fix that situation just as soon as she got home. All she had to do now was *find* home. It was still not full light, so early risers couldn't see her clearly through the falling snow. Just as well. She must make a very odd sight.

Feelings of euphoria turned to anxiety when Anna realised just what a bad state she was in physically. Every jolt shot through her injured shoulder like a burning poker, making her feel dizzy enough to faint. Several times, she almost slipped down the mare's flanks but somehow found the strength to pull herself back up again. Anna wished she could trot and get away faster, but her shoulder wouldn't stand the jolting, even if it wasn't too slippery underfoot to try it. Worse, the horse was leaving tracks in the snow since the roads were still quiet, no other traffic abroad. Anyone following her would have an easy job of it.

'Let's see if we can confuse them,' Anna said aloud to the cob, feeling a little better when she heard the sound of her own voice, albeit wobbling with cold.

Confusing them ought to be easily achieved, given she still had no clear idea where she was. She turned randomly, tugging on the halter rope with her right hand to avoid further pain to her other shoulder and using pressure from her legs to steer the cob. Fortunately, the animal responded and they continued to head in what Anna hoped was the right direction. She peered through the snow at buildings that were little more than slums, unsurprised when she recognised nothing.

The warmth she had experienced from the horse's body proved to be a transitory affair and she was now colder than ever. Cold, lost and almost at the end of her tether. She was delirious, she realised with detachment, probably suffering from something incurable brought on by the cold. She thought of all those sleeping shapes she had seen in doorways and berated herself for being so weak. With good fortune, she would not have to experience anything like this ever again. Those poor souls had nothing better to look forward to. She promised herself that if she did manage to get home, she would do something positive to help the poor.

She and the horse wandered with no clear purpose for what seemed like an eternity. The streets were gradually filling with people, and she sensed more than one curious glance being sent in her direction. Fortunately, the conditions were so bad no one paused to question her, probably because they couldn't see her too clearly. She considered asking for help, but caution held her back. She had got this far using her own wits, and she would push on for a little longer.

'We need to find a bridge,' she told the cob. 'We are on the wrong side of the river.'

Much to Anna's astonishment, just after that, she came across a bridge with dim carriage lights crossing it to show her the way. Feeling euphoria burst through her frozen body, she turned the cob in that direction. But having gained the opposite bank, she still had no clear idea of where she was and continued to wander in the hope something would become recognisable. The streets were a little wider, the buildings a little less shabby, but she was still a long way from home.

'Just one more corner,' she told the horse through chattering teeth, feeling as though she was burning up, even though she was frozen. She slid sideways again, her head pounding, and almost slithered to the ground. She clung to a handful of mane and pulled herself upright, biting her lip against the searing pain in her shoulder. 'If I don't recognise anything by then, we shall just have to ask.'

Every time she heard another horse or a carriage, she panicked, thinking it would be her captors. Anna made all sorts of bargains with God, promising to be a better person, to make good on her earlier resolve to take more interest in the poor, and not to make fun of the feuding villagers in Shawford and Compton.

The wind whipped fat snowflakes across her tired eyes, blinding her. Perhaps that was why she did not immediately realise where she was. She looked up when she reached a crossroads, wondering if she could find the strength to go on, and thought she must be hallucinating. How could she have reached Piccadilly without knowing it? Elation streaked through her.

'We are safe now,' she assured the cob, patting her neck and turning her towards Bolton Street. 'I am know where I am. Home is just a little further.'

★ ★ ★

'Lady St. John?' Winchester looked at Clarence askance. 'Are you sure?'

89

'After the wars, her late husband and I were involved in the negotiations at the Congress of Vienna, and a lot of other areas that required mediation.'

'Hmm, now this starts to make sense.'

'Lady St. John would not have been involved,' Vince pointed out. 'And her husband is dead.'

Clarence lifted his shoulders. 'Political wives are privy to more secret information than you might imagine.' He managed a mirthless smile. 'Even diplomats require a confidante.'

'The events you refer to happened years ago,' Nate said. 'Why would anyone be worried about it now?'

'A very good question,' Clarence replied, scrubbing a hand wearily down his face.

'Come on, Romsey,' Vince said, striding about the room. 'You must have some idea.'

'I can make an educated guess, but have no solid facts to back it up.'

'We won't hold you to it,' Winchester said.

'Feelings are still running high about the redistribution of territories within Europe. A lot of people feel they were not treated well. I'm guessing St. John was privy to information that would show someone in a bad light if it became public. If that person is in negotiations over territories still disputed, who knows what measures he might take to ensure that information didn't become public? Petty squabbles endure, gentlemen. Take it from one who knows.'

'I agree,' Winchester said, scowling. 'But even if someone was desperate enough to try and abduct Lady St. John, the same questions apply. How could anyone possibly know she would walk on the terrace in the middle of a society ball?'

'Anyone who knows her well would be aware,' Clarence told him. 'Frankie is claustrophobic. She hides it well, but if she's in a crowded room for too long she panics and needs fresh air. That's why she always keeps a shawl on hand wherever she goes at night, so she can have a respite, no matter the weather conditions.'

'Dear God,' Winchester said in an undertone.

'Wouldn't it be easier just to snatch her off the street?' Vince asked.

'In broad daylight?' Clarence shook his head. 'I doubt she goes anywhere unattended, and whoever is behind this wouldn't risk being associated with the abduction. No, I'd wager whoever planned this was in attendance at the ball, in view of hundreds of people when Lady Annalise was mistakenly taken.'

'We need to have Lady St. John here,' Winchester said, an edge to his voice. 'If she was the real target, then she's in danger.'

'What of Anna?' Vince voiced the question that had already occurred to Clarence. 'Once they realise they have the wrong lady, she will be of no further use to them.'

'They wouldn't . . . ' Nate swallowed. 'They wouldn't do away with the sister of a duke.'

'Let's hope we don't find out,' Vince replied grimly.

Winchester strode across to a desk in the corner of the room, and reached for pen and ink. He wrote a few lines, sealed his missive, and rang the bell.

'Have this delivered to Lady St. John at the Duchess of Bexley's residence,' he told Faraday, the butler, when he responded to the bell. 'I know it's early, but I doubt if they have gone to bed yet. The ball will still be going on. I have asked Lady St. John to join us here as a matter of urgency regarding Lady Annalise. I feel sure she will come. Wait for her and ensure she arrives safely.'

'I shall see to the matter myself, Your Grace.'

'Take Paddock with you, as well as a driver,' Winchester said, clearly not prepared to take any chances with Frankie.

The Sheridan brothers looked at one another, wearing identical scowls, but no one spoke. Clarence excused himself to go outside and check with his men. Not that he expected anything to come of it, but it made him feel as though he was doing something useful. It was still dark, and a full moon shone from a clear sky. The snow had stopped, but the air was frigid.

'Where are you, Annalise?' he said aloud, feeling the full weight of the responsibility he bore for this sorry affair.

Dear God, why had it fallen to his lot to make so many enemies on behalf of an ungrateful government? Something inside him had unlocked since dancing with Lady Annalise that evening — feelings he had previously kept under close guard, not expecting to have any use for them. He had been attracted to Winchester's lively sister when he first met her in the summer, but had no intention of taking that attraction further. Clarence had no reason to marry. He did not need a lady's fortune, had no business with emotional involvement and was already wedded to his duty.

Duty and patriotism had been his father's bywords. Those same standards had been beaten into Clarence since he was in short coats and he had spent every waking moment living up to his father's expectations of him. It was too late for him to change direction now. He knew nothing else. Besides, too many people relied upon him.

Even so, the satisfaction he had once taken from resolving sensitive international situations with tact and subtlety suddenly seemed . . . well, unsatisfactory. Clarence shook his head, watching Winchester's carriage appear around the side of the house, heading for the duchess's home. Mixing with such a close family as Winchester's — feeling the affection they entertained for one another, seeing how determined the Sheridan men were to protect their sister — had left its mark on Clarence. And made him realise just how alone he actually was. Alone, but he had never felt lonely before.

Even so, he would remain true to his duty. Lady Annalise was both lovely and highly sought-after. Always assuming she survived her ordeal, she would accept an offer soon enough and establish a life for herself as one of society's leading hostesses. Clarence could then put her out of his mind and get back to that which was really important. He ignored the virulent pang of jealousy that stabbed him when he thought of her with another man. Jealousy was not an emotion Clarence was accustomed to experiencing and assumed it had put in an appearance because he was to blame for Lady Annalise's dilemma.

He strode across the road and conferred with one of his men stationed there. As suspected, he had no new intelligence to impart.

★　★　★

Clarence and all three Sheridans stood when Frankie was shown into the drawing room at Sheridan House a short time later, still in her ball gown.

'Thank you for coming,' Winchester said.

'I could not have slept a wink anyway for worrying. What news?'

'I'd best let Romsey explain what we think happened,' Winchester replied. 'But first, can I offer you refreshment?'

'Thank you, no.'

Winchester indicated to Faraday that he could leave them. He did so, closing the double doors quietly behind him. Frankie turned to look expectantly at Clarence, who lost no time in relating their suspicions to her.

'I was the target?' Frankie clasped both hands to her face, looking deathly pale and totally shocked. 'This is my fault.'

'It is *not* your fault,' Winchester replied firmly.

'If anyone is to blame, it's me,' Clarence said.

'The blame lies with the people who took her,' Winchester said. 'And we were hoping you might be able to cast some light upon who that might be, Lady St. John.'

'We feel persuaded the abduction was arranged by one of our foreign guests,' Clarence added. 'Has anyone approached you with regard to St. John's affairs recently?'

'Actually, yes.'

Four male heads turned expectantly in Frankie's direction.

'I thought nothing of it at the time, but Count von Hessel spoke with me at Lady Trumper's ball last week.'

Vince frowned. 'He's the strutting peacock who offered for Miss Outwood?'

'Ah, that makes sense,' Clarence said, almost to himself. 'I ought to have thought of it.'

'What did he want, Lady St. John?' Winchester asked.

'He commiserated with me over Gerald's death, went out of his way to be charming, saying how much he enjoyed Gerald's society.' Frankie tossed her head. 'Not so very good as it transpired, since it got him killed. However, I thought nothing of it.'

'Presumably he said something that made

96

you change your mind,' Clarence said.

'He would keep mentioning Gerald's name, which I thought was rather indelicate of him.'

'Quite so,' Winchester muttered.

'He then asked me what had happened to Gerald's papers. He supposed they had been passed on to officials at the Foreign Office. I told him that must be the case.'

'Did he seem satisfied with your answer?' Clarence asked.

'He changed the subject but then came back to it later, sounding a little too casual, now I think of it. He asked if my husband kept diaries, or any personal papers. I thought the question impertinent, and it made me uncomfortable, so I didn't answer him. Then others joined us and he couldn't ask anything else.'

'Well then, it must be the count who has Anna,' Nate said, scowling.

'Can you think of any reason why he would be so concerned about . . . excuse me, Lady St. John, a dead diplomat's papers, Romsey?' Winchester asked.

'Not offhand but I dare say — '

The door opened and all heads turned in Faraday's direction. 'What is it?' Winchester asked.

'Mr. Pierce is here, Your Grace, desirous of

a word with Lord Romsey.'

'My secretary,' Romsey said, standing. 'Excuse me, Frankie, gentlemen. He is co-ordinating the search for Lady Annalise and might have news.'

Clarence chose to speak with him out of the earshot of the others. If the news was not good then it would be better if he heard it first. He ran down the stairs and found his secretary in a greatcoat covered with fresh snow, standing in the entrance vestibule.

'What is it, Pierce?' he asked.

'I have men asking everywhere,' Pierce replied, shaking his head. 'But the weather has kept most villains quiet tonight, and those that are about claim no knowledge of a lady being abducted.'

'Damnation!' Clarence paced the length of the hall, staring through the window at the snow falling outside. With each hour that passed, his fears for Lady Annalise multiplied exponentially. 'There must be someone, somewhere, who knows something.'

'We are still asking, but — '

'What the devil?'

He blinked, thinking at first that he was imagining things. A cob walked slowly down the middle of the snow-covered square, with what looked like a ragamuffin almost sliding off its back. Some sixth sense told him who that ragamuffin was, even though he wasn't close enough to see clearly. Clarence inhaled sharply, pulled off his coat and raced for the front door. He tore through the snow in his indoor shoes, much to the astonishment of Pierce and the men he had stationed in the square. He reached the cob and grasped its halter, bringing it to a stop.

Lady Annalise, for he knew it was her, even before she lifted her head from beneath the thin blanket that covered it, slid from the cob's back, into his waiting arms. Dear God, she was frozen to the bone, barely alive. She screamed when her shoulder touched his body. Clearly, she had injured it, so he gently lowered her to her feet, supporting her with one arm as he draped his coat around her. He then scooped her carefully into his arms again, keeping the afflicted shoulder away from his body.

'You're safe now,' he said, wondering if that was actually true. Clarence's heart lurched. Damn it, she couldn't die!

'So cold,' she muttered, her blue lips lending support to her words. 'So cold.'

And then, she lost consciousness.

7

Clarence turned to his men. 'Stable that cob in His Grace's mews,' he said curtly. 'It must belong to someone. We might be able to trace who took her if we find out where it came from. Then await my orders.'

He carried Lady Annalise into the house, thanking a God he was unsure he believed in any more for her safe return. If she *was* safe. She was suffering from extreme exposure to the elements, had injuries the extent of which he had yet to conjecture, and her recovery was far from certain.

'Faraday,' he yelled, as soon as he was through the door. 'Blankets, warm water. Warm, not hot, mind.'

Sheridan males spilled from the drawing room on the floor above to see what the commotion was about.

'My God, it's Anna!' Nate cried, leading the charge down the stairs. 'Let me take her.'

'I've got her,' Clarence replied. 'Let's get her into the drawing room.'

'Is she all right?' Winchester asked.

'Exposure,' Clarence said succinctly. 'We need to warm her up.'

'She's unconscious,' Vince said. 'How did she get here?'

'Later.'

Clarence carried her into the drawing room and sat her beside the fire. Faraday burst in, carrying the blankets himself. Clarence grabbed one, removed his coat and the tatty, soaking wet rag from around her shoulders, and replaced it with a thick, dry blanket.

'Lady Annalise,' he said urgently. 'Wake up. You can't sleep now.'

'Let her sleep, damn you!' Nate cried.

'He's right, Nate.' Winchester placed a restraining hand on his brother's arm. 'We need to keep her conscious until we're sure she's warm. If she sleeps, she might not wake up.'

'Oh, right.'

'Have the fire banked up, Faraday,' Winchester barked. 'Send someone to rouse Her Grace, and send word to Doctor Fisher.'

'Hot broth, too,' Clarence added just before Faraday left the room. 'But there's something else we need to do before we try to bring her round,' he told Winchester. 'She's put her shoulder out. It might be better if she's unconscious while I put it back again.'

'Shouldn't the doctor do that?' Vince asked.

'I've done it before. Lady Annalise will be

more comfortable if I do this before we try to warm her.'

The brothers shared a glance. 'Do it,' Winchester said curtly.

Clarence took a deep breath, then gently but firmly grasped Lady Annalise's left elbow and wrist. Slowly he rotated her lower arm until he felt resistance. When he did so, he nodded to Winchester, who placed a restraining hand on his sister's other shoulder.

'Ready?' he asked.

'Go ahead,' Winchester replied. 'I have her.'

Clarence forced his mind to go blank. This was not the lady who had occupied so many of his thoughts recently, but a stranger, and he could fix this. Thus resolved, he lifted her upper arm as far forward as possible and rotated her forearm to bring her hand towards her opposite shoulder. There was a sharp click and a louder scream from Lady Annalise. She was definitely conscious now. Her eyes flew open but appeared unfocused, hazy with pain.

'I'm so sorry,' Clarence said, crouching beside her, still holding her arm. 'But that should feel better now.'

'Clarence?' The frozen fingers of one hand clawed at his sleeve. 'Am I dreaming?'

'No, Anna. You're home.' Winchester crouched on her opposite side and stroked her wet, tangled hair. 'You're safe now.'

'So cold,' she muttered, her teeth chattering. Both wolfhounds pressed their bodies against her legs, as though instinctively trying to warm her. Lady Annalise closed her eyes and sighed. 'Everything hurts.'

'Shush, I know.' Winchester replaced the blanket over her shoulder. 'Brandy,' he said to Vince.

Clarence lifted the glass that Vince handed him to Lady Annalise's lips. 'Take a sip,' he encouraged. 'It will warm you.'

She appeared delirious, a jumble of words spilling from her lips that made no sense, and he was unsure if she even heard him. Sharing a concerned glance with Winchester, he forced the glass to her lips and tipped. A little must have trickled down her throat because she spluttered. More trickled down her face. Clarence was filled with rage when he noticed her cut lip and the bruise forming on the side of her face. Someone had obviously struck her. Clarence intended to discover who that someone was and ensure everyone involved paid a heavy price for their cowardly act. He was a diplomat, given to winning arguments through intelligent mediation. The determination he felt to resort to physical violence took him by surprise. Let the bastard responsible for hurting Lady Annalise take on someone his own size and see how he fared then.

'Frankie, we need to warm her feet,' he said, pushing aside his murderous thoughts. 'Can you remove that sacking around them, and her stockings, please?'

'Of course.'

The gentlemen turned their backs while Frankie crouched down and did as Clarence asked.

'Dear God, her shins are scraped and bloody, but I don't think the damage is too severe. There are rope marks around her ankles.' Frankie looked up, her eyes blistering with anger. 'Someone tied them very tightly.'

'Her wrists too,' Clarence said, disgusted when he saw the chafing on her delicate arms.

'Wash her lower legs and feet with a warm towel, please, Frankie. Rub them briskly to get the circulation going, and then wrap her feet in dry towels.'

Before Frankie could complete that task, the duchess came into the room. She looked haggard yet composed, until she saw the condition of her daughter. Tears then streamed down her face.

'My poor love,' she said, shooing Winchester's dogs aside and crouching to take a frozen hand in hers. 'Whatever happened to you?'

The two ladies bathed and dried Lady Annalise's legs and feet. When Clarence examined her face again, he was relieved to notice a little colour returning to it. But she still wasn't fully cognisant.

'Don't burn that!' At Clarence's sharp command, Nate's hand arrested halfway towards the fire, onto which he had been about to throw the sacking that had bound Lady Annalise's feet. 'It might lend a clue as to where she was held.'

'We know who held her,' Vince growled. 'We shall be paying Count von Hessel a visit just as soon as we're sure Anna is all right.'

'And what do you imagine he will say if we do?' Winchester asked.

'Is that who took her?' the duchess asked at the same time.

'We don't know for certain yet, Your Grace,' Clarence replied, slipping into his diplomatic persona.

'You may not be certain,' Nate snarled, 'but I am.'

'Don't jump to conclusions, Nate,' Winchester advised. 'Our first priority is to ensure Anna recovers. Then we shall decide what's to be done.'

Clarence nodded his approval as he unwound the sacking from one of her frozen hands and patted it briskly between both of his own. Winchester mirrored his actions with her opposite hand.

'She has a nasty gash on her forearm,' Winchester said.

Clarence looked and nodded. 'At least the cut on her lip is superficial and won't leave a scar.'

'Can we not warm her up in a bath?' the duchess asked.

'No, Your Grace,' Clarence replied. 'We need to warm her gradually. I would not recommend bathing until tomorrow, but the doctor will be able to advise you better.'

'Does she have frostbite?' Nate asked.

'It's a close run thing, but I hope not.'

'Then why the devil doesn't she respond?' Vince demanded to know.

'Quite apart from anything else, she's exhausted. I suspect, from the state of her, that she escaped from wherever she was being held and found her way home in the middle of a blizzard.'

The three brothers shared an admiring glance. Clarence felt inclined to join in, but was careful to keep his expression neutral. The Sheridans' initial euphoria at having their sister returned to them was quickly turning to anger at her condition. Clarence suspected blame would again be apportioned to him, which was only right and proper since that was where it belonged.

'Oh my goodness!' The duchess took in Clarence's words and looked close to losing consciousness herself. 'The poor, poor child.'

'Her determination held until she got home. Now she feels safe, her body has closed down so it can heal.' Or at least, Clarence ardently hoped that was the case.

Faraday came in with the broth Clarence had asked for.

'Make sure there's a good fire in Lady Annalise's room,' Winchester told him. 'Have the bed warmed, and put plenty of blankets on it.'

'Arrangements are already in hand, Your Grace.'

'Lady Annalise.'

Still holding her hand, which was gradually warming, Clarence squeezed it and spoke loudly to his brave, damaged, totally exhausted angel. Eventually her eyes fluttered open and this time they looked a little less cloudy.

'Lord Romsey?' She blinked. 'Where am I?'

'Sheridan House,' the duchess said, wiping away tears. 'You are quite safe now, my love. Take a little broth. It will warm you.'

When the duchess placed the spoon to her lips, Clarence was pleased to see a few sips slide down her throat.

'No more,' Lady Annalise said, pushing the

spoon away. 'I feel like I will choke on it.'

'Doctor Fisher,' Faraday said from the doorway.

The doctor introduced himself to Anna. Having examined her, he dressed her various cuts, declaring none needed stitching, and said she was warm enough to be removed to her chamber.

'She ought not to be left alone overnight,' he said. 'Call me again if her situation deteriorates.' He packed up his bag, shaking his head. 'Terrible business. I don't know what the world is coming to.'

Once the doctor left, Winchester went to lift his sister from her chair but Lady Annalise raised her arms towards Clarence instead. The brothers exchanged another of their speaking looks.

'I'll show you the way,' Winchester said curtly.

Clarence gently picked Lady Annalise up. She was as light as a feather but thankfully more aware of her surroundings than when he last lifted her. The duchess followed them up the stairs.

'Her maid and I will take turns watching her,' she said.

'What happens now?' Vince asked when Clarence and Winchester returned to the drawing room.

'We wait until later today, when hopefully Lady Annalise will be able to tell us more about who took her and where she was held. Then we will decide.' Clarence yawned. 'In the meantime, I suggest we all get some sleep.'

'I have arranged a chamber for you here, Lady St. John,' Winchester said. 'Faraday has sent round to the Bexley residence for your things. I would be happier if you remained with us until we get to the bottom of this matter. You were the target of this atrocity and I feel responsible for your welfare.'

Frankie nodded. 'I feel responsible too, despite what you say. Anna should not have had to suffer on my account.'

'I shall return this afternoon,' Clarence said, shaking Winchester's hand. 'Hopefully Lady Annalise will be in a position to talk to us then.'

★ ★ ★

Was she dead? When Anna felt an agonising pain rip through her shoulder, she wished she was. But she was fairly sure one didn't feel pain once one died. Now the pain had gone completely and she could move her shoulder again. Yes, definitely dead then, but it was almost worth it to be rid of the pain. And to feel warm again.

Strong arms lifted her, carrying her up a flight of stairs, murmuring reassurances in a melodic voice that soothed her. A rich voice that haunted her dreams. It sounded like Lord Romsey, and smelt like him too. A rich, spicy masculine aroma she would always associate with that reserved, highly intelligent, suave and sophisticated gentleman. He had a surprisingly solid chest, or at least the version of him who was carrying her up the steps to heaven could certainly make that boast. She snuggled more closely against it, clutching the lapels of a coat that felt surprisingly real.

Damnation, he had put her down. Why did good dreams always end too soon and the bad ones endure? Female hands peeled away her clothing. A warm shift and warmer nightgown were pulled over her head. Then she heard her mother's gentle voice. Surely, she wasn't in heaven, too? Her eyes flew open. The familiar surroundings of her chamber at Sheridan House came into view, as did the even more comforting sight of her mother's face.

'Oh, my dear. How do you feel?' the duchess asked. 'You gave us all such a fright. The boys were beside themselves. No one knew where to look for you, or who had taken you.'

'I feel chilled to the bone still, but not as

badly as before,' Anna replied, her voice weak and trembling. 'But I am very glad to be home.'

Mama hugged her. 'I don't know how I would have borne it if I had lost you, my love.'

Anna sniffed, feeling tears flood her eyes and emotion squeeze her heart. 'I'm not going anywhere.'

'No, you are not. Now, let Fanny brush your hair and then you can sleep. I shall be here with you all the while and when you wake you will feel much better.'

Anna groaned with pleasure when she felt a brush being pulled through her tangled hair. Nimble fingers braided it and tied it off with a ribbon.

'Come on, Anna.' Mama took her arm. 'Into bed with you.'

Anna groaned again as she slid between blessedly warm cotton sheets.

'Drink this, my dear. The doctor said it would help you to sleep.'

Too weary to put up objections, Anna obediently drank down the concoction. Every bone in her body ached and she still wasn't warm enough. Even so, she immediately felt drowsy, which surprised her. She had imagined she would be plagued by visions of her ordeal, which would prevent her from sleeping. As it was, she fell asleep almost as soon as her head hit the pillows.

★ ★ ★

When Anna woke, the curtains were closed but she sensed it was night-time. Fanny was seated beside the bed, sewing. She smiled when she realised Anna was awake.

'How do you feel, my lady?' she asked. 'We were that worried about you. The whole house was in uproar.'

'I'm hungry and in need of a bath.'

Fanny jumped up, beaming. 'Both of those things can be easily arranged.'

'What time is it?'

'Eight in the evening, my lady.'

'Where are my brothers?'

'Downstairs in the drawing room with Lord Romsey and Lady St. John. They will be pleased to know you're awake.'

'Don't tell them yet, Fanny. I want to eat, bath, and dress. Then I shall go down and they will be able to see me for myself.'

'Oh, my lady, do you think that's wise?'

'I have no intention of being interviewed in my bedchamber, Fanny.'

Anna felt weak, yet determined. All the things she thought she had dreamed were most likely true. It *was* Lord Romsey who had carried her up the stairs. She had a vague notion it was he who fixed her shoulder also. She rotated it now as she waited for Fanny to return and found it hardly hurt at all. He really was the most remarkable man, full of surprises. But he would not be permitted to visit her in her bedroom and she very badly wanted to see him. Even Zach, usually the most level-headed of men, couldn't be trusted to resolve this matter because he would be as angry as her other brothers about what had happened to her. It needed a cool, intelligent head to decide what ought to be done, especially if foreigners were involved. That was definitely Lord Romsey's forte. It most definitely did not require one of her hot-headed brothers fighting duels to avenge her abduction — something she would not put past Nate in particular.

Pleased that her cognitive powers appeared to have been restored to her, Anna sat up and reached for a thick shawl that was draped across the bed. She wrapped it around her shoulders, wondering if she would ever feel truly warm again. Fanny returned with a tray, which she placed over Anna's lap. There was more broth, fresh bread and pastries to tempt Anna's sweet tooth. She had felt hungry when she awoke but now she had food in front of her she found it hard to eat. She pushed the tray away again, having not taken very much. She did however drink two cups of tea, which revived her.

'Ah, you are awake.' Her mother and sister joined her. The duchess frowned when she saw how little Anna had eaten. 'Is that all you can manage?'

'For now. I will have something else later.'

'How do you feel?' Portia asked.

'Unlike you two, not ready to go dancing quite yet,' Anna replied, observing that she and her mother were both dressed in evening gowns.

'Zach insists we maintain appearances,' Portia responded, wrinkling her nose. 'Lady Sampson has a *musicale* this evening. Naturally, the boys would not be seen dead there, but Mama, you, and I have already accepted. We think the horrible count will be there with Miss Outwood and Zach says that if we behave as normal, it will make him wonder why we're not more concerned about you.'

Anna jerked upright. 'Lord Romsey thinks the count was the one who abducted me?'

'That is one possibility.'

And one that had occurred to Anna, also. 'It wasn't me they intended to abduct, but Frankie,' she said, gulping back her anguish.

'Shush, my dear.' Mama patted Anna's

hand. 'Don't overset yourself.'

'What excuses will you make for me?'

'You are indisposed with a sick headache.' Portia grinned. 'I dare say the event will be packed with your admirers. Men who would not normally go near such an event. They will be devastated by your absence, but will have no choice but to sit through the performance.'

'Don't tease your sister, Portia dear,' Mama chided gently.

Portia grinned, unrepentant. 'However, Zach has charged me to watch the count's reaction carefully and report back to him.'

'That will take your mind off the music.'

'I certainly hope so.'

Anna managed a brief smile. 'You are not supposed to be so jaded in your first season, Portia.'

'Shall you mind us leaving you, Anna?' Mama asked.

'Not in the least.' Anna saw fine lines around her mother's eyes that she had not previously noticed. Usually so poised and elegant, so very much in control of her emotions, tonight Mama looked every one of her sixty years. Her determination to get to the bottom of what had happened to her increased when she saw how badly her mama had been affected by the experience. Anger, she discovered, was a good way to overcome fear and physical debilitation. 'Personally, I have no intention of setting one foot outside of this lovely warm house until the temperature has risen by at least twenty degrees.'

'That's not to be wondered at.'

They spoke of general things for a few minutes more. Neither Mama nor Portia plagued her with questions about her ordeal. They must have known the gentlemen were waiting to do so and didn't ask her to relive it twice. She had sworn Fanny to secrecy and so they could have no idea she planned to go downstairs this evening. Mama would most certainly try to persuade her against it and Anna was not strong enough for arguments.

'Your bath is ready, my lady,' Fanny said, removing Anna's tray.

'Right, Anna, we shall leave you to your ablutions.' Mama kissed her forehead. 'You just relax and I'm sure that by tomorrow you will feel much better.'

'I am sure I shall. Enjoy the evening, if you can, and happy sleuthing, Portia.'

Portia grinned good-naturedly and followed her mother from the room.

Anna found her legs most reluctant to support her weight but refused all offers of assistance from Fanny. She walked the short distance to her sitting room, where a bath had been filled for her in front of a roaring fire. Anna shed her night clothes and groaned with pleasure as she sank into the warm water. Fanny washed her all over, including her hair, and Anna gladly submitted to her skilled ministrations.

An hour later, clad in her warmest gown, her hair dried and tied back with a ribbon, she glanced in the mirror and winced. She barely recognised the pale creature who stared back at her through haunted eyes. Her lip was cut and swollen where that brute had struck her, and a colourful bruise covered half of one cheek. The other was red with angry grazes where her face had come into harsh contact with the ground when she fell from the tree. Her wrists were sore from where they had been tied, her fingers fat and clumsy.

But she was still alive. Alive and ready to fight back. She pulled a thick shawl around her shoulders, walked through the door Fanny opened for her and slowly descended the stairs.

'Welcome home, my lady,' Faraday said, materialising as he always did when a member of the family was anywhere around. He smiled and opened the drawing room door for her.

'Thank you, Faraday.'

She paused on the threshold. Her brothers, Lord Romsey and Frankie were engaged in intense conversation.

'What are you five plotting?' she asked.

'Anna!' Zach bounded across the room and hugged her. 'What the devil are you doing down?'

8

Clarence stood back as the Sheridan males greeted their sister with fierce hugs and questions about her health, none of which she adequately answered. She turned to Frankie instead and as he watched them embrace, Clarence was consumed by a fresh bout of guilt. He had let her down, neglected her, and she had suffered a terrible ordeal as a consequence.

Winchester took his sister's hand and led her to a chair beside the fire, where she was greeted by his dogs.

'You should not have come down, Anna,' he said gently.

'I know you must have questions for me,' she replied, absently fondling one of the dogs' ears. 'It would be better to get them over with so you can decide what's to be done.'

'They can wait until you're feeling better,' Nate said.

'I have a slight headache, my fingers feel stiff and awkward, and I am a little shaky. But,' she added, tilting her chin defiantly, 'I am home, I am alive, and I *will* recover. I know this business has greater implications because I was not the intended target — '

'You know that?' Zach asked before Clarence could.

'Certainly I do, and I thought Lord Romsey might need to hear what I have to tell you.'

Her eyes sought him out, wide yet bruised, flaring with anger and something more fundamental. Clarence was unable to hold back a smile of admiration for her courage and quick thinking. Most females recovering from the type of ordeal she had experienced would take to their beds for a week. Lady Annalise appeared more concerned about the implications than about her own recovery. She was, quite simply, remarkable.

Something passed between them when their gazes clashed but Clarence wasn't entirely sure what that elusive emotion could have been. He had never experienced anything quite like it before. He prided himself upon understanding every nuance of a person's body language — it was a necessary qualification for any aspiring diplomat — and yet Lady Annalise surprised him at every turn. He thanked every deity he could name for her safe deliverance, simultaneously boiling with rage when he observed the damage to her lovely face. She appeared vulnerable, indescribably endearing, and resolutely determined all at the same time. Clarence had never met another woman remotely like her and found himself caught up in a web of fascination that was both distracting and dangerously addictive.

'All right then, Trouble,' Winchester said with a resigned sigh. 'I know better than to argue with you when you set your chin in that particular manner.'

'Well, of course you do.'

Everyone took seats close to her. Clarence noticed dark shadows beneath her eyes, blending in with the colourful bruise on one side of her face and angry red scrapes on the other. Her fingers were red raw, but he had seen men suffering from similar cases of exposure and was confident that she would recover — physically, at least. The demons bound to invade her mind whenever she closed her eyes would take longer to exorcise.

'Did I do something to my shoulder?' she asked. 'I remember feeling a lot of pain.'

'You put it out somehow,' Zach told her. 'Romsey here put it right for you.'

'Thank you, my lord,' Lady Annalise said politely. 'I am grateful for the relief from pain.'

Clarence inclined his head. An inappropriately capricious mood gripped him and he was sorely tempted to wink at her. Good heavens, whatever was the matter with him? Clarence did not wink at ladies, not ever, and especially not in situations such as this.

'It was the very least I could do,' he assured her, managing not to wink.

All three of her brothers glared at him, a situation to which Clarence was becoming accustomed.

'Do you feel up to telling us what happened to you?' Zach asked.

'Most assuredly.' Lady Annalise took a deep breath and explained how she had been literally plucked from the terrace. 'I was so surprised that at first I didn't do anything to resist. Then I fought like the devil but the person who had grabbed me hit me so hard that my head swam. By the time I recovered my senses, he had subdued me, and there was nothing I could do.' She pulled a disgruntled face. 'Although, I tried very hard to kick him. Then a sack went over my head and I was thrown into a carriage, tied hand and foot. I had no idea where they took me, although I tried to keep track.'

'It was incredibly brave of you, given the circumstances,' Vince said.

'It was a carriage with a single horse, probably a curricle, and we travelled mostly at walking pace for about thirty minutes. We finished up somewhere close to the river. I

122

could smell it. They took me into a warehouse and made me keep the sack over my head while they cut my bonds. They said if I saw them, it would be the worse for me.' She related events in a matter-of-fact tone, but when she got to the part about it being the worse for her, she shuddered, lending a clue to just how alone and terrified she must have felt. 'I believed them.'

'It was sensible of you not to test them,' Clarence said, nodding his approval.

'Once they locked me in I removed the sack but the room was in complete darkness. I couldn't see a single thing.' Her face drained of what little colour it possessed and she now looked truly petrified. Her brothers had not exaggerated. She really was scared of the dark. Clarence felt ready to burst with renewed anger at what she'd had to endure. 'It was the worst experience of my life,' she added simply, tears brimming.

'You poor thing.' Frankie leaned forward and grasped Lady Annalise's hand. 'I can't think how you endured it.'

She lowered her head and concentrated upon petting one of the dogs. 'My perilous situation helped me overcome my fear of the dark. I mean, I couldn't just passively sit there without trying to discover where I was. And so I felt my way around the room and found it was some sort of storeroom. There was a window but unfortunately I was on an upper floor with no obvious means of escape. My captors told me someone would be coming to talk to me later but they did not say whom. I was relieved to discover they didn't mean to . . . ' She gulped, her eyes hazy with suppressed fear. 'Well, to . . . you know, but couldn't think why anyone would go to so much trouble just to speak with me. I assumed they wanted a ransom and couldn't understand why they didn't just say so immediately.'

Her eyes were huge, unfocused, and her hands trembled. Clarence ached to go to her, to wrap her in his arms, apologise until his voice gave out and comfort her in any way that he could. But, of course, that was impossible. He was glad when Winchester got up and poured a glass of water. He handed it to his sister, placing a hand on her shoulders and gently massaging them until her body ceased to tremble. She sipped at the water and gradually regained her composure. Putting the glass aside, she continued to speak.

'I heard the two men speaking in low voices on the other side of the wall but I couldn't make out what they were saying. I was frozen to the marrow, with both cold and fear, but unbelievably I must have dozed off. When I awoke, I was able to see a little. The storm had passed and the moon shone through the window. I was then able to confirm I was definitely in a warehouse and there was a tree right outside the window.'

The brothers exchanged another of their looks that rendered words unnecessary.

'Please tell me you didn't try to climb out of the window,' Vince said for them all.

'Not at that point, no.'

She went on to explain how another person had arrived. 'He was furious because they had abducted the wrong lady, which was when I realised this wasn't about me and there must be graver implications that you would understand, Lord Romsey.'

'They wanted me,' Frankie said. 'I am so very sorry you got caught up in this, Anna.'

She flashed a brief, mirthless smile. 'I doubt you have much experience at climbing trees. I, on the other hand, had the example of four older brothers to guide me.'

'She followed us around like a shadow, insisting upon involving herself in our pursuits,' Nate said, leaning down to ruffle Lady Annalise's hair.

'Your pursuits were far more interesting than the ones Portia and I were supposed to follow,' she replied, the dullness in her eyes replaced by a brief glimpse of mischief.

'What else did the new arrival have to say for himself?' Clarence asked.

'I heard him berate his men for their foolishness. They defended themselves by saying he had told them to abduct a lady wearing a colourful shawl who would be walking on the terrace at some point. That's how I knew it was you they wanted, Frankie.'

'Yes. My habit of taking the air is no secret.'

Winchester muttered something unintelligible and probably unrepeatable in mixed company.

'Then I heard him tell them to dispose of me, as though I was a piece of unwanted merchandise.' Lady Annalise shuddered, her expression a combination of fear and outrage. 'I was of no mind to sit obligingly by and allow them to dump me in the river. I cannot swim, you see. Nate tried to teach me when we were children but I seemed determined to sink. Be that as it may, desperation can make one inventive.'

All three brothers turned accusatory glances towards Clarence when she calmly explained how she had escaped by climbing through the window, negotiating a snow-covered tree and then promptly falling from it, dislocating her shoulder.

'Oh for the love of God!' Lady Annalise glowered at her brothers. 'Will the three of you please stop frowning at Lord Romsey. This is not his fault, and you are being most unreasonable in blaming him. He tried very hard to return me to the ballroom before speaking with his secretary but I was determined to remain outside. If I went back inside Lord Roker would have cornered me and recited more of his terrible poetry.'

'Better that than — '

'*You* have never had to listen to Lord Roker's odes, Vince. If you had, you would understand.'

Her brothers all smiled. 'Well, I suppose that did give you a legitimate reason to linger out of his reach,' Nate said grudgingly.

'Quite so. What happened to me was unfortunate but no one is to blame, except perhaps me for being so stubborn.'

'I must disagree,' Clarence replied. 'If you wish to claim responsibility then you must join a queue, Lady Annalise. I agree with your brothers and blame myself, you see, and Frankie blames herself. We are both ahead of you. But in actual fact, the blame lies with the person who ordered Frankie's capture.'

'Quite so,' Lady Annalise said with a wan little smile that near broke his heart.

'And so, little sister,' Nate said, 'you found

yourself inadequately clothed, in the dead of night, in a district of London you didn't know. You must have been terrified. How the devil did you find your way home?'

Lady Annalise explained about the inn, and *borrowing* the cob.

'You didn't think to ask for help?' Winchester asked.

'You saw how I was dressed.' She lifted her shoulders with apparent caution, as though expecting pain. Clarence was pleased none appeared to be forthcoming when she visibly relaxed. 'It seemed too risky. I didn't know whom to trust, especially when my captors appeared and bribed the night porter at the inn. I suspected he would be more likely to support their cause than mine, even if I could prove who I was.'

'Good thinking,' Vince said, nodding his approval.

'I'm glad you took the horse and had the sense to head west,' Clarence said. 'I shall make enquiries at inns close to the wharf, find out who is missing a horse and arrange for its return.'

'No!'

'I beg your pardon, Lady Annalise?'

'No, please don't return the horse. Don't let him do that, Zach,' she cried passionately. 'That horse saved my life and I promised her that if she carried me safely home she would have oats and fresh grass for the rest of her life.' Lady Annalise brushed a tear from her swollen cheek, showing more emotion at the prospect of losing the cob than she had while recounting her entire ordeal. 'I want to keep her. Recompense the owner, by all means, but please don't send her back. She and I have formed a bond, you see.'

'Certainly you may keep her, Trouble,' Winchester replied.

'Thank God Amos taught you to ride bareback,' Nate said.

'I knew that skill would serve me well one day,' Lady Annalise replied with a flash of her former spirit. 'I was able to guide the horse, mostly just using the pressure of my legs.'

'I will find the owner, smooth matters over and make the necessary recompense from my own pocket,' Clarence said.

Lady Annalise treated him to a radiant smile, even though it probably hurt her swollen lip to do so. Being the recipient of enticing feminine smiles was not a new experience for Clarence. He was popular with the ladies and had his needs, just like any other man. But he was as diplomatic in his romantic liaisons as he was in every other aspect of his life. He didn't boast about his conquests and *never* even thought about forming attachments to unmarried ladies. In spite of that, Lady Annalise's uncontrived smile affected him in the time-honoured manner. He turned briefly away, hoping the evidence was not . . . well, evident to her, or to any of her brothers. They were already looking for a reason to flog his hide.

'Thank you, Lord Romsey,' she said. 'That is very generous of you.'

'My pleasure.' He returned her smile. 'Once we find the inn, we will have a better idea where you were held. Do you know how long you walked before you came upon the tavern? Would you be able to find it again?'

'She's not going back there!' Vince sent Clarence a murderous glare. 'She has been through quite enough already.'

'It's possible,' Lady Annalise replied, ignoring her brother's outburst. 'It would look very different in daylight, I dare say, but I do remember one or two of the places I passed.'

'Vince is right,' Winchester said. 'It would serve no purpose to return, other than to upset you. Besides, there cannot be many warehouses with large trees growing beside them.'

'There are more than you might think,' Clarence told them. 'But you are right, it would be inappropriate for Lady Annalise to return there. Forgive me. I should not have made the suggestion.'

'Actually, I would like to go.' Lady Annalise's eyes clouded again and she appeared very upset. 'Zach, you can have no idea of the sights I saw. Such wretched creatures sleeping outside in those freezing temperatures. It was actually the sight of them that gave me the courage to carry on. I found myself exposed to the elements for one night. They live like that the whole time and somehow manage to survive. But for how long?' She gave her head a determined toss. 'We have so much. We must do more to help people who cannot help themselves.'

'Our mother is already involved with all manner of charitable causes,' Winchester reminded her. 'I am sure she would welcome your help.'

'Bah, it is not enough! When we visit institutions for the poor in Winchester, they know we are coming and we see only that which they think we ought to. Last night I saw real poverty, real desperation.' She shook her head. 'Those sights will never leave me.'

'We can discuss it, by all means,' Winchester replied softly. 'When you are feeling stronger.'

'I thought perhaps a foundation set up by the family to help the very neediest children.'

Clarence came as close as he would ever allow himself to falling in love at that moment. After all this delicate young lady, cosseted and protected for her entire life, had been through, her thoughts were not for herself but for those less fortunate. Remarkable!

'So, there you have it.' Lady Annalise shared a glance between them. 'That is all I can tell you about what happened to me. Now, perhaps you will have the goodness to explain why you think Count von Hessel was behind my abduction, which is what Mama implied earlier. What did he think to gain by forcibly taking Frankie captive?'

Anna watched Zach pour drinks for them all. She was the only one to refuse. She observed Lord Romsey in the periphery of her vision, looking as suave, as handsome as always. But the worry lines etched in his forehead told a different story, as did the stormy set to his features. No doubt her abduction — a case of mistaken identity — had its roots in some diplomatic disaster or other he would be required to untangle, ensuring the British government didn't become embroiled in some unseemly situation or, God forbid, somehow compromised. Anna felt for him excessively. It seemed very unfair he should have to do so much.

'The count spoke with Frankie a few nights ago, asking about her late husband's papers,' Lord Romsey explained.

'You think they contain something to his detriment?' Anna asked, frowning.

'That I have yet to discover.' Lord Romsey stood, looking magnificent in his blue coat and superbly tied neckcloth. He also looked tired. She suspected he had not slept much since her abduction. Working, always working. She was quite determined to do something to change that situation. 'I have people looking into his family's circumstances in the new Prussian territories.'

'Do you actually have any of your husband's personal papers, Lady St. John?' Zach asked.

'Yes, but I have never looked at them. They are in a locked box in Farrington House.'

Poor Frankie, Anna thought. She had not been widowed for very long. If she was unable to look at her husband's papers it was probably because it upset her too much, or because reading his diaries would invoke painful memories.

'Would you object if I looked at them, Frankie?' Lord Romsey asked. 'You have my assurance that I won't snoop into St. John's personal affairs more than is absolutely necessary.'

'By all means.' Frankie spread her hands. 'After all the trouble I have inadvertently caused, I can hardly refuse.'

'I shall send an express to Amos,' Zach said, 'asking him to bring them to London himself.'

'Oh, but he and Crista didn't wish to come to London,' Anna said. 'I'm sure a servant could collect the papers.'

'No,' Lord Romsey replied. 'If the count is as determined as we suppose, it can only be a matter of time before he thinks to look to your country estate, Frankie. If he is desperate enough to resort to abduction, there's no telling what lengths he might go to in order to obtain St. John's papers. You ought to write a note to your servants, advising vigilance and giving Amos permission to collect that box.'

'I shall do so immediately.'

'Are things really that dire?' Anna asked, reluctant to accept the fact.

Lord Romsey fixed her with a smouldering look that made Anna's heart beat a little faster. 'You know they are,' he said softly.

'I am sure money must be part of the problem,' Anna said, feeling heat invade her face.

'What do you mean?' Nate asked.

'Well, the count thinks very well of himself, am I right?'

Everyone nodded. 'People either adore him, or are disgusted by his pride,' Frankie said.

'I am willing to wager those who do the adoring are mostly impressionable young ladies.'

'What are you getting at?' Vince asked.

'I'm not entirely sure.' Anna wrinkled her brow. 'The count's engagement to Miss Outwood will make him a very wealthy man. She was widely courted because of her huge dowry, details of which her mama ensured were circulating the *ton* before her daughter made her come-out. Yet she chose to accept the count and appears infatuated by him.' Anna paused. 'The same most definitely cannot be said of the count. Ergo, he must need her money.'

Zach seemed impressed by her reasoning. 'Very possibly,' he said.

'Perhaps Portia will learn something more about him at the *musicale*,' Anna mused.

Zach laughed. 'I very much doubt he will give anything away in public. I only suggested our mother and Portia watched him to ensure they went out this evening and didn't hear the particulars of your ordeal, Anna.'

Anna smiled up at her brother. 'That was thoughtful.'

Lord Romsey stood. 'You must all excuse

me. Now I know in which district you were held, Lady Annalise, I must prepare for searches to be made at first light.'

'Keep me informed,' Zach said.

'Certainly, and you must let me know the moment Frankie's papers arrive.' Lord Romsey turned to Anna, took her hand and kissed the back of it. 'I am so very glad to see you looking better,' he said softly, holding her captive with his eyes for a prolonged moment.

'I hope I shall see you again very soon. I would like to find the location where I was held.'

'Let's see how you feel tomorrow,' Zach said. 'Then we can decide.'

'I shall call tomorrow for the same reason,' Lord Romsey told her before turning to Frankie and taking his leave of her also.

'Try to stay out of trouble, Clarence,' she said drolly. 'I know you when you get your teeth into a problem. Nothing and no one will divert you until you find a solution.'

'Which makes me very good at what I do.' He pushed a silky lock of dark blond hair away from his scowling eyes. 'The count would do well to remember that.'

The suave diplomat was permitting his emotions to show. Anna watched his broad back as he turned to leave the room, wishing for an excuse to make him stay. Nothing sprang to mind. She abruptly looked away from Lord Romsey. Unless . . . until she was sure her feelings were returned, she would not humiliate herself by making them apparent to her relations.

The object of her affections reached the door, looked back over his shoulder and sent her another of his disarming, lopsided smiles. Anna's insides melted.

'Anna,' Zach said, sounding amused when the door closed behind Lord Romsey and she was still staring at it. 'You ought to return to your room and rest.'

9

Talking about her ordeal had driven away the residue of Anna's fear, and she was now every bit as determined to expose the perpetrators as her brothers and Lord Romsey were. Exhaustion washed through her as she slowly climbed the stairs and returned to her room. Fanny was waiting to treat her scrapes with Doctor Fisher's ointment and then helped her into bed.

'I have another sleeping draft the doctor left for you.'

'No thank you, Fanny.'

'Her Grace said to be sure you took it.'

'I don't want it. You may leave me. I won't need you again tonight.'

'No, ma'am, I cannot. Her Grace gave strict instructions that you were not to be left unattended.'

'And I am telling you otherwise. Refer the duchess to me if she tries to blame you.' She clapped her hands. 'Now shoo, off to your own bed.'

'Very well, my lady.' Fanny looked undecided. 'If you are sure.'

'Perfectly sure. Good night.'

'Good night, my lady.'

In spite of feeling so weary, Anna lay wide awake for a long time, staring at her bed's canopy, counting her blessings in a way she hadn't done since she was a child. Unlike the wretched souls she had seen shivering in the streets last night, she now felt snug, safe, and blessedly warm. She wriggled her toes and pulled her knees up to her chest, nestling more comfortably beneath her pile of covers. She was battered and bruised, but those bruises would heal. The mystery as to why the count was desperate enough to resort to kidnap would endure, but finer minds than hers were working to unravel that particular riddle.

Anna's thoughts dwelt instead upon the delicate matter of winning Lord Romsey's heart; something she was now quite determined to attempt. She was sure he enjoyed her society and seemed genuinely upset by her ordeal, but that wasn't enough to satisfy Anna. She required him to let his guard down, put his admiration for her ahead of his duties and admit to his feelings. Always supposing he entertained any.

Anna thumped her pillows into a more comfortable nest and scowled with determination. There was only one way to find out. Even if he was aware of the attraction he felt, which was far from certain because men could be so silly about these things, Anna knew he wouldn't act because ... well, because he was too serious, too honourable, too everything that she wasn't. Well, they said opposites attracted. There, she had diagnosed his problem. Now, all she had to do was make him equally aware of it. Unfortunately, her freedom would be severely curtailed until the marauding count and his underlings had been arrested, and Anna had no idea how long that would take.

On the brink of falling asleep, an idea occurred to Anna: a rather reckless manner in which she and Lord Romsey could be thrown together. If being kidnapped had taught her nothing else, at least she had learned life was precious. It most definitely ought to be grasped and lived to the full.

Anna drifted off to sleep with a smile on her cut lips and a plot incubating in her brain.

The rattle of the drapes being opened woke her the following morning. Judging by the brittle sunshine that flooded the room, it was another crisp, cold day. Conscious of another person close by, she blinked sleep from her eyes and found her mother seated beside her.

'Mama, what time is it?'

'Good morning, Anna. It's gone eleven.

How do you feel?'

'Goodness, I must have slept for more than twelve hours.' Anna sat up and stretched. 'How unusual.'

'Heavens, child, after what you went through, I'm not in the least surprised. I only asked Fanny to open the curtains because it's time to dress your poor wrists and ankles.'

'I'm glad you woke me, Mama. I don't want to sleep the day away.'

'I hear you went downstairs last night,' the duchess said on a note of mild censure.

'I knew my brothers would be anxious to learn all the particulars of my adventure.'

Mama shuddered. 'I would hardly call it an adventure.'

'Well, anyway, it seems it is all to do with some diplomatic business that Lord Romsey is working to unravel.'

Anna's mother sent her a probing, speculative look. 'I am sure he is.'

'Would you care for some breakfast, my lady?' Fanny asked.

'Yes please, Fanny.' Anna still didn't have much of an appetite, but pretended otherwise to please her mother.

'I shall be back directly,' Fanny said, beaming.

'How was the *musicale*, Mama? Did Portia get anywhere with her investigation?'

'Unfortunately not. The count and Miss Outwood sent their apologies. A last-minute invitation to dine at Carlton House kept them away.'

Anna wrinkled her nose. 'I had heard the count was a favourite of the prince's. I dare say they deserve one another.'

'Lord Roker was all for dashing round here last night when he heard you were indisposed,' Mama said, fighting a smile.

Anna rolled her eyes. 'I hope he didn't go home and compose more of his dire poetry.'

'You are being unkind, my dear. He means well.'

'You wouldn't say that if you had to listen to his poetry.'

Mama's smile defied her best efforts to contain it. 'Most likely not.'

Fanny returned with Anna's breakfast.

'I shall leave you to eat in peace,' Mama said, standing. 'I suppose it's pointless to suggest you remain in bed today?'

'Absolutely.' Anna clasped her mother's hand. 'Don't worry, Mama. I feel so much better. I can even flex my fingers, *and* they have been reduced to their normal size again. Well, almost.'

'That is something, I suppose.'

Once her mother left her, Anna toyed with her food while plotting her next move. When she had eaten sufficient, she had Fanny remove the tray, attend to her scrapes and help her wash and dress. Anna then seated herself at her escritoire and reached for pen and ink. She had written this letter many times in her head last night, and now committed those words to paper with the same single-mindedness she had employed as a child when determined to join in her brothers' games.

Lord Romsey, she wrote. *I woke disgustingly late this morning, having slept through the night with no bad dreams to disturb my repose. Mama tells me the count and Miss Outwood dined at Carlton House last night. Clearly, the count is intimate with the prince. I'm not sure if that is significant and, anyway, I don't suppose I'm telling you anything you did not already know.*

Mama also tells me I must expect a visit from Lord Roker this afternoon and I fear that more terrible poetry will set back my recovery. Besides, how am I to explain away the state of my face if I am seen by any of society's elite? A solution to both problems occurs to me. I am more determined than ever to revisit the East End and discover the location of my prison in the hope that it will aid your investigation. It is in this respect that I write to beg your intervention.

If you have any desire to be of service to me, can I prevail upon you to call immediately after luncheon and conduct me to that district? Don't worry about my brothers causing difficulties. Vince and Nate make themselves scarce in the afternoons, taking refuge at their club to avoid the ladies who call on the pretext of seeing my mother, Portia and me, but whose real purpose is to show themselves to my brothers. Zach will probably keep guard over Frankie, leaving us at our leisure to explore to our hearts' content.

If more pressing matters prevent you from keeping the engagement I shall, of course, be pleased to excuse you from it. Although she had no intention of giving up that easily.

With best wishes, Annalise Sheridan.

Anna took a deep breath before sealing her missive, feeling as though she was sealing a very great deal more than a letter of questionable validity written to a single gentleman. Mama would be horrified if she knew, but given the circumstances, Anna felt the usual rules seemed rather stringent.

Besides, she really couldn't face receiving callers when she was still so battered and bruised. Rumours would abound as to the cause of her injuries and all the trouble her family had taken to keep her abduction secret

144

would have been in vain. More than one young lady resented Anna's popularity and would be happy to orchestrate her downfall by spreading rumour and innuendo that had no basis in truth.

But what if Lord Romsey refused her? Well, Anna decided, if he didn't grasp this chance to be alone with her, he wasn't the man she thought him to be and she would forget all about him.

'Fanny,' she said. 'I need your help.'

'What is it, my lady?'

'I need you to have this note delivered to Lord Romsey in Moon Street.'

Fanny's eyes widened. 'My lady!'

'Don't look so shocked. It is to do with what happened to me, but I don't want the duke or any of my brothers to know about it. They will only make a fuss. Can you trust that nice young footman you walk out with to deliver it for me without Mr. Faraday finding out?'

'How did you know . . . ' Fanny blushed scarlet. 'How did you know about Peter, my lady?'

'I saw you together in the park on your afternoon off. You looked very happy.'

Fanny's blushed deepened. 'I hope you don't think I'm acting improperly.'

'Not in the least. The duke doesn't mind

what his servants do in their own time, just so long as they behave respectably.'

'I don't allow Peter to take liberties.'

Anna bit her cut lip to hold back a smile. 'I am very glad to hear it.'

'This letter you want Peter to take . . .' Fanny dithered for a moment, then nodded decisively. 'Leave it to me, my lady. I shall make sure Lord Romsey gets it. Should Peter wait for a reply?'

'Yes please.'

Fanny slipped the letter into her pocket and left the room. Anna remained where she was, reading a book. She didn't want the reply to arrive when she was with the rest of her family. They would want to know who was writing to her and she would prefer not to indulge in an untruth. As it transpired, Portia joined her in her room just before Fanny returned with the promised response from Lord Romsey.

'A secret admirer?' Portia asked, raising a brow.

'Shush, Portia, you mustn't say anything. I'm plotting a little investigating with Lord Romsey, but if Zach were to find out before I'm ready to tell him — '

'I understand.'

'You are not going to try and talk me out of it?'

Portia laughed. 'I know you too well to waste the energy.'

'Good, because I mean to discover where it was that I was held. Always assuming Lord Romsey isn't too frightened of Zach to agree to the scheme.'

'I can't imagine him being intimidated by anyone. Mind you, he lost his composure completely when you went missing, which is not something I expected to witness.'

'What did he do?' Anna propped one elbow on her knee and leaned towards her sister, keen for any snippet of information about the object of her affections.

'He didn't fume and rant in the way Vince and Nate did, but something very dark and dangerous moved behind those intelligent eyes of his. His voice became very quiet, very clipped, and he had people running all over London trying to locate you. I expected, at any moment, for him to call out the guard in his quest to find you. Were it not for Zach insisting the particulars of your abduction be kept confidential for fear of ruining your reputation, I believe that is precisely what he would have done.' Portia grinned. 'I am convinced he must be in love with you.'

'Lord Romsey only loves his occupation. I expect he was frantic because I was in his care when I was abducted; nothing more.'

'Oh, Anna, you goose!' Portia sighed. 'Well, are you not going to open your letter?'

'When I have some privacy.'

'Ah, I see.' Portia's smile was full of satisfaction.

'You see nothing at all. Now go away and tell Mama I shall be down directly.'

'I do hope I am right, about Lord Romsey's intentions, I mean. If you were to accept his offer, I could then enjoy myself without being compared to you the entire time and being found wanting.'

Anna elevated one brow. 'Fishing for compliments, Portia?'

'Not at all. I just wish nature had been a little fairer in the distribution of her favours between the two of us, that's all.'

'If that had been the case, I might be cleverer and I would then be able to bandy words with Lord Romsey on more equal terms.' Anna clapped her hands at her sister, shooing her from the room. 'Now, go!'

Finally alone, Anna broke Lord Romsey's seal and read his letter, written in the neat, legible hand she expected of him.

Lady Annalise, she read. *I rejoice to learn of your swift recovery, although I cannot persuade myself you are yet completely well. Be that as it may, I fully intend to call at Berkeley Square this afternoon to update*

Winchester on the intelligence I have gathered thus far. Provided your brother does not object, and always assuming I consider you equal to the strain, and I shall not know whether you are until I have seen you for myself, then it would be my pleasure to drive you to the East End this afternoon.

After all you have been through, the very least I can do is offer my services in an effort to save you from yet more poetry.

Yours etc., Clarence Vaughan.

Anna read the letter twice, nodded with satisfaction and hid it away inside the cover of her journal. That was the first part of her plan accomplished. Now for the difficult part. She was well aware she could not go with Lord Romsey unless Zach permitted it and she hadn't wanted to ask his permission until she knew his lordship was willing.

She left her room and ventured downstairs in search of Zach. She noticed her mother, sister and Frankie ensconced in the small sitting room that overlooked the snow-covered back garden, deep in conversation. She slid past the entrance without being seen and headed for Zach's study, hoping to find him there without any of her other brothers to join forces against her. She was in luck. Zach was seated behind his desk, studying a pile of papers. He looked up when she walked in and smiled at her, then walked round the desk to take both of her hands in his.

'You look far better this morning,' he said, examining her face closely. 'Your eyes are brighter and there is more vitality about you.'

'My bruises are brighter, too,' she said with a small laugh, touching the one on the side of her face that had turned various shades of purple, yellow, and black.

'It means you are healing. Come and sit beside the fire. How are your fingers?'

She held them up and wiggled them about. 'Much better.'

'You're here for a reason,' he said after a brief pause. 'I can tell. I suppose you know there was never a better time to ask a favour of me, if that is your intention. We are all so pleased to have you back with us that there is little I could refuse you.'

Anna fiddled with the tail ends of the shawl she had knotted over her shoulders. She focused her eyes on her fingers, fearful of revealing too much about her personal feelings when she was unsure if they were reciprocated.

'He is quite the most intelligent man it has ever been my privilege to know,' Zach said into the ensuing silence, a smile in his voice.

Anna's head shot up. 'Whatever do you mean?'

150

'You came here to talk to me about Romsey.'

'First Portia, now you. Am I that transparent?'

'Your reaction to Romsey when you met him in the summer was remarkable enough to stick in my memory. You are inundated with attention from gentlemen, none of whom seem to interest you. But Romsey held you in awe right from the first.'

Anna saw no point in denying it. 'You say he's intelligent, but then so are you.'

'Romsey is in a class of his own. He has no siblings, and his mother died when he was quite young, so he had nothing to distract him from his studies.'

'That must have been very lonely for him.'

'He excelled in every subject at school,' Zach said with a wry grin. 'He didn't even seem to make any effort, which was very annoying for the rest of us. He joined in with our escapades, but also kept himself apart, if that makes any sense. He told me once that he couldn't remember a time when he had not been destined for the diplomatic service.'

'He seems to be very good at what he does.'

'Oh, he is. That's why he is so indispensable to the government.'

'That hardly seems fair. He is entitled to a

life of his own too. Apart from his diplomatic efforts, he also has to try and keep the peace in Hampshire. It is too much for one man.'

'I doubt whether Clarence sees it that way.'

'Perhaps if he spent some time with a close, loving family such as ours he would begin to understand what he has missed all these years.'

'What are you scheming now?' Zach shook his head. 'Romsey is much older than you.'

'But so much more interesting than the vacuous men of my own age. Besides, he is the same age as you, which is not so very much older. Frankie's husband was twenty years older than her.'

'Lady St. John, as I understand it, was pushed into the union by her parents when she was still only seventeen. Unlike you, I very much doubt if her passions had been aroused.'

'Zach!' Anna felt colour flood her cheeks. 'What a thing to say.'

Zach chuckled. 'If I can't tease my own sister — '

'I want to go and look for the warehouse, Zach,' she said in an abrupt change of subject.

Zach's relaxed attitude, his easy smile, instantly faded. 'I'm not sure about that.'

'I need to put what happened into perspective.'

'I understand that, but don't you think it's too soon?'

'If you want to catch the people behind the plot, then the sooner the better. Best not give them time to cover their tracks.'

Zach rubbed his chin, quiet for a long time. 'All right, Anna. I shall take you this afternoon.'

'Thank you, Zach, but I want to go with Lord Romsey.'

Zach elevated both brows. 'And you know he will be free to take you, how, precisely?'

A capricious smile flirted with Anna's lips. She made no attempt to remove it, partly because she knew Zach would find it harder to refuse her if she allowed pleasurable anticipation to show. 'Oh, something tells me he will call early this afternoon, and I need your permission to go with him. Quite apart from establishing the location of the warehouse, there is the matter of my lovely cob to be resolved. And, I have also decided to teach Lord Romsey how to relax. It's quite shocking what a slave he is to duty.'

Zach shuddered. 'God help him.'

Anna beamed at her brother. 'Precisely.'

Zach stood up and ruffled her hair. 'Very well, Trouble.'

Anna blinked. 'Are you agreeing? Just like that?'

'There are few men in England I would permit you to be alone with, but it just so happens I would trust Romsey with . . . well, with my own sister.'

10

Lady Annalise's letter took Clarence completely by surprise. Her willingness to flout convention by writing to him said much about her independent character, and more still about her determination to get to the bottom of this matter. He imagined her concern would be for Frankie, since it was she who would remain in danger until the puzzle had been solved.

The prospect of driving her to the East End was more enticing than it ought to have been. But it would not be wise, simply because he didn't trust himself to behave with decorum — a difficulty he had never before encountered in his admittedly limited dealings with unmarried innocents. He did not have time to waste on flirtatious dalliances, and restricted his relationships to females who were in a position to receive his advances without expectation of permanency.

But there was something about Lady Annalise that got beneath his defences. For the first time in his recollection, the appeal of putting his own interests ahead of duty and responsibility was truly compelling. He blamed those plump lips of hers that just cried out to be kissed, her beguiling smile, her lively wit — everything delicious thing about her. Damnation, he had so many important affairs to attend to in this politically unstable time, and absolutely did not require such distractions.

He had been careful not to agree to her suggestion, having already persuaded himself that she would not be well enough to undertake such an emotionally distressing excursion. Besides, Winchester would never permit it unless he accompanied them. Clarence would then be obliged to disregard his lustful intentions and they might actually discover the location of her imprisonment. God alone knew, he had not yet managed to unearth a single piece of information regarding the identity of the abductors and was starting to feel a little desperate.

The door opened to admit Pierce.

'What news do you bring me?' he asked, guessing from Pierce's dour expression that he wouldn't wish to hear it.

'Still no word of a missing cob, and we are no closer to identifying the warehouse where Lady Annalise might have been held. The wharf is so extensive. It would help if we had some idea which part of it she was taken to.'

'No word from any of our contacts?'

Clarence stood up and paced the room. 'I find it very difficult to believe that no one knows anything about the abduction. Keep the pressure up, Pierce. Make sure all the ne'er-do-wells understand they will not be left alone until we learn something that will help us. Increase the cash rewards on offer for information. Something has to break.'

'Has anyone at the Foreign Office found anything to Count von Hessel's discredit?'

'Quite the reverse.' Clarence ran a hand through his hair and sighed, unable to maintain his composure. He had faced far graver situations than this one, especially during the war years, and had always remained icily calm. But, despite what the lady herself insisted, no one would convince Clarence he was not responsible for her capture. That made this personal. 'The damned man is highly regarded in all quarters. The prince loves him, which is good reason for the current government to find something to his detriment if they possibly can, but so far he appears to be the war hero he claims to be.'

'Are we absolutely sure he was behind the abduction? He was not recognised, has been behaving perfectly naturally in the interim, and if we cannot discover why he thought it necessary to kidnap Lady St. John, then I'm sure no one can.'

'I'm not entirely sure about anything.' Clarence threw up his hands. 'There are other foreigners in London, the damned place is packed with them. But Lady St. John doesn't think any of them, apart from von Hessel, knew of her habit of walking terraces in colourful shawls. I am just now reading through some of my own papers to see if I can find cracks in his background.' Clarence picked up the depositions he had taken from various soldiers under von Hessel's command after Waterloo and waved them about in frustration. None of them revealed anything to the man's detriment. 'But no one is that perfect!' Clarence slapped the papers back down on his desk and sighed. 'There must be something.'

'If there *is*, we will find it eventually.'

Clarence's manservant, Sampson, put his head round the door and announced that luncheon was ready. Clarence walked through to the dining room with Pierce. Both men sat and ate quickly, Clarence's mind now focusing on his forthcoming visit to Berkeley Square.

'I shall be visiting Winchester immediately after luncheon,' he told Pierce. 'Have the town coach brought round, drive it yourself and arrange for a reliable man to be up behind. It is possible Lady Annalise will return to the East End with us to see if she can identify her prison. I don't want to take any chances with her wellbeing on this occasion.'

'I will make the arrangements immediately,' Pierce replied.

Clarence kept only one permanent man-servant in his Moon Street apartment, his bachelor needs being simple. Sampson fulfilled many roles, including that of valet, employing as many other servants on a daily basis as he saw fit. Clarence stabled his horses, and kept his carriage, in a nearby mews.

Pierce took himself off as soon as he had eaten and organised the carriage. A short time later, it arrived outside Clarence's front door. Clad in his greatcoat, Clarence accepted his hat and gloves from Sampson and walked the short distance to the conveyance. The temperature had risen by a few degrees and winter sunshine was rapidly thawing the snow. At least the roads were now clear. The man Pierce had chosen to ride behind opened the carriage door for Clarence. He climbed aboard and Pierce encouraged the horses forward.

Clarence was inexplicably nervous about seeing Lady Annalise again, which was perplexing. He was *never* nervous. She was a chit of a girl — spirited, beautiful, and lively enough to make him feel dull by comparison — but that hardly explained the desperate determination he felt to earn her respect. Clarence shook his head. It made no sense. No sense at all.

The ride to Berkeley Square was a short one, affording Clarence little opportunity to settle upon an explanation that *did* make sense. A methodical, rational man, Clarence disliked being unable to account for any part of his behaviour almost as much as he disliked not being in control of his reactions. His father had routinely taken a strap to his backside for acting impetuously, effectively beating all impulsiveness out of him.

'Facts, my boy,' he could still hear his father booming. 'Facts are the only things that signify. Establish those and do not be swayed by emotion.'

Clarence never had been. Until now.

Faraday admitted Clarence to Sheridan House and conducted him to the drawing room. To his considerable surprise, only Winchester and Lady Annalise were in occupation of it. Clarence had expected to be confronted by three angry Sheridans and the duchess, all demanding to know what progress he had made. He glanced at Lady Annalise, wondering if she was responsible for the reprieve, recalling how she had taken her brothers to task for blaming him for her abduction. She was dressed in a stylish, warm-looking walking gown and her hair had been dressed partially to cover the injuries to her face.

The lady sent him a radiant smile that caused all other considerations to flee from Clarence's head. *Do not be swayed by emotion,* he heard his father caution. Clarence ignored the warning and concentrated on Lady Annalise, allowing intense feelings that were as pleasurable as they were inexplicable to course through him. The look she sent him was recklessly sensual and it was quite beyond Clarence not to react to it. She looked so much better today but the sight of her ugly bruises, visible in spite of her maid's best efforts with her hair, made him frown.

'I am pleased to see you looking much more like yourself,' he said, bowing over her hand. 'And your fingers are better, I see.'

'Thank you, Lord Romsey. I feel a great deal better and quite ready to help find the location of my prison, if only to remind myself of the obstacles I overcame. How very annoyed my captors must have been when they discovered I was missing.'

'A perfectly natural reaction.'

'What news do you bring for us?' the duke asked.

'Frustratingly little.' Clarence spread his hands as he selected the chair on the opposite side of the fire to Lady Annalise. 'So far, the count is proving to be everything he purports to be. I have people combing through my

161

archives. If that proves fruitless, I hope the papers Amos brings from Frankie's home will throw some light on the matter.'

'Let us all hope for that,' Winchester replied with feeling.

'I saw the Foreign Secretary this morning and informed him of your abduction, Lady Annalise. He was most put out about it, sends you his apologies, Winchester, and wants to be kept informed. He has given me free access to just about any record I need to examine.'

Winchester nodded, looking grim. 'Whatever concerns the count will not be held on record anywhere,' he said, echoing Clarence's own thoughts. 'You would have found a clue of some sort by now if it was, Romsey.'

Clarence nodded. 'I keep coming back to his Prussian roots. Do you have any idea, Lady Annalise, where Miss Outwood and the count plan to live when they are married? Do they intend to settle in England or Prussia?'

'I'm sorry, no. Miss Outwood and I are not intimate, but I can ask her the next time our paths cross.'

'You can't return to society until your bruises are healed,' Winchester reminded her.

'No, but Mama and Portia plan to attend Mrs. Davis's party this evening. I expect Miss Outwood will be there. Portia could ask her.'

'That wouldn't be wise,' Winchester said. 'If von Hessel overhears the conversation, he will know we suspect him. He knows you were abducted in error, Anna, and will expect us to try and discover why.'

Lady Annalise wrinkled her pert little nose. 'How very disobliging of him.'

Winchester laughed. 'Romsey will get to the bottom of this affair. I have every confidence in his abilities.'

'As do I.'

'Then I shall endeavour not to disappoint you both.'

Lady Annalise indulged her enticing habit of biting her lower lip, seeming to forget it was cut. Clarence found the gesture very sensual and hoped she didn't notice his inappropriate reaction to it. Damnation, he had no right to entertain the possibilities that sprang to mind but, for once, was unable to discipline his thoughts to matters of actual fact. Or rather, he was. Lady Annalise biting her lower lip was exceedingly arousing.

Fact.

'Botheration, I so wanted to suggest something that would be of use,' she said.

'She wants to go to the East End and see if she can identify the warehouse where she was held,' Winchester said. 'Are you willing to take her, Romsey?'

Clarence was surprised by Winchester's readiness to go along with the plan. Astonishingly, it did not sound as though he planned to be a member of the excursion. 'Her suggestion has your approval?'

Winchester slanted a resigned glance in Clarence's direction. 'She can be very determined.'

'Do you think she's well enough to withstand the emotional trauma?'

Winchester lifted his shoulders. 'She can be insufferably stubborn when she decides upon a course of action.'

'Well then, if I have your permission, we might as well attempt it.'

'Even if you find the warehouse, the owner is probably ignorant about the use it was put to.'

'You are probably right, but perhaps the men who actually carried out the abduction have some connection with it.'

'That's true enough, but with regard to Anna — '

'Oh, for goodness sake, you two! Please stop talking about me as though I was not in the room, or perfectly capable of speaking for myself.'

Clarence's lips quirked. 'I apologise, Lady Annalise.'

'Apology accepted. Now, we are wasting

time. I would like to leave before Mama discovers our plan. She's bound to make difficulties if she learns of it.' Lady Annalise stood up. 'If you will give me a moment, Lord Romsey, I shall fetch my outdoor garments and we can leave at once.'

Clarence stood also, watching her as she bustled from the room, wondering what he had just committed himself to.

'Try not to lose her this time, Romsey,' Winchester said in an indolent tone.

★   ★   ★

Fanny awaited Anna in the adjoining small sitting room, Anna's bonnet and warmest pelisse at the ready. The bonnet she had selected sported a small half-veil that partially concealed Anna's bruises and, hopefully, added an air of sophistication to her appearance. She was already wearing her thickest wool walking gown and warm half-boots. Her pelisse was fur-lined vivid blue velvet with matching muff.

With her gloved hands tucked into her muff, she was as ready as she would ever be for her first sortie outside since her abduction. Was that only two nights ago? It felt like half a lifetime. Well, she thought, as she adjusted the angle of her bonnet, at least one good thing had come out of it. She would never have been permitted to ride in a carriage with Lord Romsey — alone with Lord Romsey — under any other circumstances.

She found Zach and Lord Romsey awaiting her in the vestibule.

'Are you warm enough, Trouble?' Zach asked.

'Yes, don't worry. I am perfectly sure Lord Romsey will take care of me.'

'He had better,' Zach muttered in an undertone.

Faraday's expression was impassive as he opened the front door, but Anna knew him well enough to discern disapproval beneath his bland features. Why was everyone in this household so determined to blame Lord Romsey for the fate that had befallen her? It was most unreasonable of them. His only crime was dedication to King and country; a circumstance which Anna fully intended to alter, starting with this opportunity she had created for herself.

'The weather is a little warmer today, Lady Annalise,' Lord Romsey said, taking her elbow and escorting her down the front steps. 'And my carriage is very warm.'

He led her to the conveyance and helped her inside. Naturally, he took the seat with his back to the horses, having first insisted upon tucking a blanket over her knees.

'Thank you,' she said as the person she recognised as Lord Romsey's secretary drove the carriage off at a steady trot. Clearly, he was a man of many talents. She was equally sure the tough-looking individual who had opened the carriage door for them and then hopped up behind was more than a mere groom. Lord Romsey was taking every possible precaution.

'Are you comfortable?' he asked.

No! 'Perfectly so, except it might serve better if you sat beside me.' She waved a gloved hand in dismissal of the protest she sensed him formulating. 'Oh, I know that is not the accustomed way, what with your not being related to me. It's just that I want you to see the same view as me at the same time, just in case something looks familiar.'

He sent her a speaking look, and she thought he would refuse. Then, with one of those lopsided smiles of his that gave his normally impassive, albeit brutally handsome countenance the boyish appearance that so appealed to her, he did as she asked. She was immediately conscious of his muscular thigh in very close proximity to her own, of the breadth of his shoulders, and the raw masculine power that emanated from him.

Anna's insides churned with a bewildering paradox of pleasure and deep longing. Far from being too cold, she suddenly felt in danger of overheating.

'Is everything all right, Lady Annalise?' he asked in a provocative tone that implied he knew perfectly well the effect he had upon her.

Anna tilted her chin, prepared to play him at his own game. At least for now. 'Indeed. You have made me very comfortable.'

His gloved hand briefly covered one of her own. 'I realise just how difficult this must be for you, but if it becomes too much we can turn back at any time. You have nothing to prove to anyone.' He lowered his voice to a compelling purr. 'Certainly not to me. I admire your courage, and your bravery.'

But not me?

Anna swallowed. 'Perhaps I need to prove something to myself,' she said softly.

'That is perfectly understandable.' He held her gaze for a moment longer, then turned away to stare at the passing streets. 'You say you found yourself and your cob in Piccadilly. Can you recall which street you approached it from?'

'Unfortunately not. I must have been delirious by that point and cannot recall much about it. It was Betty who found the way.'

'Betty?'

'That is what I have decided to call my cob.'

He smiled. 'Betty it is then.'

They left the smarter part of town behind them and Pierce slowed the carriage to walking pace as the streets got progressively narrower. Anna's breath hitched in her throat, her fear palpable as the reality of what she had agreed to do was brought into startling clarity by the scenes outside the carriage window. Sensing her anxiety, Lord Romsey removed one glove and ran his forefinger down her bruised face with a feather-light touch that made her insides melt with raw desire.

'My brave Annalise,' he muttered softly. 'So beautiful. You do not deserve this.'

'Anna,' she replied. 'Everyone calls me Anna.'

'But I shall not. You have a beautiful name.' The pad of his thumb traced the line of her lips so gently she could almost have imagined his touch. 'Why would I wish to shorten it?'

He thinks I am beautiful. His words imbued Anna with renewed courage. She tore her gaze away from the blazing intensity in his eyes. The streets were crowded with vendors, urchins, people bundled up against the cold, hurrying about their business, and all imaginable forms of transport — everything from handcarts to fine carriages. The roads were noisy, dirty and very different to her recollection of the cold misery two nights previously. Even so, she knew that misery was still lurking there, waiting for the sun to go down so it could continue to wreak havoc.

'We really have to do something,' she said, shaking her head and brushing aside tears.

'We will. Your brothers and me. You can involve yourself as much as you wish.'

She sent him a disbelieving gaze. 'Do you mean that?'

'I never say anything I don't mean.'

She laughed. 'I'm sure you are far too diplomatic to be so rash.'

Lord Romsey sighed. 'Most likely.'

'I'm sorry, Lord Romsey. I didn't mean to mock your achievements, or imply criticism of who you are.'

'Of course you did not.' He sent her a devastating smile. 'Now, we are getting closer to the wharf. Do you recognise anything?'

'Will this carriage not stand out in such a district?'

'At night-time it would, if I was foolish enough to bring it here. But at this time of day, all manner of people go to and from the docks, transacting business. No one will think it odd.'

Satisfied on that score, she peered through the window but shook her head. 'Nothing looks familiar. How could it not?'

'You had more pressing matters on your mind at the time of your escape.'

'Yes.' She paused, conscious of the street smells permeating the inside of the carriage, and wrinkled her nose. 'I recognise the putrid smell, but I don't suppose that helps much.'

'Not a great deal, unfortunately.'

They turned another corner, and Anna could actually see the river, its water grey and angry-looking as melting snow drained into it. Several ships swung on their anchors, waiting to offload their cargos. She could also see lines of warehouses dotted along the wharf and instinctively stiffened. So many of them. It was sheer folly to imagine she could recognise one when she hadn't even seen it properly. There were more trees than she had expected interspersed between the buildings, too. Even so, a sense of *déjà vu* gripped her. She had been in this spot before, and very recently, too. She knew it without understanding why.

'Ask Pierce to turn left,' she said, sitting forward expectantly.

Lord Romsey leaned out of the window and gave the instruction.

'And now right,' she said, her excitement

increasing. 'I think this is the way I came. I recognise that doorway. The most wretched creature was asleep there. I shall never forget that.'

'How long after you escaped?'

'Almost immediately.' She peered through the window, and pointed. 'There!' she cried triumphantly. 'That tree there is the one I climbed down. I would know it anywhere.'

11

Clarence tapped twice on the roof of the carriage with his cane, the signal for Pierce to drive back to a smarter district.

'Are we not going to get out and make enquires?' Lady Annalise asked.

'You are not going anywhere near the place. Nor am I for that matter. We don't want whoever owns it to know we are on to them. I shall send one of my people to ask questions later on.'

'I suppose that would be best.' She sent Clarence a wide-eyed look. 'But how will you find it again?'

'I asked Pierce to drive in this direction for a specific reason. Given the amount of time you said the carriage took to bring you here, it seemed as good a place as any to start.' He glanced out of the window. 'Did you really climb down that tree, in the snow, in the dark with nothing but sacking on your feet?' He shook his head. 'Quite remarkable.'

'Certainly I did, and there was nothing remarkable about it. I was very adept at climbing trees when I was younger.'

Clarence smothered a smile. 'Evidently.'

'I was vexed to slip and displace my shoulder. How did you know how to fix it?'

'I was not always a safe distance away from the fighting.' Clarence spoke with a lightness he didn't feel as he recalled some of the horrors he had witnessed. 'The battle of Château-Thierry was a total disaster for the allied forces. I happened to be there. The field hospital was overrun, and I did what I could to make myself useful. A harried doctor showed me how to put various joints back into place.' He shook off the images conjured up by that battle's name, recalling Prussian forces had played a leading, not especially heroic, role in it. 'Don't worry. You were not my first victim.'

'I am very grateful to you.' She looked away from him. 'But you still have not told me how you will find this warehouse again.'

'We are at New Gravel Lane now and the tree you used as a staircase is in Cotes Gardens. We shall find it easily now we know where to look. And, if I am not much mistaken, there is an inn along here on the right which must be the establishment from which you liberated Betty.'

Lady Annalise was quiet as the carriage made slow progress along the busy thoroughfare. Her hand trembled and he instinctively clasped it in one of his, but only because she required comfort. The fact that he had been fighting the urge to touch her ever since he foolishly agreed to sit beside her had absolutely nothing to do with his decision.

'It's all right,' he said softly. 'You are perfectly safe in this carriage.'

'You make me feel safe, Lord Romsey,' she said, her eyes luminous, compelling. A man could drown in such captivating eyes if he didn't have a care.

'Even though I have already let you down?'

'It is you who ought to be disappointed in me. I never did learn to do as I am told.'

Clarence was at a loss to know what to say, a circumstance so unusual as to give him pause. In his time as a diplomat he had dealt with disquieted monarchy, heads of state who wished to tear one another to pieces, squabbling politicians of all persuasions, and had always known precisely what to say to defuse sensitive situations with tact and humour. And yet, a mere slip of a girl had left him speechless. Remarkable!

'There, up ahead, is the Three Bells,' he said pointing, glad of the opportunity to speak about something more mundane. 'Does it look familiar?'

She bit her lip again and nodded. 'That is where I concealed myself when I heard my captors talking to the night porter.' She pointed to a pile of barrels at the edge of the mews. The hand he was clasping continued to tremble. 'I am absolutely certain about that.'

'Then I shall be able to make the appropriate recompense for the loss of Betty and you will then own her.'

'Thank you, but I am sure Zach will be happy to pay.'

'Perhaps, but I insist.'

'Very well,' she said softly. 'Have it your way.'

Clarence tapped his cane twice on the roof and Pierce pushed the horses into a trot, taking Lady Annalise away from the scene of her nightmare as quickly as possible. Her captors had taken her a considerable distance from familiar territory and she never would have made it home on foot, even in good weather, without being accosted. Or worse. The fact that she managed it on horseback still astonished Clarence.

'I assume you and Betty crossed a bridge at some point.'

She smiled. 'Betty found the way without any help from me.'

'Westminster Bridge, I dare say.'

'Perhaps. Does it matter which?'

'Not in the least.' He smiled at her, seeing no reason to release her hand. 'You have been a great help this afternoon, Lady Annalise, and I know it has not been easy for you. But at least now we have something, a clue, to work with.'

'Then I'm glad. But I must be keeping you from important matters of state.'

'My *only* concern at present is discovering what von Hessel is up to. Others are hard at work in that regard even as we speak.'

'Then I must be keeping you from your leisure pursuits.'

What the devil was she asking him? 'Not at all.'

She fixed him with a penetrating gaze. 'You do have leisure pursuits that help you relax, do you not, Lord Romsey?'

'I don't have a great deal of time to please myself.'

'That is so sad. Surely, you belong to clubs, like my brothers do, and . . . well, do whatever they do in those clubs. Play cards, drink more than you should and relax without having to mind your manners because you are in all-male company.' Her lips quirked. 'But I suppose you belong to all the political clubs, so you are never really at your leisure.'

'Something of that nature,' Clarence replied in an absent tone he hoped would discourage further probing on her part. Naturally, it did not.

'When you are in Southampton, please tell me that you hunt, and fish, and shoot.'

'Unfortunately I cannot often spare the time.'

Mischief danced in her eyes. 'Shame on you, Lord Romsey.'

No one had ever asked him about his leisure pursuits before. Nor had it occurred to him to mind that he didn't have any. He wasn't about to tell her that he couldn't remember the last time he had driven in the park purely for pleasure, only using the location for meetings with diplomatic contacts whom it wouldn't do to be seen with in society.

'You will wear yourself out if you do nothing but work.'

'I am not working now,' he pointed out mildly.

'In a sense you are, because we would not be here if it were not for what happened to me. And I wager the moment you return me home, you will bury your head in your dull papers again.'

It was the truth and so he saw little point in denying it. 'I am entirely at your disposal, Lady Annalise,' he replied.

'I understand just how occupied the wicked Foreign Secretary keeps you nowadays, my lord, but what about when you were

178

younger? What pleasures did you enjoy then?'

Clarence turned a splutter into a cough, convinced she could not realise what she had asked him. 'The same things as your brothers, I dare say.'

'I saw you play cricket at the park last summer but I don't suppose you make a habit of it. Do you enjoy long rides, just for the pleasure of riding? Did you swim in lakes during your holidays, or indulge your pugilistic tendencies? My brothers did all of those things, very frequently, and others besides.'

'You forget I am an only child.'

'But you must have had friends to stay.' When he shook his head she frowned, seemingly concerned about his lonely childhood. A childhood that had not seemed lonely until that moment. 'Surely you did not spend the holidays alone?'

Images of sitting at one end of a long dining table with his austere father at its head filled his memories. His father conducted conversations with Clarence in Latin or Greek, or whatever language happened to take his fancy. Woe betide Clarence if he failed to understand or fluffed his responses. The parental punishments could be brutal, always humiliating, and often very public. Clarence felt his face flush with anger as he recalled the times he had been obliged to lower his breeches and bend over the table while his father birched his backside for some minor incorrect response, always in full view of the servants.

Often the questions would be on delicate political situations of the day, his pater demanding to know how Clarence would resolve them. Training, always training. It had seemed perfectly normal at the time, simply because Clarence didn't know any better. The prospect of being punished, of failing to meet his father's expectations, turned him into a diligent student who took pleasure from excelling.

'I ought to take you home,' he said abruptly.

'I didn't mean to speak out of turn. Sometimes, especially when I am nervous, my tongue runs away with me.'

'Do I make you nervous, Lady Annalise?' Clarence realised he had been scowling and softened his expression. 'That was not my intention.'

'No, not nervous precisely.' But she didn't elaborate. 'Please don't return me home quite yet,' she said softly.

Clarence fixed her with a look of polite enquiry. 'There is something else you wish to do?'

'I would like to drive in the park, if you can spare the time to escort me.' Her eyes burned with an unfathomable emotion. 'I need time to recover my composure before I face my family.'

'Of course.'

Clarence leaned from the window and gave Pierce instructions. He released Lady Annalise's hand in order to do so and thought it wise not to recapture it.

'I doubt too many fashionable people will be in the park in this weather,' he remarked, just for something to say. 'Shall you mind?'

'Not in the least.' She turned to face him, her eyes bright with expectancy. Expectancy of what precisely? 'I need to do normal things, to feel alive, to . . . oh, I don't know. Being at Sheridan House is not exactly a hardship, but I still feel too confined sometimes. City life does not agree with me. I miss the freedom of the country, you see.' She clapped a hand over her mouth. 'Goodness, how can I complain about my privileged lot when I saw for myself how the wretched creatures in the East End have to live day in and day out? How quickly I seem to have forgotten their plight. Well, not forgotten precisely. Still, whatever must you think of me?'

Clarence couldn't possibly answer her

question without being economical with the truth. 'Here, we are at the park,' he said, as the carriage reached Hyde Park Corner and turned in through the gate. 'And, as I suspected, we have it almost to ourselves.'

The paths were clear, but snow still covered the grass. He noticed Lady Annalise's expression brighten as she observed it.

'Shall we walk?' she suggested.

'Are you sure you are well enough?'

'I need exercise.'

'Very well.'

Clarence tapped on the roof again and the carriage rattled to a halt. He helped her alight from it, proffered his arm and they strolled along the gravel walk.

'Be careful. It's slippery underfoot.'

She threw her head back, breathed deeply of the crisp air and sent him a radiant smile. 'This is so much better.'

'I am glad it pleases you.'

'I imagine your head is full of the important things I am keeping you from doing.'

'There is nowhere else I would prefer to be.'

Her trilling laughter rang through the air. 'Gallantly said, Lord Romsey, but I don't believe a word of it.'

'You think I lie?'

'I think diplomacy is second nature to you.' Her eyes twinkled up at him from beneath her silly little veil. 'There is a difference, I feel sure.'

'How do you occupy your time when you are in London, Lady Annalise?'

'Oh, doing the usual things. Making and receiving calls, attending all the right soirees, seeing and being seen. I am permitted to ride in the park, but always with a groom.' She turned up her nose. 'And always at a sedate pace.'

He smiled, endlessly amused by her frankness, so at variance to the way he had been taught to think and behave. 'How tiresome.'

'Precisely. Last year was my first season and so I found it quite interesting. This year I am already bored.'

'And yet I saw for myself just how ardently you were pursued by your horde of admirers at the duchess's ball. Is that not what every young lady desires?'

'Not this young lady.' She tossed her head. 'Most of the men who take an interest in me do so because they need my money.'

Clarence smothered a smile. That frankness again. 'And write dreadful poetry in celebration of your eyes.'

'Precisely so. I have yet to find any

gentleman who is intelligent enough to hold *my* interest for more than five minutes. Men of my own age are insufficiently mature to satisfy something inside of me.'

Once again, Clarence was obliged to smother his reaction with a cough. Was she hinting at an interest in him, or was her frankness once again making her indiscreet? In case it was the former, it seemed only right to warn her off.

'And yet age disparity in matrimony can create more problems than it resolves.'

She canted her head and peered up at him. 'What a very strange comment to make. I know of many successful marriages in which the age difference is quite considerable.'

'Be that as it may . . . ' Clarence broke off when Lady Annalise's hand left his sleeve and she darted onto the snowy grass. 'Have a care! You may slip and fall.'

'Nonsense.' She stretched her arms wide and whirled in a circle. 'I already told you, I love snow.'

And it was evident that she did. Colour had returned to her face and her bruises no longer seemed quite so stark against her alabaster skin. Her eyes came alight as she continued to dance through the crisp piles of snow, not seeming to mind that the hem of her gown was getting sodden. Her joy communicated itself to him and it was all Clarence could do not to join in her celebration of life. Given the ordeal she had just survived, he did not have it in him to try and prevent her.

'I am sure you have never enjoyed a snowball fight.'

Before he could formulate a response, a heavy mound of snow struck his shoulder with pinpoint accuracy. She laughed aloud and bent down to collect more ammunition. Clarence felt recklessness overtake caution. Such actions could not go unrevenged. He bent to collect snow for his own arsenal and slowly moulded it between his gloved hands.

'I never have,' he replied, laughing. 'But I am willing to learn.'

Without giving her time to take evasive action, he let his snowball fly. It caught her arm and slithered slowly down her skirts, rapidly melting as it hit the ground. She laughed louder.

'Is that the best you can manage?'

Her next missile whizzed past his ear, and Lady Annalise let forth with an unladylike curse.

'I don't need to ask where you learned such language.'

'Oh, don't blame my brothers.' She executed a careless shrug. 'Portia and I used

185

to sneak up on them when they were home from school and eavesdrop on their conversations. It was the only way to learn anything interesting.'

She swirled in another circle and stumbled. Clarence was at her side in an instant, grabbing her arm to prevent an accident for which he would be held responsible. He pulled her upright and her body collided with his. Hard. Her laughter faded and her lips parted in a startled *oh*. Clarence cursed as his arms slid around her to keep her safe, quite without his permission, and suddenly time stood still. He sensed the rapid beating of her heart and felt her glorious curves pressed inappropriately against him through the multiple layers of their clothing.

'I did warn you,' he said softly, lowering his head until his breath peppered her face. Her expression was wary yet curious, as though she expected him to kiss her. As though she hoped he would. Never had he wanted to do anything more and he almost certainly would have forgotten himself, except for the sound of carriage wheels on the gravel path that caused them to jump guiltily apart.

Too late.

'Damnation!' Clarence muttered beneath his breath.

The carriage slowed almost to a halt, its

occupants staring at him and Lady Annalise with a combination of excitement and almost certainly faked censure.

'Oh Lord.' Lady Annalise clapped a hand over her mouth. 'Unless I mistake the matter, we have just been observed having a snowball fight by Mrs. Anderson and her daughter.'

12

Clarence felt momentarily disadvantaged. He prided himself on having lightning-quick responses in sensitive situations. But this particular sensitive situation could not be fixed with diplomacy. Mrs. Anderson had not seen the innocent consequences of a snowball fight. Instead, she had observed Clarence holding Lady Annalise in his arms. He had no difficulty imagining what she would make of that delicious *on dit*.

'Come,' he said tersely. He grasped Lady Annalise's elbow and conducted her back to his carriage.

'I'm sorry, Lord Romsey. Once again I have caused difficulties for you.'

She had caused difficulties for both of them but didn't appear to have grasped the ramifications of her actions quite yet. As they re-entered the carriage, Clarence ordered Pierce to drive around the park. This time he seated himself across from Lady Annalise, even though the damage was already done and he could have legitimately enjoyed sitting beside his beautiful, wilful and impetuous companion. But what he had to say to her required no such distractions.

'You look very severe,' she said when they had driven for a while in tense silence. 'We were only having a snowball fight. It was unfortunate that Mrs. Anderson happened to come along, especially because she resents me, but she cannot make anything out of what she saw.'

'Why does she resent you so much?'

'Absolutely nothing . . . well, she wants Lord Roker for her daughter. But his lordship pursues me and Mrs. Anderson has got it into her head that I encourage him.' She rolled her eyes. 'Ridiculous woman!'

Perdition, she really didn't understand. 'Annalise,' he said softly. 'Regardless of Mrs. Anderson's reasons for resenting you, I was holding you in my arms — '

'Only to prevent me from falling.'

'Mrs. Anderson does not know that. Nor would she believe it if we tried to convince her. You know how society ladies enjoy spreading gossip, she already resents you and will be out to make mischief for you.'

'I don't care!'

'Perhaps not, but your family most assuredly will.'

Her face paled. 'Oh!'

'Winchester went to considerable trouble to protect your reputation when you were abducted — '

'Only for me to undo all his good work. Oh heavens, Zach will be furious with me.' She shrugged. 'Still, it cannot be helped. It will blow over.'

'Unfortunately, it won't. And it isn't just you who will suffer. Portia's reputation will be tainted by association.'

She looked on the verge of tears. 'Surely not?'

He had been angry with her for behaving recklessly — angrier still with himself for being drawn into her childish games and enjoying them a little too much. Now, watching her reaction as reality struck home, he felt nothing but an urgent desire to comfort her. Such unbridled spontaneity should never be tempered by society's rules, and the desire to banish the bruised expression from her eyes became more compelling by the minute. The desire to kiss her temptingly plump lips had never left him. He was fairly certain he would have given way to it, right there in the centre of the park, had Mrs. Anderson not driven along. And so he was as much responsible for this situation as she was. More so, since he understood the dangers of being alone with her.

'We can make it right,' he said, reaching for her hand.

Her head shot, hope replacing the feral

look in her eyes. 'How? What must I do?'

Clarence took a deep breath. 'If you would do me the very great honour of becoming my wife, then society will turn a blind eye to our escapade.'

Her eyes widened to an impossible degree, and he could see she was genuinely shocked, perhaps even insulted, by the suggestion. Foolish child! Could she not see he was offering her a way to salve her family's reputation? Her mouth fell open, and she appeared incapable of speech. Clarence waited for her to recover her composure, nervous about how she might respond. He had not intended to embrace matrimony. Now that he had been boxed into a corner, instead of feeling trapped, he was surprisingly ambivalent about his changed circumstances. Life with Annalise would certainly never be dull.

'That was *the* most unromantic proposal in the world!'

Clarence's lips twitched. 'You require romance?'

'No, because I don't have the slightest intention of marrying you, Lord Romsey.' She crossed her arms defensively. 'There must be another way to resolve this misunderstanding.'

'I can imagine the nature of the thoughts

running through your head,' he said.

'I very much doubt it.' She turned away and looked out of the carriage window.

'You are very beautiful, Annalise,' he said softly.

'Harrumph!'

'You might at least look at me when I pay you a compliment.'

'The time for compliments is *before* you propose.'

'Is it? You must excuse me if I am doing this all wrong. I have never proposed to a lady before, and did not anticipate doing so today, so I have not had time to prepare pretty words.'

'Do you prepare everything you say in advance? Of course you do,' she said, answering her own question. 'Spontaneity can have no part in a diplomat's life.'

'Whereas you have received countless addresses,' he continued, ignoring her interruption, 'so are in a position to point me in the right direction.'

'You want *me* to tell *you* how to propose?' She sent him a damning look. 'This just gets better and better.'

He drilled her with an intensely profound gaze. 'If you would be so kind.'

★ ★ ★

Anna could scarce believe her ears. Her world was falling apart and he was jesting with her. Could he not see just how much she adored him? How desperately she needed to hear him say he felt the same way about her, even if it wasn't true?

'I will not do your work for you, my lord. Besides, nothing you say could persuade me to accept you. You are proposing for all the wrong reasons.' She tossed her head, conscious of a headache threatening, brought on by the storm that would explode at home when they learned of her latest escapade. 'Just take me back to Sheridan House.'

'Drive round again, Pierce,' Lord Romsey called through the window.

'Just a minute, Pierce,' she called out. 'I wish to go home.'

'Drive on, Pierce.'

Clearly satisfied his order would be obeyed, Lord Romsey returned his attention to Anna. 'Now, where were we? Oh yes, about the reasons why we ought to marry. You are beautiful, talented, intelligent, and from one of the best families — '

'And I have a good dowry.'

Lord Romsey's smile faded. 'Which I do not need,' he said, clenching his jaw.

'I'm sorry. I should not have said that.'

'I know you think that is why so many

gentlemen have pursued you, but I can't accept that. They could not help but fall for your charms, I'm absolutely sure.'

And yet, you appear immune to them. 'Nevertheless, it's true.'

'You were a sensation last season and have every right to expect to be romanced.' Lord Romsey spread his knees, rested his forearms on them and stared at the carriage floor. 'Unfortunately, I don't know how to be romantic.'

She widened her eyes. 'You do not?'

'I have never had time for romance, just as I have never had time for any of the pursuits you enjoy so much.'

Anna was aghast. 'I think that is the saddest thing anyone has ever said to me.'

He looked up at her again, effortlessly capturing her gaze and holding it, such was the power he wielded over her. 'I am older than you, Annalise, but not so much older that it would make things awkward for us. I am wealthy in my own right, I can offer you a comfortable home and I will do my very best to make you happy.'

Tears trickled from the corners of her eyes. 'Thank you, but the answer is still *no*.'

'Don't be difficult. We really don't have any choice.'

'You may not, but I — '

'Love will come, I am perfectly sure of it.'

'And I am not prepared to take the risk of . . . '

'Of what?' he asked when her words trailed off.

'It doesn't matter. Please take me home. I shall tell Zach what happened and make sure he understands it was not your fault. Once he stops scolding me, he will think of a way to fix things. Zach always knows how to fix things. It is what dukes do.'

'Very well.' Lord Romsey tapped on the roof and gave Pierce new orders. 'It just so happens that I need to speak with Winchester as well.'

By the time they reached Berkeley Square, Anna still had not recovered from the shock of Lord Romsey's cold, practical proposal. Faraday took her outdoor garments and informed her the duchess wished to see her in the small sitting room the moment she returned home. Mama probably wished to ring a peal over her for going out with Lord Romsey alone. She could have no idea how richly that dressing down was deserved but Anna had rather hoped it could wait. She desperately wanted to speak with Zach before Lord Romsey got to him but could not defer a direct request from her mother.

'Is the duke in his study?' Lord Romsey asked Faraday.

'I believe so, my lord. And he wishes to see you, immediately.'

'Not as much as I wish to see him.'

Lord Romsey sent her the ghost of a wink, a gesture that was as surprising as it was uncharacteristic. It proved to Anna there might yet be hope for him, but that did not alter her firm determination not to accept him under the current circumstances.

'You're enjoying this,' she hissed at him.

'I am not enjoying oversetting you, Annalise. But I *will* do the honourable thing by you and there is no more to be said on the matter.'

'On the contrary, there is a very great deal to be said.'

He touched her face, just fleetingly, and then headed in the direction of Zach's study. She felt his fingertips searing into her skin long after he removed them. These brief glimpses of the sensitive man lurking beneath all those years of training and dedication to duty made her want to call after him. Beg him to pour out his heart. Find a way to convince him he had nothing to fear from loving her. And . . . that it was perfectly acceptable to fall in love, even for someone with his rigid standards. But she didn't think he would ever do so. Damnation, why could he not love her? What had happened to him as a child to make it impossible for him to feel emotion, or openly display it even if he did? Her poor, damaged Clarence was a complete enigma.

The man she had fallen in love with had proposed to her. It ought to be the happiest day of her life, even if that proposal had been made grudgingly. It ought not to matter if her love was not returned. She was sure Lord Romsey *liked* her and enjoyed her society. She made him laugh. Not the polite, social laugh she had heard him deploy — the one that did not reach his eyes. But a real, genuine laugh that lit up his handsome features with a wicked humour that made her insides melt with desire. Many marriages had been built upon considerably less.

But, unfortunately, it did matter to her very much indeed.

Sighing, she turned in the direction of the small sitting room and found her mother there alone. She looked up when Anna entered the room, put her book aside and smiled at her.

'Bring us some tea, please, Faraday.' Mama patted the seat beside her on the settee. 'Now, tell me what you have been up to this afternoon, my dear. But first, tell me you feel better.'

'Oh, Mama, I have made such a mull of everything!'

To her horror, and her mother's obvious consternation, tears flooded Anna's eyes and trickled down her bruised face.

'My love, whatever is wrong?'

The duchess clutched Anna's hand, much as Lord Romsey had in his carriage. Anna accepted the handkerchief her mother handed her, mopped her eyes with it and did her level best to compose herself. Then she told the duchess everything that had happened that afternoon, starting with the trip to the East End and her recognition of her prison, finishing with the events in the park. Her mother, instead of appearing horrified, merely smiled.

'Oh dear,' she said. 'Mrs. Anderson will cause all sorts of mischief for us now.'

'Yes,' Anna replied glumly. 'And it's all my fault. I just wanted Lord Romsey to have some fun. Do you know, he has never done anything for his own pleasure? Or anything reckless.' She wrinkled her nose. 'Not before he met me anyway, and I am sure he regrets that day now.'

Mama laughed. 'And I am equally sure he does not.'

'I doubt whether he has ever read a book for enjoyment rather than self-improvement.' Anna waved her mother's discarded novel in the air to lend emphasis to her words. 'It is so very sad.'

'How does he plan to fix the problem he created?'

'He did not create it. I did.' Anna ground her teeth. 'I have been a terrible trial to him these past few days. And now, I have damaged not only my reputation but Portia's also.'

The duchess waved Anna's statement aside. 'It will blow over.'

'That's precisely what I said, but Lord Romsey doesn't agree.'

'Then what does he propose to do about it?' Anna shook her head and said nothing. 'Anna, what are you not telling me?'

'He asked me to marry him,' Anna replied, addressing her words to the rug beneath her feet.

'Well, my love, that is what you want, isn't it?'

Anna looked at her mother askance. 'What do you mean?'

Mama chuckled. 'You have had eyes for no one else since you first met him. A mother always notices these things. I knew immediately that Crista was right for Amos the moment I saw them together.'

'Just as you think Frankie is right for Zach.' Anna wrinkled her brow, momentarily diverted from her own problems. 'And yet Frankie is living here and you do nothing to promote the match.'

'Your brother is the most stubborn one of you all. If I try to push him in a particular direction by pointing out what he is not ready to admit to himself, he will most likely run the opposite way.'

Anna managed a weak smile. 'You are very wise, Mama.'

'I have six children, my love. Of course I am wise because I care so very much about the happiness of you all.' Mama smiled. 'Now tell me again why it's such a bad thing that the man you adore proposed to you?'

'I want him to marry me because he loves me, not because he feels compelled.'

Mama's soft smile was full of understanding. 'Why do you imagine he doesn't love you?'

'He didn't say he did. If fact, he made no mention of his feelings. Actually, I don't believe he has any,' she added with a mutinous toss of her head. 'I imagine they were beaten out of him by his brute of a father. What little he has said about him makes him sound like a cold, heartless ogre.'

'Many fathers are like that. Not everyone is as lucky as you were.'

'So I am finding out. Lord Romsey spoke

about duty, about his house and giving me a comfortable home, but nothing about his feelings. How can I possibly marry a man who does not feel?' Anna rested her head on her mother's lap, as she had often done when she was a little girl and felt unwell. Her mother's comforting hand gently stroked her hair. 'I want what you and Papa had, Mama. It is all I have ever wanted. I saw daily just how much you loved one another and I can't settle for anything less. Zach is not the only one of us who can be stubborn.'

'Your papa and I were not always as close as you remember.'

Anna's head popped up. 'You were not?'

Mama smiled at Anna, a faraway look in her eye. 'When I was your age I was plain Miss Ascot, daughter of a wealthy but untitled family. I had no brothers or sisters and was my father's only heir, which made me that much more attractive to the fortune hunters.'

Anna laughed. 'Mama, you were a beauty. It cannot only have been money that made gentlemen admire you.'

'Perhaps not. You are in a similar yet better position than I was. Just as you are, I was pursued all the way through my first season, mainly for my fortune. Your papa needed a wealthy wife. His father had run the

201

Winchester duchy almost into the ground with his gaming habit. I knew that was why your papa took an interest in me, but I liked him, and I liked the idea of being a duchess. I won't deny that. Besides, my family put a lot of pressure on me to accept him.'

'Oh Mama, I have put Portia's reputation as well as my own in jeopardy, and you have yet to issue a single word of censure, or put any pressure on me to accept Lord Romsey.' Anna sat up and threw her arms around her mother's neck. 'I don't deserve you.'

'In my case, not much pressure was necessary. I decided I would marry your father and that I would make him fall in love with me.'

'You certainly succeeded in that ambition.'

'And that is what you must do with Lord Romsey.'

'I wouldn't know how.' Anna shook her head. 'How did you achieve it with Papa?'

'Ah, there is only so much help I can give you. The rest you must work out for yourself.'

A footman brought their tea and neither Anna nor her mother spoke again until he withdrew.

'You have no choice but to accept Lord Romsey, my love,' Mama said, handing Anna her tea. 'He is quite right about that.'

'But I — '

'Mrs. Anderson is bound to be at the Pettigrews' party this evening. Vince doesn't know it yet, but he will escort Portia and me to it. I shall tell Mrs. Anderson in the strictest confidence that you have accepted Lord Romsey. She will be delighted because that will leave the field clear for her daughter and Lord Roker. I shall tell her that you and his lordship will make your announcement at Lady Ancel's ball in two nights' time. Your bruises ought to be healed enough by then for you to be seen in public. If they are not, I am sure Fanny will be able to conceal them with your hair and a little face powder.' Mama flashed a mischievous smile that caused the years to fall away from her face. 'Naturally, Mrs. Anderson will spread the word and everyone in the room will know within the hour.'

Anna laughed in spite of herself. 'But I am still not sure I wish to marry Lord Romsey under such circumstances.'

'You don't have to. You merely have to enter into the engagement. If after a few weeks you still feel the same way, we shall find a way to break it off.'

'Mama!'

The duchess executed a delicate shrug. 'It might cause a little scandal, but what is that compared to your happiness?'

'What indeed?' Anna thought she was the most contrary creature on God's earth. She really did not want to marry Lord Romsey unless he loved her. But having been talked into the engagement by her wise mother, she was now reluctant to consider breaking it off again.

'The important thing is that no reputations will be ruined. Engagements are broken for all sorts of reasons. I am sure we will think of something to satisfy the tattle-mongers.'

'And if Mrs. Anderson does mention seeing his lordship and me in an ... er, compromising position, it will not matter since we are engaged.'

'Precisely.'

'Mama, you are a miracle worker.'

'That she is,' Zach said from the doorway, Lord Romsey lurking at his shoulder.

'Listening at doors, my dear?' Mama asked indolently.

'I hear you have had quite an afternoon and lived up to our name for you, Trouble,' Zach said in a mildly reproving tone. 'Romsey has seen fit to offer you a way out of it and I have given him my approval. The rest is up to you, Anna.'

'Mama and I have been talking about that.' Anna stood up and faced Lord Romsey. 'I have had a change of heart, Lord Romsey, and will be happy to become engaged to you.'

Clarence took her hand and kissed the back of it. 'I am delighted to hear it.'

'As to marriage, however . . . ' She sent him a teasing smile, ideas about how to follow in her mother's footsteps already percolating through her mind. ' . . . I have yet to decide about that.'

13

Within ten minutes of entering the Foreign Office the following morning, Clarence had been congratulated upon his forthcoming nuptials by three different people. Others smiled and shook his hand cordially. Aware that the duchess would have stuck to her plan and told only Mrs. Anderson of the engagement, Clarence was pleased to have it confirmed that the *ton*'s gossip machine was working as efficiently as ever.

Having committed himself to enter a state he had always planned to avoid, a largely sleepless night had left him none the wiser as to the true nature of his feelings. The prospect of matrimony, of having his carefully organised life disrupted by a person who would have every right to make demands upon his time and seek his attention, ought to have petrified him. And, to a degree, it did. He was not qualified to be a good husband simply because he didn't have the first idea how to go about it. He had no example to emulate. His parents' idea of domestic felicity had left much to be desired. Dear God, supposing he turned out to be no better at it than his father was? The thought filled Clarence with abject horror. He could never be that cold, callously single-minded and unfeeling. Could he?

Certainly not intentionally, but he had seen countless examples of children turning out to be mirror images of their parents. It was precisely that possibility Clarence had been hoping to avoid by remaining single. Annalise deserved to be happy. Her spirited character could not — should not — be tamed by society's mores. It was a charming aspect of her personality that set her apart from other young ladies of her age. Unfortunately, it also meant she was far too outspoken to be a diplomat's wife.

Annalise's last comment before he had left Sheridan House the previous day still rang in his ears. *As to marriage, however, I have yet to decide about that.* Surely, she didn't intend to break off the engagement? Given his concerns about entering into matrimony, being released from the commitment ought to have given him relief. Instead, it filled him with a firm determination to ensure she did not renege on their agreement.

Clarence readjusted his position on the uncomfortable leather seat he occupied while waiting for the Foreign Secretary to see him. He shook out his newspaper and turned the page without being aware of what he actually read, his mind still occupied with Annalise's unwillingness to marry him. Did she love someone else? Jealousy surged through Clarence in virulent waves, which in itself was unusual enough to make him snort. He had never had reason to be jealous in his entire life and ought not to feel that way now. After all, he did not actually love Annalise. Did he?

Love had no place in his life. His father had beaten any such whimsical notions out of him before he reached puberty. He *liked* Annalise very much. Her company was engaging, showing him a different side of life he seldom had much contact with. But love? Clarence shook his head, chuckling to himself, determined to overcome Annalise's doubts. Perhaps he would court her. She had complained that his proposal was not romantic and it was as clear as day to him now that she possessed a romantic soul. The problem was, he had never courted a woman before and wasn't too sure how to go about it. Those he played with were willing and didn't require pretty words or declarations of undying love.

But Annalise was different.

Very well then, a'courting he would go. It would be no hardship, putting aside his duties for an hour or two at a time and making himself agreeable to Annalise.

'The Foreign Secretary will see you now, Lord Romsey.'

Clarence put his newspaper aside and walked into Castlereagh's inner sanctum.

'Romsey.' Lord Castlereagh stood up, hand outstretched. 'What's all this I hear about you nabbing the Sheridan girl?'

'You are very well informed, sir. The official announcement has not yet been made.'

'Didn't know you had it in you,' Castlereagh replied bluntly, subjecting Clarence to a candid appraisal it was difficult not to take exception to. 'Diamond of the first water, is Lady Annalise. Everyone's after her, but I never figured you for one of 'em. Thought you were a cold fish, like your father.'

Cold, like my father? 'I have my moments,' Clarence replied offhandedly.

'Obviously, if you've snared the catch of the season. Anyway, congratulations. I expect an invitation to the wedding.' He motioned Clarence to a chair. 'I suppose this business with von Hessel abducting Lady Annalise brought you together.'

When Viscount Castlereagh summoned him, Clarence suspected he would require an explanation. He hadn't wanted to tell him until he knew more and would be careful what he told him now. Information leaked out of all government offices in torrents, almost as efficiently as the *ton*'s gossip machine manufactured the latest *on dits*, but seldom as accurately.

'Von Hessel has been badgering Lady St. John about her late husband's papers.'

Castlereagh's head shot up. 'Why?'

'That is what I am attempting to find out.'

'Hmm. What the devil has Lady Annalise to do with the matter?'

'An unfortunate case of mistaken identity, although I cannot prove von Hessel took her. Yet.'

Castlereagh rubbed his whiskered chin between his thumb and forefinger. 'I hear von Hessel has secured the affections of the Outwood girl. That will keep his nest well feathered. Her father is as rich as he is a thorn in the prime minister's side, and the girl gets the lot when he goes.'

'So I understand.'

'He and the Prince Regent are tighter than bugs in a rug, but I can't stand the blighter myself.'

Nor could Clarence, but he had good reason to feel that way, given what the man had done to Annalise. 'I haven't found anything to date that paints him in a bad light. I have people trying to find out how things stand for him back in Prussia.'

'Good thinking.' Castlereagh paused. 'Does Lady St. John have any of her husband's personal papers? Papers that ought to be in our archives?'

'She doesn't know. She does have some things of his but has never looked at them. They are being sent up to town. Should arrive today or tomorrow.'

'I don't like it when our Prussian friends become furtive.' Castlereagh stood up, indicating that the meeting had come to an end. 'Keep me advised if you find anything interesting, Romsey. Damned rum affair this and I don't like it above half.'

'That I will, sir.'

Clarence walked briskly back to his apartment, glad that the weather had improved. All signs of snow had disappeared from the streets and the world had returned to normal. A perfect afternoon to commence his campaign to win Annalise's affections.

'What news do you have for me, Pierce?' he asked as he walked into his sitting room, throwing his outdoor garments at Sampson.

'We have made a little progress, my lord.'

'Good. Let's hear it, then.'

★ ★ ★

'What shall you wear this afternoon to receive Lord Romsey?' the duchess asked.

Surprised, Anna looked up from the book she was reading. 'I am not expecting him to visit, Mama. I assumed he would come to the ball this evening, since we are supposed to be seen together there, but there is no occasion for him to put aside his duties for my sake before then.'

Frankie laughed. 'You are an engaged couple, Anna. Of course he will call this afternoon.'

'You don't look terribly happy about being engaged,' Portia remarked. 'I thought you would be delighted by the turn events have taken.'

'I would be, if he had offered for me because I am his heart's desire.' Anna shrugged. 'Still, he is trying to protect my reputation, so I ought to be grateful, I suppose.'

'We will be inundated with callers this afternoon, coming to see if the rumours I started, or rather Mrs. Anderson started, are true,' Mama said, smiling. 'Your poor face will not stand up to close scrutiny in daylight. Besides, I feel persuaded Lord Roker will be one of the first visitors.'

Anna groaned.

'If Lord Romsey is half as perceptive as I

believe him to be, he will come to your rescue.'

'And do what with me?'

'Anna!' Mama actually looked shocked. 'What a thing to say.'

'Sorry, Mama.' Anna smothered a giggle. 'What I should have said was that Lord Romsey spends all his time working and won't have the first idea how to entertain me.'

Anna noticed her mother and Frankie exchange an amused glance. 'I think you underestimate your future husband,' Frankie said.

'He is not my future husband,' Anna replied stubbornly. 'I have only agreed to become engaged to him, nothing more.'

Portia and Frankie shot Anna identical shocked looks. Anna realised she ought not to have said anything but was saved from explaining by the sound of the luncheon gong. Vince and Nate were out somewhere, so only Zach joined them at the table. He seemed to be doing that a great deal more than usual since Frankie had come to stay with them, Anna noticed. And yet, he made no particular attempt to single her out. He looked at her frequently, though, and always listened politely to whatever she had to say.

Anna had absolutely no idea what her suave brother's intentions were regarding

Frankie, nor could she ask. But nothing would give her greater pleasure than to see a lady who was fast becoming one of her closest friends assuming the mantle of Duchess of Winchester. And yet, she had been married for eight years before Lord St. John died and had no children to show for it. Anna knew there could be all sorts of reasons for that. Her husband had been twenty years older than Frankie. Perhaps he had been incapable of . . . well, of whatever he was required to be capable of doing. Anna was rather hazy on that point. There again, poor Frankie could be barren. The same thought must have occurred to Zach. Could that be what was holding him back?

'When can we expect Amos to arrive, Zach?' Anna asked.

'I hope to see him by tomorrow. Perhaps even later today,' Zach replied. 'The sooner we can resolve this business, the sooner Lady St. John can return to her normal life.'

'Tired of my society already, Your Grace?'

'Not in the least, but I don't like to think of you being in danger, or to see your enjoyment curtailed because of this business.'

'Oh, I feel perfectly safe here, and have enjoyed my respite from the social whirl. It quickly becomes tiresome, I find. Besides, we have agreed I shall attend Lady Ancel's ball this evening in company with the rest of you.'

'But you must promise me not to walk outside unescorted or to have anything to do with von Hessel.'

Frankie elevated one elegant brow. 'Must I?'

'Excuse me, I did not mean to give you orders, but you must see the logic behind my — er, request.'

Frankie smiled, perfectly compliant, now she had made her point. 'Since you ask me so persuasively, Your Grace, I shall be happy to do as you ask.'

'Thank you.'

Anna looked up and observed her mother watching the verbal sparring between Zach and Frankie, a satisfied half-smile playing about her lips. But for Anna's abduction, this business with von Hessel had played right into her gently manipulative hands.

'Run along and change,' Mama told Anna as soon as luncheon came to an end. 'Lord Romsey will be here any moment.'

Anna wasn't convinced but did as she was told anyway.

'The new sprigged muslin, Fanny,' she said as she walked into her chamber. 'The green with the cream spots.'

Dressed in a gown that, in vogue with the current fashion, fitted tightly to her form,

Anna felt ready to do battle with her poor, misguided lord. There was nothing like a new gown to give a lady confidence in her abilities, Anna thought. She sat still while Fanny tidied her hair, fashioning it to hide her rapidly fading bruises.

She had not been down for more than five minutes, seated with her mama, Portia, and Frankie, before Lord Romsey was announced. Her mother sent her a speaking look that implied Anna should have known better than to doubt her.

'Good afternoon, Lord Romsey,' Mama said.

'Your Grace.'

Romsey bowed over Mama's hand, and then turned his attention to Anna. She bobbed a curtsey as he took her hand and was pleased to see his eyes widen at the sight of her in her new gown. She lowered her eyes and noticed, belatedly, he was dressed for riding in tight-fitting breeches and shiny Hessians. That clothing *did* surprise her. The fact that he looked magnificent in it — all hard muscle, broad shoulders and unimpeachable masculinity — did not. She moistened her lips, thinking to herself it was a great pity he did not love her. She would so very much like to marry him.

'Are you on your way somewhere else?'

Anna asked when Lord Romsey had greeted Frankie and Portia.

'I was hoping to persuade you to ride with me in the park.'

'Me? You? Together?' Anna hoped she didn't look as stupid as she sounded, astonishment having robbed her of the ability to string two coherent words together. 'Are you sure you can spare the time?'

'Perfectly sure,' he said, his lips twitching.

Zach joined them at that moment and shook hands with Lord Romsey.

'What news?' he asked.

'With regard to the warehouse, it is as we suspected. The place is unused at present, the owner looking for new tenants. He is a person of good character and I have no reason to suspect him of duplicity. It is our belief the two villains who abducted Annalise were recommended to von Hessel by a third person. They must work at the wharf, but finding them without knowing what they look like would be next to impossible.'

'I would like to get my hands on them,' Zach replied, 'but they are not important.'

'My thoughts exactly,' Lord Romsey replied. 'I saw the inside of the warehouse myself less than an hour ago. It is just as you described.' He turned to Anna with a sympathetic smile. 'We found the room you were held in. The remnants of the sack you tore apart were still on the floor, along with a few scraps of pink silk from where you ripped your gown. It is definitely the place, but it lent us few clues.' He shook his head. 'I examined the tree you climbed down. It would be a perilous descent in daylight in reasonably good weather. I am astonished you only dislocated your shoulder.'

'You see, Lord Romsey — ' She sent him a sparkling smile. ' — Having four brothers to rough and tumble with is not such a bad thing.'

His lips quirked. 'Evidently not.'

'Nothing more than that?' Zach asked, frowning. 'You have thus far only confirmed what we already knew. Surely, with all your contacts . . . '

'Patience, Winchester. I have a small army of men combing through every document the Foreign Office possesses, as well as people making enquiries about von Hessel's personal circumstances. Something will come to light before much longer. In cases of such close scrutiny, something always does.'

Zach nodded. 'Right. I'm sure you know your business best.'

'I do have some good news for Annalise.'

'Oh, what is it?' Anna asked.

'We located Betty's owner. The landlord at

the inn you liberated her from also acts as a horse dealer. He had acquired the mare with a view to selling her on and was not best pleased to learn that she had been startled by something and broke free of her halter rope. That is the explanation the grooms put about to cover up their incompetence. Pierce invented a story about the mare being found wandering in the nearby streets. Anyway, suffice it to say the landlord was happy to accept payment for her and leave the matter at that.'

'I am sure you paid more than she's worth,' Annalise replied. 'You must allow me to compensate you.'

Lord Romsey appeared affronted. 'Certainly not!' His scowl gave way to one of his lopsided smiles. 'Look upon her as a wedding present.'

'I thank you for the gift of Betty,' Anna replied, without agreeing to look upon her in the manner he suggested. 'I have been to see her every day and she is settling very happily into her new home. She and I already get along famously and I am longing to ride her. However, I thought it best not to let her be seen until I was sure I would not be taken in charge for horse theft.'

'There is no danger of that now.' Lord Romsey's indulgent smile heated the air between them. Or was that just wishful thinking on her part? He really did have *the* most beautifully suggestive smile. 'That is why I thought you might enjoy riding with me this afternoon.'

'Yes, I would like that above all things. How thoughtful of you.'

'Run up and change, Anna,' Mama said. 'I dare say callers will soon arrive and I don't suppose you want to be held up by them.'

Thoughts of Lord Roker and his poetry saw Anna scampering for the stairs. She heard Zach giving orders for Betty to be saddled. Did she *have* a saddle? Presumably, that was something Zach had thought of and organised on her behalf. How fortunate she was to have such a caring family. Poor Lord Romsey. It was such a shame that he had no first-hand experience of the closeness Anna had enjoyed, and occasionally fought against, all her life. In spite of the fact that her brothers infuriated her sometimes with their overprotective ways, she knew she could talk to any of them about absolutely anything, secure in the knowledge that they would keep her confidence. When . . . *if* she married Lord Romsey, she would immediately set to work convincing him that everyone needed a soulmate and that he had found his.

A short time later, she ran back down the

stairs, clad in her emerald-green habit and a matching hat with a plume that fell across her face.

'I am sorry to have kept you waiting, Lord Romsey.'

He devoured her with his eyes, taking in every inch of her and appearing to like what he saw. 'The short wait has been very worthwhile.' He offered his arm. 'Shall we?'

'I do hope you will dine with us this evening, Lord Romsey,' Mama said. 'And escort Anna to the ball afterwards.'

'Thank you, Your Grace. It would be my pleasure.'

14

Annalise appeared delighted when they walked into the mews and Betty gave her a little whinny of recognition.

'You see, she knows me already.'

'I dare say you kept your side of the bargain and she is getting all the oats she can eat.'

'Fie, Lord Romsey, are you suggesting it is merely cupboard love?' Annalise stroked her mare's nose in a possessive fashion. 'Betty is not that shallow.'

Clarence's lips twitched. 'I am sure she is not.'

'Doesn't she look well?' Annalise stood back and admired the mare's sleek coat that had been groomed until it shone. 'Thank you, Harry,' she said to the hovering groom. 'This is your work.'

The lad blushed. 'It was a pleasure, m'lady.'

Harry led Betty to the mounting block. Annalise slid elegantly into her side saddle, adjusted the single stirrup to her satisfaction and took up the reins. She looked entirely at home on horseback. Clarence shuddered when he recalled her sorry state the last time he had seen her on Betty's back, just a few short days ago. Both rider and horse were different creatures now, no thanks to his investigative skills.

He and Annalise walked their horses from the mews side by side.

'It is very kind of you to make the time for me, Lord Romsey.'

'The weather is so much finer today and the park will be full of people promenading.' He grinned across the space that separated them. 'It wouldn't do for anyone to doubt the accuracy of the rumours started by Mrs. Anderson.'

She bit her lip, but a smile escaped anyway. 'Indeed not.'

'Betty appears to be enjoying herself.'

'She is a pleasure to ride, and to own.' She patted the cob's sleek neck. 'Thank you so much, Lord Romsey. I am quite delighted with my gift.'

'It is the very least I can do for my intended bride.'

'There's no occasion to pretend we will actually follow this sham engagement through to matrimony.' She tossed her head, sending her ridiculous plume dancing across her eyes. How the devil could she see where she was going? 'At least, not when it is just the two of us.'

'I never make false promises,' he replied languidly.

'I cannot accept that. You are a diplomat.'

'A diplomat, not a deceiver.'

'Is that not one and the same thing? You must forgive me if I am being obtuse, but I do not have your sharp mind.' Clarence swallowed back the denial that sprang to his lips. 'You are called in to arbitrate between two or more warring factions. Is that not what a diplomat does?'

'In simplistic terms, I suppose it is.'

She sent him an arch smile. 'Those are the only terms I understand.'

She was teasing him. Clarence couldn't remember the last time a person had teased him. Everyone took him seriously — as seriously as he took himself, because that was the only way he knew. Having this lively beauty taunting him with frivolous repartee was as enchanting as the desire to retaliate was compulsive.

'I know what you are about, sweet Annalise,' he warned softly.

'I cannot imagine what you mean.' She sent him a convincingly innocent look. 'I was merely attempting to demonstrate that by dint of your occupation, you cannot help bending the truth when attempting to bring two opposing factions together. Both parties,

I am sure, believe their view is the correct one. Otherwise, your services wouldn't be needed. Therefore, you must disappoint one or the other, or both, or resort to subterfuge to make both sides think they have won.'

'Has it occurred to you that I might allow both parties to maintain their views, and find alternative middle ground satisfactory to both?'

'There, you see, that proves my point. You are much cleverer than I am. I should never have thought of that. I would most likely scold both sides for being so obtuse, bang their heads together, and tell them not to be such babies.'

Clarence laughed aloud. 'And *I* had not thought of that.'

'Oh look, there's Lady Makepeace.' Annalise pointed to a carriage that had slowed almost to a stop so that its occupants could peer at them. 'She is one of the biggest gossips in town. The rumours of our engagement have just been well and truly substantiated. It would be perfectly safe for you to return me home now.'

'Is that what you would like me to do?'

'If we are going to simply trot along this path, then it seems like a waste of your valuable time. I *know* you have more important things to do.'

'And yet I cannot think of anywhere else I would prefer to be.'

'I appreciate the compliment, but there is no need for them when we are alone, since we are only pretending.'

'Are we?' He elevated both brows, suspecting that she was waiting for him to ask her why she felt that way. Clarence would never be so direct. 'And who said anything about simply trotting? Just have patience, Annalise. I know what you really want to do.'

'Oh look, there's Lord Jenkins. I promised to dance with him at the duchess's ball. I hope he does not think I deliberately cut him.'

They halted their horses and exchanged a few words with Jenkins.

'You are in my debt to the tune of one dance, Lady Annalise,' he said, ignoring Clarence to the point of rudeness.

'I apologise for that. I was taken suddenly unwell.'

'So I understood from the duchess. I hope tonight at Lady Ancel's you will honour me.'

'It will be my pleasure.'

Clarence quietly seethed through the entire exchange. It only lasted for a minute or two, but seemed more like a year. How could she smile and flirt with the rogue quite so openly? She never behaved in that fashion with him, or anyone else as far as he knew, up until now. They were engaged to be married, damn it! Everyone knew Jenkins was in dun territory and probably only wanted Annalise for her dowry. *Hands off, she's mine!*

'Romsey.'

Jenkins inclined his head to an insulting degree before taking his leave of Annalise with warmth that bordered on liberty-taking.

'Shall I have to endure those sorts of episodes frequently?' he asked, wishing he didn't sound quite so jealous.

'Whatever can you mean, Lord Romsey?'

'Firstly, you ought to call me Clarence. Engaged couples address one another less formally, do they not?'

'Don't you know?' She looked surprised. 'Have we hit upon a subject upon which you are not fully informed?'

He smiled at her. 'I have never been engaged before.'

'How did your mother address your father?'

'I barely recall. I was only six when she died but, now that you ask, I don't think she ever called him anything other than Lord Romsey.'

Her eyes widened. 'What, even in private?'

'Yes, even then.'

'And I suppose he addressed her as Lady Romsey.'

'Either that or madam.' Clarence shrugged, uncomfortable with the sympathy in her expression. He had not, up until that point, considered there was anything strange in the way his parents had communicated. 'It is not *that* unusual.'

'If you say so.' She sent him a wicked smile. 'And you are right. I really ought to address you as Clarence. It will make this pantomime that much more convincing.'

Clarence fixed her with a condemning look, the one that usually sent his underlings scurrying for cover. On Annalise, it had no discernible effect.

'Where are we?' she asked. 'I am not familiar with this part of the park.'

'You wish to canter?'

'I am keen to discover what Betty is made of and she seems anxious to stretch her legs.'

'Well, we can do so here without fear of mowing anyone down.'

She sent him a probing gaze. 'How do you know of such out-of-the-way places, Clarence? Is this where you meet your informants to exchange secrets of state?'

He chuckled. 'You have an overactive imagination.'

'I know that very well. All of my brothers have complained about it over the years, but it's not my fault. It is simply the way I am.'

She shrugged, looking adorable in her tight-fitting habit and with the light of mischief dancing in her remarkable eyes. 'I don't see how I can be held accountable for the way my mind works. Although my old governess, were she here, would probably say things would be different if I had applied myself more diligently to my lessons. Portia did precisely that. She is so very clever, you know. I, on the other hand, never could see the point of some of the obscure subjects I was required to study.'

'I am very glad for your quixotic mindset. It is endlessly enlightening.'

'Then I am pleased to be of service.'

Clarence removed one hand from the reins and placed it over hers. 'You are a very great deal more than that to me.'

She arched a brow. 'Why, Clarence, I do believe you are being romantic.'

He removed his hand and concentrated on controlling his thoroughbred. Having placed his hooves on the gallops, he was anxious to speed off.

'Shall we?' he asked.

'With the greatest of pleasure.'

They gave the horses their heads and sped off along the wide path left muddy by melted snow. Clumps of sodden earth flew into their faces, churned up by flying hooves. Clarence knew better than to make allowances for her. His horse was built for speed, but Annalise appeared to have acquired the same competitive streak that all her brothers possessed. Light in her saddle as she leaned forward over Betty's withers, her beautiful face lit up with an uncontrived smile of pleasure. Clarence was so enraptured, so caught up with watching her that he missed a turn in the path and almost came to grief. Her musical laughter rang out as she watched him right himself in his saddle and she sped ahead, reaching the end of the gallop fractionally ahead of him.

'Well done,' he said, reining his mount in.

'You were not concentrating,' she said in an accusing tone. She was breathing hard and his attention was caught by the swell of her breasts pressing against the fabric of her bodice. It took a monumental effort of will to tear his gaze away from such a compelling sight.

'Something distracted me,' he replied evasively. 'How did Betty go? A stupid question really, since the pair of you beat one of the finest thoroughbreds in town.'

'She was wonderful and you did not really try!' Annalise patted the mare's sweaty neck as they slowed the horses to a walk, giving them time to cool off before returning to Berkeley Square.

'I am glad she gives you pleasure.'

'It is not so very hard, is it?' she asked a short time later.

'I beg your pardon?'

'Riding simply for riding's sake, and taking pleasure from the experience.'

'That rather depends upon whom one rides with.'

'Really?' She arched a brow. 'I notice you did not agree to having enjoyed yourself. I dare say you are thinking about all the ways you could more profitably be employing your time. That is most unflattering! I hope you are not dissatisfied with my company already.'

'Dissatisfied, yes, but never with your company.'

'My, Clarence, have a care. You have paid me several compliments this afternoon *and* done something reckless.' Her sultry, teasing smile added to his dissatisfaction, but not for reasons she was likely to comprehend. 'I do believe there is hope for you yet.'

'I must take your word for that since I have no idea how you want me to behave.'

'I want you to be yourself,' she replied, so quietly that he almost didn't hear her. 'The person you are supposed to be, not the one your father turned you into.'

'Then we both have surprises in store. And I am entirely at your service.'

'Hmm, until an affair of state calls for your attention.'

'I hope I will not prove to be such an inconstant husband.'

She took one hand from the reins and shook a finger at him. 'You are getting ahead of yourself again.'

'Here we are,' Clarence said, turning his horse in the direction of Winchester's mews. 'I shall see you safely inside and return to dine this evening.'

They left their horses in the care of the grooms and entered the house through a side door. Annalise's face broke out into another wide smile when she noticed the paraphernalia of arrival in the entrance vestibule.

'Amos must be here!' she cried.

She dashed ahead of Clarence into the drawing room, where the entire family was gathered. Amos Sheridan and his new wife Crista were in their midst, still wearing their travelling clothes.

'Amos!'

Annalise threw herself into his arms. Amos, having turned at the sound of his name, smiled, picked his sister up and swung her around.

'I hear you've been living up to our name for you again, Trouble,' he said, placing her back on her feet.

Clarence already had a fair notion how her

brothers had come to christen her *Trouble*.

'It was *not* my fault!'

Amos chuckled. 'It never is.' He held her at arm's length and examined her face, tutting when he saw her fading bruises. 'Are you sure you're all right?'

'Yes. I was frightened, but it all worked out for the best.'

'So I understand.' He looked towards Clarence and held out his hand. 'Congratulations, Romsey. I hope you know what you have agreed to take on.'

'I am rapidly discovering the truth,' Clarence replied calmly.

Annalise was now in close conversation with Crista and so Clarence quizzed Amos about the papers he had brought with him.

'No idea what's in them,' Amos said. 'But it's just as well I got them when I did.'

Everyone in the room was now listening to them.

'What do you mean?' Winchester asked curtly.

'I sent someone to the Crown to see if any strangers had been asking questions about Lady St. John's estate, just as you asked me to, Zach. It seems a couple of foreigners had done so just that day.' Frankie gasped and Clarence noticed Winchester place a reassuring hand on her shoulder. 'Jeggins was suspicious and didn't tell them anything. They took themselves off, probably to Compton village to ask similar questions there.'

'They will find out where I live easily enough,' Frankie said, looking distressed. 'I do hope my servants aren't at risk.'

'I asked Amos to send four of my strongest men to your estate until this business is over, for that very reason,' Winchester said. 'I hope you don't mind.'

Frankie's expression was a combination of gratefulness and annoyance. 'I can hardly object to your thoughtfulness, Your Grace, but would have liked to know of your intention in advance.'

'It might have proved unnecessary,' Winchester replied. 'And then I would have worried you for no reason.'

Frankie opened her mouth as if to argue the point, then shook her head and closed it again without speaking.

'He can be annoyingly dictatorial,' Annalise told Frankie. 'All of my brothers share that tendency, but they mean well.'

The duke sent Annalise a reproving glance but refrained from comment.

'Anyway,' Amos said. 'The papers are in a box in the hall. I assume you want to take them with you, Romsey?'

'Yes, if you have no objection, Frankie.'

'None whatsoever.'

'I will only read the personal documents if absolutely necessary.'

'Nothing Gerald committed to writing will be of a personal nature,' Frankie replied.

Winchester looked at her askance, probably as intrigued as Clarence was by her remote expression and cryptic remark. He had long wondered about the circumstances of her marriage to a man so much older than she was. It seemed like a perfectly convivial match to outsiders, but Clarence knew appearances counted for little.

'I'll have someone carry the box round to your rooms, Romsey,' Winchester said.

'Thank you. In that case, I shall take my leave and return in time for dinner.'

He bid *adieu* to the ladies and shook each of the gentlemen's hands. He was unsure what to make of it when Annalise treated him with offhand courtesy. And yet he was conscious of her gaze boring into his back as he left the room.

The lady he was now determined to make his wife was something of a mystery. She was far more intelligent than she let on, and was playing some sort of game by pretending she had no intention of going through with the marriage. What was it she wanted him to say or do to convince her? She had dropped less than subtle hints the entire time they were in the park, but Clarence was too good a strategist to fall for such an obvious ruse and ask outright what she wanted of him.

He reclaimed his horse and rode briskly home, keen to have at Frankie's papers. All he knew about Annalise was that she was testing him in some way. It was up to Clarence to work out why.

15

'Where is everyone?' Crista was the only person in the drawing room when Anna walked into it that evening. 'Am I early?'

'They are all tardy.' Crista smiled up at Anna and gasped. 'You look lovely!'

Anna's anxiety was partially relieved by Crista's spontaneous reaction to the sight of her in her new blue changeable silk ball gown, complete with overskirt of silver sarsenet. The tight-fitting bodice was cut daringly low and trimmed with pretty seed pearls. Flemish lace adorned the capped sleeves and hemline. She had taken especial care with her toilette, and changed her mind three times before she was satisfied with Fanny's efforts with her hair. It was ridiculous to feel nervous, she repeatedly told herself. Clarence's head was so full of stuffy government business that he probably wouldn't even notice the trouble she had gone to.

'Do you really think so?' Anna chewed her lip. 'The neckline is rather lower than I am comfortable with, and — '

'And Lord Romsey will be enraptured. Stop being such a goose.' Crista stood up and hugged Anna, careful not to crush her gown. 'Being engaged agrees with you. You look as though you have been lit up from within. I am so glad you have achieved your heart's desire.'

Anna wrinkled her nose. 'I would be glad, too, if it had been for the right reasons.'

'This sounds intriguing.' Crista sat forward. 'What have you been up to, apart from getting yourself abducted from society balls?'

Grimacing, Annalise told her just that.

'Oh, Anna!' Crista laughed aloud. 'Only you could land yourself in such a mess.'

'I'm glad you find it amusing,' Anna replied, sniffing.

'Excuse me.' Crista wiped tears from her eyes. 'I am not laughing at you but at the circumstances that landed you where you have always wanted to be, which is engaged to Lord Romsey. Something good has come out of your ordeal.'

'Perhaps, But I didn't plan to coerce him into marrying me against his will.'

Crista shook her head. 'Lord Romsey didn't look like a condemned man when you returned from your ride this afternoon. In fact, he looked rather pleased with himself.'

'Looks can be deceiving. Which is why I am absolutely determined not to be left to stew in his mausoleum of a house while he gallivants around the globe, righting all the wrongs done to the British government.'

Once again, Crista's lips twitched. 'What makes you so sure his house is a mausoleum? You have never set foot inside it.'

'True, but his father sounds like he was an ogre, his mother died when Clarence was still a child, and I would wager no effort has been put into maintaining the house.'

'Then you will have a lovely time righting that situation. And come to that, why would he leave you in the country? Frankie went everywhere with her husband.'

'Presumably that was because *her* husband loved her and wanted her with him.'

'You don't know that any more than you can be sure Romsey doesn't love you.'

'I *do* know. He would say so if he did.'

'Perhaps he doesn't know how. You need to give him a little encouragement, that's all. But I can understand why you feel the way you do. I would not have married Amos if I was not assured of his complete and absolute devotion, even though I was desperately in love with him.'

'Well, anyone with eyes in their head could see your feelings were reciprocated.'

'Everyone except me.' Crista took Anna's hand and smiled at her. 'And now that situation is reversed, and it is I who must persuade you to open your eyes. Some things transcend mere words. Besides, I think your handsome earl will not take much persuading to put aside his serious ways.'

'We did ride out at his suggestion this afternoon, which was an encouraging sign. He doesn't usually waste time riding for no reason. He paid me several compliments and was very charming.'

'He is a diplomat. Of course he's charming, but I have always thought charm comes naturally to Lord Romsey.'

'Possibly.' Anna wrinkled her brow. 'But I want his compliments to be spontaneous, from the heart, as opposed to acts of diplomacy.'

Crista smiled. 'Rome wasn't built in a day, my dear.'

'I dropped numerous hints that I didn't plan to go through with the marriage but he ignored them; infuriating man!'

'He probably doesn't think you're serious.'

'He ought to be glad I don't want to hold him to the commitment when his feelings are not engaged.' She tossed her head. 'Clarence never intended to marry, you know.'

'Then you will have to change his mind about that.' Crista became serious. 'If you love him, Anna, it will be worth the effort. Lord Romsey is entirely sure of himself when negotiating affairs of state, but completely at sea when it comes to untangling his feelings for you.' Crista smiled. 'No matter how intelligent they are, men are not nearly as clever about affairs of the heart as we ladies naturally are.'

'Because we have nothing better to do than daydream about finding our heart's desire.'

Crista smiled. 'Possibly.'

Anna felt guilty. Until she married Amos, Crista had had plenty to do with her time, working all the hours God sent to stave off the enemies her father had made through foolish decisions. 'Thank you. I fully intend to follow your advice. Clarence is definitely worth fighting for.' Anna perched carefully on the edge of a settee. 'Why are you not dressed for the ball?'

'Oh, Amos and I shall not go. We were up at the crack of dawn in order to get here and we are exhausted.'

'Of course you must be. How thoughtless of me not to have realised it.' Anna canted her head and examined Crista more closely. 'There is something different about you. Something about your eyes, your complexion. Your skin positively glows. Are you quite well?'

'Never more so.'

When Crista's face broke out into a beatific

smile, Anna gasped. 'You and Amos are going to make me an aunt?'

Crista nodded. 'We have only just found out and haven't told anyone yet. We planned to do so at dinner this evening.'

'I am so delighted!' Anna hugged Crista, this time not caring about the welfare of her gown. 'Mama will be beside herself with joy. So will Zach. It will take the pressure off of him to marry.'

Crista laughed. 'I doubt your mama will see things that way.'

'No, I am sure she won't.' Anna sighed. 'You should not have come tearing up to town in your condition.'

'You're worse than Amos. I insisted upon coming so I could assure myself you were all right.'

Others joined them and their private discourse came to an end. Anna gave Amos a huge hug, making it clear that she knew his secret. He squeezed her waist, put her aside, and went to stand behind Crista. Without preamble, he then told them all their news. Everyone was excited by it. The duchess actually cried.

'I am to be a grandmama at last,' she said, hugging Crista and simultaneously wiping her eyes.

Amos received hearty backslaps from his

brothers. Crista was kissed and fussed over by everyone. Champagne was served and the hubbub had only just died down when Clarence was announced. Anna inhaled sharply when she looked up and their gazes locked. She was conscious of colour flooding her face as a fine tremor of expectation lanced through her, causing her to wonder briefly how she could possibly expect such an intelligent sophisticate to take an interest in a dunce like her. What would they find to talk about that wouldn't bore him rigid? It occurred to her suddenly, his fierce intellect was one of the things that had attracted her to him.

He was so debonair in his evening clothes, thick hair falling over his brow — every movement and gesture poised and elegant — that just looking at him robbed her of the ability to think straight. She wanted to run to him and throw herself spontaneously into his arms. Physical demonstrations of affection came as naturally to her as they were alien to her intended. With that thought in mind, she made do with inclining her head, somewhat coolly, in his direction and then turned back to her conversation with Frankie. He might be cleverer than she was but she had her feminine wiles to aid her cause, which made this battle of wills more even.

'What game are you playing?' Frankie asked in an undertone.

'I will tell you later.'

'You have totally confused Clarence.'

Anna flashed a smug smile. 'Good. Then it's working.'

Frankie laughed. 'The next few weeks will be entertaining. Clarence isn't familiar with confusion. His existence revolves around orderly control and intellectual reasoning.'

'Whereas mine is entirely spontaneous.' She grinned at Frankie. 'One of us will have to make concessions.'

A large hand came to rest on her waist. She felt the heat searing through the silk of her gown, flaming her blood.

'Good evening, Clarence,' she said, not needing to turn to know who owned that hand.

'You look adorable,' he whispered. 'Good evening, Frankie,' he said in a more normal voice. 'Will you please excuse us for a moment? I have something to say in private to Annalise.'

'By all means,' Frankie replied.

With his hand still on her waist, Clarence steered Anna into the small salon.

'Whatever do you wish to say to me that cannot be said in front of my family?' she asked, somewhat breathlessly.

'It is more a case of what I have to give you.'

Before she could ask what he meant, he produced a box from his pocket. Obviously a ring box. She had not thought of that, hadn't expected a token to seal their supposed engagement. He opened it and she gasped loud enough to draw attention from the adjoining room. A superb, very large sapphire circled by exquisite diamonds sparkled against the black velvet lining of the box.

'It is beautiful!' Anna said, awestruck.

'It reminded me of the colour of your eyes.'

'Clarence, that was a very romantic thing to say.'

'You see, I am learning. You will find me a very responsive pupil.'

He extracted the ring from the box and slid it onto her finger. It was a perfect fit. She waggled her finger about, admiring the light refracted by the stones from all angles.

'It is a Ceylon sapphire,' Clarence said. 'The very best they had.'

'Was it your mother's?'

Anna regretted the question when a cloud darkened his expression. Up until that point, he had been like a little boy, rare excitement cutting through his suave exterior in his anxiety for her approval.

'No,' he said curtly, his eyes flat and hard.

'I would not have you wear anything of hers. All the jewellery I give to my wife will be selected to suit her personality.'

'Then she will be very fortunate. And you may rest assured I will take very good care of this ring and return it to you when the time comes.'

Anna smiled up at Clarence, expecting him to finally ask what she meant by that comment. He did not. Instead, he lowered his head and their lips collided, briefly. Far too briefly for Anna's liking, but the contact was still sufficient to send soaring excitement spiralling through her veins, heightening her perceptions and making her long for a mysterious something that had thus far been lacking in her life. An omission she was absolutely sure Clarence would be able to rectify, *if* she went through with the marriage.

'I have wanted to do that since first setting eyes on you,' he said softly. 'And, just so you are aware, I intend to do a more thorough job of it the next time we are alone.'

Anna gulped, too overcome by surprise at the raw intensity evidenced in his expression to point out this was his second romantic comment in as many minutes. She bit her lower lip, which still tingled from its brief contact with his, and remained silent.

'Come,' he said briskly, once more placing

a hand on her waist. 'We ought to rejoin the others so you can show them your ring.'

* * *

Clarence escorted Annalise into the crowded ballroom where many pairs of eyes followed their progress with varying degrees of interest. Many of the gentlemen would be disappointed. A large number of them had fixed their interest on Annalise, and not only because she possessed such a large dowry. Clarence had no need of her money, but an alternative use for it was already formulating in his brain.

Their hostess was positively bursting with joy because Annalise appeared at her ball on Clarence's arm, confirming the rumours that had been circulating. Clarence's training saw him through the interlude with a gushing Lady Ancel as he said and did all the right things with charm and grace.

Annalise had never looked more beautiful or composed. She played her part superbly, sending him frequent adoring glances that had been conspicuous by their absence at Sheridan House. But he could sense that she was actually a tangle of uncertainty and nervousness. Nervous with him, of facing von Hessel, or disappointing her myriad admirers? Clarence wished he knew.

'You look radiant,' he said, tightening the muscles in his forearm upon which her hand rested, his ring glistening on the outside of her glove. 'Half the men in this room want to detach my head from my body at this precise moment, for which I can scarce blame them.'

'You are getting very good at paying me compliments, Clarence. Be careful. I might grow to expect it.'

'I shall do my humble best not to disappoint.'

'Harrumph, there is absolutely nothing humble about you.'

'Why, thank you.'

'That was not intended to be a compliment.'

'Nevertheless, I shall take it as such.' He chuckled at her affronted expression, aware that she was still on edge. Hardly surprising. The last time she had set foot in a ballroom, she had been abducted from it. 'Relax. This is your night to shine. Forget about everything else and enjoy yourself.'

'Is that not what I should be saying to you?' She flashed him an adorably wicked smile. 'After all, I *know* how to relax. You do not.'

'Then I rely upon you to teach me.'

The crowd swirled around them as they made slow progress across the room. Many congratulations were sent their way, some people even applauded. Twice he was briefly accosted by politicians keen for a private word. He frowned, making it clear that this was neither the time nor the place. He could see Annalise did not appreciate the interruptions. It occurred to Clarence that he could hardly blame the men who tried to stop him since he had made a habit of entering society specifically to speak with such people away from the hotbed of gossip at Whitehall.

'There is von Hessel,' Annalise said, tensing again.

Clarence tapped the fingers of the hand still resting on his arm. 'Ignore him, smile, and let him wonder.'

'Oh no. Lord Roker is heading our way. I'm not sure I can face him.'

'Then you shall not.'

Clarence effortlessly steered her in another direction. The crowd swallowed them up, and Lord Roker disappeared from view.

'Thank you,' she said.

'My pleasure.' They continued to stroll and Clarence sensed her relax her rigid pose, just fractionally. 'Are you familiar with the layout of this house?'

'No, I have never set foot in it before. Why do you ask?'

'I ask because you look far too anxious. I have many skills, but relieving young ladies of needless anxiety is not one I recall being called upon to employ.' He smiled at her. 'Frankly, I don't have the first notion how to go about it.'

Her eyes widened and she sent him a teasing smile. 'I have discovered something you do not excel at?'

'That we have yet to establish. Just because I have never had to do it before, it does not follow that I'm inept.'

She rolled her eyes. 'Modesty becomes you so well.'

Clarence chuckled. 'This might sound desperate, but the only way I can think of to remove the haunted look from your lovely eyes is to take you somewhere private and kiss you witless.'

'Lord Romsey!'

'I did warn you I'm a novice at this, but admit it, sweetheart,' he said, offering her a wicked smile, 'you are intrigued.'

'I am not sure how to answer such an arrogant assumption.'

'Ah, but you are now so cross with me that you have forgotten to be anxious.' This time his smile was imbued with smug satisfaction. 'I rest my case, *and* reserve the right to claim my kiss. We must do everything we can to maintain appearances.'

She tossed her head. 'If you say so.'

'Oh, I do.' A rich chuckle rumbled in his chest. 'I most assuredly do.'

Lord Jenkins appeared before them and bowed. 'I understand I am to congratulate you both,' he said stiffly.

'Thank you, Lord Jenkins,' Annalise replied with the sweetest of smiles.

'You are a lucky man, Romsey.'

'I am well aware of that.'

'With your permission, Romsey, may I have the pleasure of this dance, Lady Annalise?'

Clarence was most reluctant to let her go, but had no choice. He surrendered her to Jenkins' care and stood at the side of the room, watching them. Amelia Hardgraves appeared at his elbow without his noticing her approach.

'So, Clarence, you have fallen prey to the parson's mousetrap. She is an enticing package, but still, I must confess to being surprised.'

'Thank you for your congratulations, Amelia.'

Amelia's smile lacked warmth. 'I was unaware your tastes ran to virginal heiresses.'

Clarence was sorely tempted to point out that was because it had been so long since she had been one herself. Naturally, he didn't give voice to such a vulgar thought. He and Amelia had enjoyed a casual affair some months previously. Clarence had ended it. Amelia had wanted it to continue and had been a thorn in his side ever since.

'You know where to find me when the bloom fades from the rose,' she said, sounding a little desperate. 'Shall we join the dance?'

'Thank you, but the sets are already complete.'

'I shall not take offence.' Amelia deployed her fan somewhat aggressively, possessive jealousy imbued in the gesture. 'I can understand why you no longer want your name to be associated with mine. I also know marriage will not suit you. You are not cut out for it, which is why you and I rubbed along together so well.'

'We had an enjoyable time, Amelia, but both understood it wasn't permanent.'

'Precisely my point. Neither permanency nor monogamy form part of your character.'

'Perhaps you don't know me as well as you imagine,' Clarence replied curtly.

'On the contrary, I understand you perfectly.' She paused. 'I must say, I am surprised Winchester allowed you to address his beloved sister.'

Clarence was grateful when others joined them, saving him from responding. Von Hessel held him in a death glare from the opposite side of the room. Whimsically, Clarence nodded in his direction. The gesture was so out of character he wondered what had come over him. Annalise's influence must be rubbing off on him, he supposed. Von Hessel acknowledged him in similar fashion and finally averted his gaze.

The dance came to an end and Jenkins returned Annalise to Clarence, expressing polite thanks before walking away. Clarence glanced down at her face, glowing with animation. She did not glow in a similar fashion for him — a situation Clarence had every intention of rectifying in the near future.

'Miss Anderson must be delighted,' Annalise remarked, nodding across the room to where she was being entertained by Lord Roker. 'I do hope she enjoys poetry.'

'You really are a romantic,' Clarence observed.

'Certainly I am. Everyone deserves to find true love.'

Clarence wanted to laugh at her naivety but refrained since it was evident she really believed what she said.

'Ah, a waltz,' he said. 'And so early in the evening, too. May I have the pleasure?'

'Of course you may, my lord.'

Clarence led her onto the floor and swung

her into his arms. Was she, like him, thinking of the previous occasion upon which they had waltzed together, and all that had happened subsequent to that?

'Don't!'

'What have I done?' she asked.

Clarence held her a little closer as they circled the floor. 'You are not permitted to think about anything other than enjoying yourself this evening. As your future husband, I absolutely forbid it.'

'Ah, so you intend to be a tyrant. Thank you for the warning.'

'Not a tyrant, my dear. Just a man who cares very much about your wellbeing.'

'Only cares?'

What the devil did she want him to say? Before he could decide, she spoke again.

'Oh look, Vince is waltzing with Frankie. I had thought Zach would take the opportunity.'

'He cannot take the risk.'

Annalise arched a delicate brow. 'Why ever not?'

'He waltzed with her at the last ball they attended. Were he to do so again today — '

'Ah, of course, the wagging tongues.'

'One or more of your brothers has not left Frankie's side since we arrived at this ball.'

'You noticed that when I did not?'

'I am trained to notice things.'

'What have you noticed about von Hessel?'

'He is behaving just as he should, but is intrigued by your presence, and wondering about our sudden engagement.'

'He is not the only one,' she replied sweetly.

God's beard, he had had enough of this. The dance ended and he all but dragged her from the room.

'Where are you taking me?' she cried breathlessly.

'Somewhere to make you see reason.'

He pulled her along behind him, opening doors randomly on either side of the corridor until he found an unoccupied sitting room. He took her into it and locked the door behind them. Then he pulled Annalise into his arms and subjected her to the searing kiss she so richly deserved.

16

Anna felt a surge of power ripple through her when Clarence lost his composure and dragged her from the ballroom. But that was nothing compared to the swirling mix of sensations she experienced when his strong arms closed around her and his lips claimed hers with such bold assurance that her senses reeled. He didn't ask permission, kissing her as though he had earned the right. After all the trouble she had caused him, he very likely had. In any event, Anna had no intention of putting up protests. She had never been kissed before and was anxious to discover what all the fuss was about.

She wasn't left in ignorance for long.

He slanted his mouth above hers and kissed her with heart-stopping precision. Well, she was almost certain the ambiguous ecstasy flooding her body, as his hands roved her back and he coaxed her lips apart with his skilful tongue, was sufficient to stop her heart from beating. Her breasts were pressed against his coat, her nipples raised, solid and sensitive against the friction caused by his movements. She wound her arms around his neck, tangling her fingers in his thick hair as she, probably inexpertly, attempted to return his kiss.

Her reaction appeared to be all the encouragement he required. His tongue slid past her parted lips and explored the contours of her mouth with lazy expertise as he deepened a kiss that appeared to go on forever. Anna wasn't complaining about its quality or its length, even when her head started to swim and her breathing fractured. In fact, she couldn't seem to breathe at all and boldly stole air from his mouth. With her lungs no longer protesting, she pushed herself closer against Clarence's body. She savoured the tingling exhilaration that cascaded through her, already wanting more, much more of him.

A small moan of protest slipped past her lips when he finally broke the kiss.

'I did warn you what to expect if you provoked me,' he said, his eyes flashing with a silent message of conquest as he gently untangled her arms from around his neck.

'I didn't intentionally provoke you.' Her voice sounded shaky and most unlike her own. 'But if that is to be my punishment, I cannot give my word I won't deliberately do so in future.'

He sent her a wicked smile. 'The next time you provoke me I shall put you across my knee and spank you.'

She gasped. 'You wouldn't dare!'

'You've spent the entire evening smiling at other gentlemen,' he told her in a low, stirring voice containing a hint of censure. 'Unless you want to discover that I don't make idle threats, it's not a course of action I would recommend.'

'I have not!' But she had. She had done so quite deliberately, simply to evoke his jealousy. 'I always smile. It is what ladies are supposed to do in ballrooms.'

He wagged a finger at her. 'Not in the way you smiled at Jenkins when you danced with him.'

'How would you know? You were talking to one politician after another and didn't spare me a glance.'

'You mistake the matter,' he said, somewhat coldly. 'Suffice it to say, if you wish to flirt, then confine your activities to me. I am not a patient man and don't share what is mine.'

'You have endless patience. You are a diplomat.'

He shrugged. 'Not when it comes to you, apparently.'

'No, when it comes to me, you seem to think you can dictate my every move. I advise you against such a course. Ask my brothers if you doubt me. They christened me *Trouble* for a reason.' She sent him the sweetest of smiles. 'I think it only fair to warn you, I don't take orders well. That is why we can't go through with this farce of a marriage. You will want to control everything I do, stifle my character, and that would make us both miserable.'

'I don't understand what it is you want from me, Annalise,' he said, softly running a finger down the curve of her face. Her heart melted when she saw the tenderness and bewilderment in his expression. 'You have me, we shall be married soon, and there's an end to the matter.'

She looked at him for a long time without speaking, nibbling absently at her index finger as she did so. He really didn't understand and she found that unendurably sad. He was a very passionate man. She knew that after having been kissed by him. And yet he was incapable of committing to her emotionally by telling her that he loved her. That was all she needed to hear. Was it so very much to ask? At that moment, she wished his father had been alive just so she could tell him precisely what she thought of him for the damage he had inflicted upon his highly intelligent, beautiful, yet emotionally deprived son.

'Tell me about growing up with your father,' she said, turning away from him. 'What was it like? What was he like?'

'Demanding,' he replied succinctly.

When he said nothing more, she swung around to face him again. 'Is that all you can say?'

'Annalise, you really don't want to know, and I don't want to talk about him.' He sighed. 'He is gone, and I hope I am a better man than he ever was. God knows, that wouldn't be a difficult ambition to achieve.'

'He beat you?'

'For the smallest of reasons. He enjoyed it.'

She gasped when he told her about having to speak down the length of the dining table in a foreign language and being flogged in front of the servants if he made the smallest mistake. 'He did it for the last time when I was fourteen. I was as tall as he was by then, and considerably stronger. I grabbed the birch from his hands, snapped it in two, and told him that if he ever laid a finger on me again, I would use a birch on him. After that, I only had to suffer from the lash of his tongue, and that was hard enough to endure.'

Anna went to him and took one of his hands in both of hers. That small explanation told her so much about his character, and made her love him even more as a consequence.

'He sounds perfectly horrible,' she said lightly.

Clarence's eyes were clouded with the pain of remembering, but Anna suspected talking about his dark secrets might help him to put the past behind him.

'He did what he thought was right.'

'No, he took sadistic pleasure from being a bully.'

Clarence twitched a brow. 'Very possibly, but it doesn't matter now.'

'Is that why you decided not to marry? Because you thought you might be like him?'

Clarence sighed. 'We should not be having this conversation. Not here. Not now.' He shrugged. 'Perhaps not ever. I cannot think why I spoke about it at all. It does no good to dwell upon the past.'

'I disagree.' She was still holding his hand and ran her thumb across his palm, drawing intricate patterns upon it as she tried to formulate exactly the right words of reassurance. 'You are not your father. Never think for a moment you are anything like him.' She stood on her toes and grasped his face in both of her hands. 'I did not know him, but I don't need to have to be aware of that. You are a far better man than he ever was.'

'And yet, I just threatened to beat you,' he said lightly.

'You did not mean it, and even if you did, I

261

wouldn't permit it.' She laughed. 'All of my brothers have made similar threats at one time or another. I probably gave them good reason.'

'No.' The corners of his lips lifted and the grip of winter left his eyes. 'I don't suppose you would permit it.'

'Is the table your father misused still in the dining room at Romsey House?'

'I believe so.'

'Then it ought to be replaced.'

Anna was careful not to say she would see to its replacement. She was not yet ready to agree to the marriage. Now that he had revealed so much of his inner self — especially because he had — she was more determined than ever that he would tell her he loved her. Until he could do that, he would never shake off the spectre of the father who haunted him and live his life on his own terms. Anna accepted it would take more work, more stratagems, than she had anticipated. But at least now she knew what she was fighting against. Having been kissed by Clarence, she also knew it was a fight well worth undertaking.

'You may do whatever you like with Romsey House,' he replied, misinterpreting. 'It is long overdue for redecoration.'

Oh, Clarence!

'We are still a long way from that stage.'

He sent her a curious glance, obviously not understanding. 'Much as I would like to remain here with you, we ought to return to the ball before your family wonder what has become of us.' He reached out a hand, looking far more in control of himself. 'And no flirting with anyone other than me, Lady Annalise.'

'Lord Romsey, I would not dare.'

He chuckled. 'I think there is little you would not dare to do.'

'I can't deny that. I have an impulsive nature but can't expect *you* to understand the joys of reckless behaviour.'

'You do me an injustice. I am engaged to be married to one of the most impulsive ladies in London, who is rapidly teaching me all there is to know about impulsiveness. I hope I am proving to be a diligent student.'

'More effort is required yet.'

He tucked her hand into the crook of his arm. 'I am entirely at your disposal. What would you like to do tomorrow?'

She probably looked as surprised by the question as she felt. 'You are giving up part of your day for me, again, when you have Frankie's papers?'

'I am well able to delegate. I will only read the most sensitive ones myself. I shall spend the morning doing precisely that. In the afternoon, we could — '

'I want to see your apartment in Moon Street,' she said, demonstrating the impulsiveness she had just assured him was a large part of her.

He looked shocked. 'I can't take you there.'

'Why ever not? We are, as you keep pointing out, engaged.'

'Even so, why would you wish to see it?'

'I want to learn more about your character. A person reveals a lot about himself through his living arrangements.'

'I don't think your brother would approve.'

She smiled. 'I won't tell him if you don't.'

'We shall see. Now come, the dancing.'

Satisfied to have planted the seed, Anna walked willingly along, this time at his side and not dragged by the wrist.

'Excuse me for a moment,' she said when they reached the chamber set aside for use by the ladies.

'I will wait here for you.'

'There's no need.'

He fixed her with a look. 'There is every need.'

'Very well, if you insist.' A small part of Anna was glad he insisted upon taking such good care of her. 'I shall not keep you waiting for long.'

He leaned a broad shoulder against the wall and sent her one of his heart-melting lopsided smiles. 'Take all the time you need.'

Anna walked into the withdrawing room with a light step. She felt she had made huge progress with Clarence in the past half-hour, and already understood him so much better. She ran her tongue across her lower lip. It felt pleasantly bruised from the passionate nature of his kiss. She fell into the nearest chair, reliving the feel of those lips upon her own and the quite extraordinary way her entire body had reacted to him. God's beard, if that was passion then she wanted to know a very great deal more about its potency.

She wanted to know what happened next.

That was why she had suggested going to Clarence's apartment. If she could rouse his passions, perhaps he would reveal what was in his heart. It was certainly worth trying. She would not surrender to all his demands if she could possibly stop herself. If she did, it would leave her with no bargaining tools. But she was already discovering her half-formed plan to employ her feminine wiles was the very best way to break through Clarence's reserves.

She roused herself and attended to her reasons for visiting the room. There was another lady in the outer chamber when she returned to it. One whom she did not know. Anna nodded politely as she washed her hands, pulled her gloves back on, and carefully adjusted her ring.

'Congratulations,' the other lady said, her eyes focused on the ring. 'It is magnificent.'

'Thank you very much.' Anna paused, wondering why the lady was looking at her so intently. 'Excuse me, but I don't think we have been introduced. I am Annalise Sheridan.'

'Amelia Hardgraves.'

Hardgraves? Anna knew that name. Frankie had mentioned it once or twice, and not in a complimentary manner.

'Your husband worked in the diplomatic service with Lord St. John, I collect. I am sorry for your loss, ma'am.'

'Thank you, but it was several years ago now.'

'Even so, it must have come as a terrible shock.'

Anna went to leave the room, but Mrs. Hardgraves stopped her by placing a hand on her arm. 'I would strongly advise you to think carefully before marrying Lord Romsey.'

'I beg your pardon!' Anna stopped dead in her tracks and frowned at Mrs. Hardgraves. Who the devil did this woman think she was? What right did she have to offer advice?

'Clarence is not an easy man.' *Clarence?* 'Some men are destined for matrimony, others are not. Clarence falls into the latter category. Trust me when I tell you he does not have it in him to make you happy.'

'How can you possibly say such a thing? You do not know me.'

'But I know Clarence very well. He carries demons in his soul that will never give him peace.'

'He told you that?' *Please say he didn't. I so want to be his only confidante.*

'He didn't need to. It is obvious to anyone who studies him in unguarded moments. Oh, he covers it very well with those charming manners and that devastating smile, but beneath it all he is a very troubled man.'

'He is not his father,' Anna said, wishing the words back as soon as they slipped past her lips, implying she shared Mrs. Hardgraves' concerns.

'Ah, I see you already understand, although I doubt you ever had the misfortune to meet the previous earl. He was poison, Lady Annalise. Wicked, brutal and unfeeling.' She shuddered. 'I dread to think what poor Clarence suffered at his hands as a boy. He never speaks of it.'

And yet he told me a little about it. That thought gave Anna heart. She turned her attention back to Mrs. Hardgraves. When it occurred to her that she spoke with spite rather than sympathy in her tone, Anna realised the truth.

'You want him for yourself,' she said accusingly.

'*I* do not want matrimony. I tried it once and have no wish to repeat the experience. And so I can give Clarence what he needs, which is comfort and company when he requires it, freedom when he does not. You, my dear, are too young and inexperienced to know the difference, or to understand his needs. You are very beautiful and have half the *ton* worshipping at your feet. My advice, for what it's worth, is that you select a husband from that band, someone closer to your own age.'

'You don't know what you are saying.' Anna was furious, but the need to escape from this woman's viper tongue superseded the desire to put her in her place. She looked down at her arm, which Mrs. Hardgraves was holding in a vicelike grip. 'I don't think we have anything else to say to one another. Please allow me to pass.'

'By all means, but remember what I have said. Clarence will not remain true to you for more than five minutes, and you strike me as the type who will demand fidelity.' The woman turned her attention to the mirror and patted her curls into place. 'Don't say I didn't warn you.'

Anna flew out of the room as though it was on fire. She had thought for a moment earlier, when Clarence confided in her, she would be able to make a marriage between them work. Now, with a few spiteful words, all her uncertainties had resurfaced. Mrs. Hardgraves was right. Anna was young and inexperienced, while Clarence was a complex mix of authority and uncertainty. How could she have supposed she possessed the means to keep his demons at bay? She knew so little about him, so little about men in general, in spite of having four older brothers. Tears blinded her as she let the door swing closed behind her and ran straight into Clarence's arms.

'What is it?' he asked, frowning. 'What has happened to overset you so?'

'It's nothing. Let us return to the ballroom.'

'Not until you tell me what's wrong,' he replied, wiping a tear from her cheek.

Anna sensed a presence behind her, and felt Clarence stiffen. 'What did she say to you?' he asked in a mordant tone.

17

Recollections of Clarence's passionate kiss, tempered by the intensity of his controlled anger when he realised Mrs. Hardgraves had cornered her, ensured Anna slept fitfully. Mrs. Hardgraves' intimate knowledge of Clarence and her proprietorial attitude towards him haunted her, making her wonder quite what she had become involved with. She was prepared to do what she could to make Clarence fall in love with her. But she had neither the will nor the experience to fight off his lover. Nor was she willing to share him. On that point, she was fiercely determined. She was aware how many gentlemen entered into dalliances while their wives looked the other way.

Anna was not prepared to be such a wife.

She tossed and turned for much of the night and woke late the following morning, a headache threatening. When she found the energy to venture downstairs the house was unnaturally quiet and only Frankie was in occupation of the drawing room.

'Good morning, Anna,' she said, smiling up at her. 'Did you enjoy being the centre of attention last night?'

'Morning?' Anna laughed. 'It is almost time for luncheon. I don't normally sleep so late after a ball. Where is everyone else?'

'Your mama, Portia and Crista are shopping.' Frankie grinned. 'I suspect the duchess is already thinking about things for the baby.'

Anna smiled, imagining that would explain why Frankie had not accompanied them. Intimate as they now were, Anna had never found the courage to ask Frankie if she was saddened not to have had a child of her own. She suspected it must be the case. Every lady aspired to be a mother, did she not? Presumably shopping for baby apparel would be too painful to endure.

'I am perfectly sure she is. She has waited very patiently for this moment.'

'Lord Nathaniel has accompanied them, not very graciously, I might add.'

Anna laughed. 'I can well imagine.'

'I believe the duke is in his library and your other two brothers have taken themselves off to their club.'

'That's good. I was hoping for a quiet word with you.'

'What is it?' Frankie put her sewing aside and looked more closely at Anna. 'You don't look as though you slept well. Has something happened to overset you?'

'What can you tell me about Mrs. Hardgraves?' Anna asked, seeing no point in prevarication.

A flash of anger passed through Frankie's eyes. 'I noticed she was in attendance last night. I hope she didn't make a nuisance of herself.'

'As a matter of fact, she warned me against marrying Clarence. She said I could never make him happy and implied I was too young for him.'

Frankie ground her teeth. 'The vindictive witch!'

'Frankie!' Anna was shocked, and a little alarmed, by her friend's reaction. 'I have never heard you speak like that about anyone before.'

'That's because you don't have the dubious pleasure of being acquainted with Amelia Hardgraves.'

'I know she is very beautiful.' Anna paused, too embarrassed about the subject matter to meet Frankie's gaze. 'And . . . er, experienced.'

'Bah, she is very loose.'

'She is a widow. She is allowed to be.'

'I am a widow.'

'Yes, but you are nice.'

Frankie laughed. 'Thank you, but not

always. If people cross me or behave in a manner I don't approve of, then I cannot always hold my tongue.'

'I shall warn Zach.'

'The duke? What does this have to do with him?'

But Frankie's cheeks turned pink, confirming Anna's suspicions that Frankie was not quite as indifferent towards Zach as she made out. She was always fastidiously correct in her terms of address towards all of her brothers and her mother too, as they were with her. And yet, to Anna, it already felt as though she was a part of the family. It would be very interesting to see if her slightly detached attitude towards Zach, the fact she made a point of not pursuing him and didn't necessarily agree with every word that fell from his lips, worked to her advantage. Anna ardently hoped she would succeed where so many before her had failed.

Anna smiled in response to Frankie's question. 'I cannot think.'

'Regarding Amelia, she had her sights set on Clarence while her husband was still alive, but I happen to know Clarence would never come between a man and his wife, no matter how much encouragement he was given. However, Hardgraves wasn't cold in his grave before she struck, caught Clarence at a weak time, and . . . well, I also happen to know he broke the affair off some time ago but she is reluctant to let him go.'

'Ah, so they are no longer involved?' Anna felt relieved, but also a little perturbed by Mrs. Hardgraves' persistence.

'My dear, even if they had been, he would have set her aside the moment he offered to marry you.'

'I don't see why.' Anna shrugged. 'I don't know much about these matters, but I do know it is not unheard of for married men to keep a mistress.'

'Some married men, certainly, but not Clarence, if that's what concerns you. He is far too honourable, so you may rest easy on that score.'

'I have never seen him as angry as he was when he realised she had spoken to me. His face lost all expression, and his eyes took on a hard shine that quite startled me. He took a moment to collect himself, and then wanted to know what she had said, but I couldn't tell him. It was too excruciatingly embarrassing, so I brushed his concerns aside.'

'It wouldn't require much imagination for Clarence to work it out for himself. I think he regretted going anywhere near her very soon after he instigated the affair. Or rather, after she did.'

Anna was intrigued. 'You appear to know a great deal about it.'

She smiled. 'The diplomatic community is very close-knit.'

'Then it is hardly diplomatic for its members to become intimately involved. If this happened fairly recently, your husband was dead and you were no longer moving in those circles, and yet you still know of it.' Anna shook her head. 'Definitely not diplomacy at its finest.'

'I still have a lot of friends from the days when I was married. They keep me apprised of any interesting . . . er, developments.'

'Very delicately put,' Anna said, wrinkling her nose.

'Bear in mind even diplomats are human, my dear, and have the same needs as lesser mortals.' Frankie's wicked smile was infectious and Anna found herself smiling too. 'They just have to be careful where they turn to satisfy those needs.'

'If you say so.'

'Stop pretending to be shocked.' Frankie wagged a finger at Anna. 'You are not *that* innocent. Not if you spent so many hours trailing around after your brothers, spying on their activities.'

Anna laughed. 'That is undeniably true.'

'So tell me, what happened next?'

'Well later, when I was dancing with Mr. Brigstock, I noticed Clarence in a corner, in very intense conversation with Mrs. Hardgraves.'

'Well, of course he was angry, and of course he would take her to task for approaching you. It is the height of bad manners for a mistress — although she was never that to Clarence, more a dalliance — '

'There is a difference?'

'A huge difference.'

'Goodness.' Anna puffed out her cheeks. 'I have a lot to learn.'

'A man sets up a mistress in a property. He pays all the expenses, gives the lady an allowance as well as generous gifts, and usually undertakes to look after any children resulting from the liaison. Quite often, there are written agreements to that effect. A dalliance, on the other hand, such as Clarence had with Amelia Hardgraves, is simply . . . well, physical. I dare say Clarence gave her gifts, but nothing more. You have nothing to worry about. Amelia wants Clarence. Her feelings are not reciprocated, and that's an end to the matter. No one, but no one, will make Clarence Vaughan do anything he does not wish to.'

'I hope you're right about that. The woman made me feel very foolish. I didn't know what to say to her.'

'That was what she was relying on. She was trying to shock you into not taking Clarence. Pay her no heed.'

'Thank you for the reassurance. I shall try not to think about her again.' Anna paused. 'But what if I *do* marry Clarence. Is he likely to have another dalliance, or take a mistress?'

Frankie smiled. 'I doubt that very much indeed.'

'But gentlemen do.' She tilted her head, blushing as she asked Frankie a very personal question. 'Did your husband?'

'Goodness no. Gerald was many things, not all of them nice, but he most definitely did not look to other women.'

'It must have been very reassuring to have so much confidence in your husband's love.'

Frankie looked down at her folded hands, varying shades of irritation and dismay etched in her expression. 'Gerald and I understood one another very well,' she said in a tone that discouraged further questions on the subject. Anna sensed she had touched a nerve and regretted discomposing her friend.

'There is so much more to worry about when considering matrimony than I had at first realised.' Anna sighed. 'I mean, when we came out, every single girl had one subject and one subject only on her mind, which was snaring a rich and charming husband. None of us were warned of all the pitfalls along the way.'

Frankie smiled, seeming to have shaken off the reflective mood. 'Half the battle is working these things out for oneself. Besides, if a lady knew all the foibles pertaining to her heart's desire, she would probably run in the opposite direction, screaming.'

'It can't be so very bad, can it?'

'What cannot be?' Zach asked, joining them, both dogs at his heels.

'Your sister and I were discussing the joys and perils of matrimony,' Frankie replied.

Zach flexed his brows. 'Then I am interrupting.'

'Not at all, Your Grace. I believe we have exhausted the subject.'

'That I cannot accept.' He fixed Frankie with a challenging smile. 'It is a subject upon which most ladies always have too much to say.'

'How would you know, Zach?' Anna asked, sharing a wry smile with Frankie as she bent to scratch Phantom's ears. Frankie supplied a similar service for Phineas.

'I am a duke. I know everything.'

Anna shook her head. 'He always says that when he can't think of a better reply.'

Zach laughed as he took a seat beside the fire. 'That's because it is true.'

'Did I also mention that my brother numbers modesty amongst his many attributes?'

Zach looked down his nose at Anna in an exaggerated attempt to appear superior, only to succeed in making her laugh. 'I have something to be modest about?'

'I see what you mean,' Frankie said to Anna.

'Are you expecting Romsey to call today?' Zach asked.

'He said he might.'

'And so he should,' Frankie replied.

'I would prefer him to concentrate upon finding out what Count von Hessel is playing at, rather than dancing attendance upon me,' Anna said. 'I won't feel comfortable until that situation is resolved. I sensed him watching me at the ball last night and his presence made my skin crawl.'

'Don't worry,' Zach said, leaning forward to pat Anna's shoulder. 'I know you're still haunted by your ordeal. Romsey knows it too, and is determined to get to the bottom of it.'

'If he can spare the time,' Anna muttered under her breath.

'Did you say something, Anna?' Zach asked, looking a little bemused by her attitude.

'Oh, don't mind me.' She flapped a hand. 'I am quite out of sorts today. I must be more tired than I realised.'

'But still, something concerns you.' Zach sat forward and focused a concerned look upon Anna's face. 'Tell me.'

She shrugged. 'There's nothing specific to tell, other than that Clarence is too secretive for his own good. He won't tell me anything, and I keep seeing shadows where none exist as a consequence.'

'He's a diplomat,' Frankie said softly. 'It's how they operate. Don't blame Clarence, my dear. It is such instinctive behaviour, he can't help himself.'

'Yes, I'm sure it is. But I would feel so much better if he told us everything he knows, or suspects, about von Hessel's intentions. I can't help feeling he is holding something back, as though he is trying to protect me.'

'Better late than never,' Zach replied, scowling.

'Zach, we have already been through all that,' Anna said in a tone of exaggerated patience. 'I don't need protecting from the truth. It just makes me more nervous.' She sighed. 'Has Clarence confided in you?'

'No, you know everything I do.'

Anna drummed her fingers on the arm of her chair, but before she could challenge Zach, Faraday entered the room and announced Clarence.

'Well then, Anna,' Zach said mildly. 'Perhaps you will get your answers after all.'

'We shall see.'

Anna was surprised by Clarence's appearance. She had not expected to see him until after luncheon, if at all. He had said he would call, but he had so many other claims upon his time that were more pressing. She had lost count of the number of times he had been accosted the previous evening by serious-looking gentlemen who clearly were not there to dance. But here he was, and Anna felt her face heat as he headed straight for her. He sent her an infectious smile, took her hand and kissed the back of it.

'Are you all right?' he asked softly.

She knew he was referring to the incident with Mrs. Hardgraves, which was the real reason for her unsettled mood, and appreciated his sensitivity. She summoned up a smile of her own and nodded.

'Yes, I am perfectly well, thank you.'

Clarence greeted Frankie and Zach and took the chair opposite Zach's, which just happened to be next to hers. Phantom roused himself, sniffed Clarence's hand and then flopped back down on the rug again, next to his brother.

'I am glad to find you here, Winchester,' he said, 'because at last I have some positive news to impart.' He sent Anna a prolonged look. 'I thought you would want to know immediately.'

'We are all ears,' Zach replied, sending Anna an *I-told-you so* glance.

'It seemed to me a day or two ago that von Hessel's military record really must be as clean and heroic as all the reports I have read indicate. Believe me, if there was anything known to his detriment I would have found a reference to it by now. Therefore, his actions must have been for some other reason. I know little of his background in Prussia, or where he plans to live when he is married to Miss Outwood. The second part of that conundrum was easily resolved. I had someone ask Miss Outwood, who was more than happy to talk about it. It seems the couple are to live permanently in Prussia as soon as they are married, and von Hessel will put his wife's fortune to good use in filling his depleted coffers.'

'Miss Outwood told your people about his financial situation?' Zach asked sceptically.

'No, that intelligence came from elsewhere,' Clarence smiled, waving Zach's question aside with a negligent and very elegant flip of his wrist, 'but more of that directly. Discovering more about von Hessel's family circumstances required a less direct approach. Since we are fairly sure he is the person who ordered Frankie's abduction and took Annalise by mistake, and given he now knows Annalise and I are to be married, I could not approach anyone in his entourage and show an interest in his situation. It would have got back to him immediately and he would know we suspect him. And so I sent some of my people, people who cannot be connected directly to me, to speak to the Prussian community in England. And what they learned made for very interesting listening.'

'Are you planning to enlighten us?' Anna asked when Clarence paused for breath.

'Most certainly,' he replied, smiling at her impatience. 'Von Hessel has an uncle, a very powerful uncle, Count Brandenburg.'

'I have heard the name,' Zach said thoughtfully. 'But I had no idea he was connected to von Hessel.'

'To be honest, I only discovered that fact for myself a day or two ago.' Clarence shook his head. 'An unfortunate oversight. Had I known, I might have put it together sooner. However, where was I? Ah yes, Brandenburg. He has no children of his own, but three nephews. Von Hessel, then a man called Heinrich, who never served in the military. He has a twisted leg, but is Brandenburg's eyes and ears everywhere. Apparently nothing escapes his notice, and he has made himself indispensable to his uncle. The third nephew is a very interesting chap. His name is Wahlstadt. He served during the war and also enjoys a distinguished record.'

A footman appeared with refreshments and nothing more was said until he left the room.

'The uncle is the power broker in this drama,' Clarence continued, thanking Anna for the cup of coffee she handed him and taking a sip. 'Brandenburg's name is well known to me, although I have never met the man. It seems he's amusing himself by playing his three nephews off against one another. As a result of the Congress of Vienna, Prussia has regained much of her annexed territories, including the disputed Partition of Poland, which has been granted to them under Russian rule.'

'The Polish issue is a thorn in Prussia's side, I gather,' Zach said. 'Royal Prussia was disbanded in '06 and . . . ' Zach's eyes came alight. 'Brandenburg wants to recreate it!' Clarence nodded. 'How the devil will he achieve that with the Russians breathing down his neck?'

'He obviously thinks he can, and plans to put the best nephew for the job in charge of the scheme. Titles and riches will be poured upon that person, who will also be named as his heir.'

'And von Hessel loves being the centre of attention,' Anna said, finding the excitement flying between Zach and Clarence contagious. 'We also know he is no coward, in spite of his dandyish appearance.'

'Precisely.' Clarence briefly touched her hand. 'But his cousin's claim is equally valid, and he is married to a well-born Prussian woman, which finds favour with his uncle. Von Hessel was forced to look to England to find an heiress to finance his ambitions.'

'They will never get away with it,' Zach said.

'You underestimate patriotic fervour,' Clarence replied.

'But, even if they can achieve it, it will start a war against Russia.'

'I doubt whether they care.' Clarence shrugged. 'What is the sacrifice of a few more of their countrymen for the sake of their ambitions? Napoleon thought that way, and the French flocked to follow him.'

'True enough.'

'Are you absolutely sure about this?' Anna asked. 'Surely, such a daring plan could not have been missed by those watching the situation. We all know just how volatile matters are in Europe at the moment.'

Clarence fixed her with a look that implied he was impressed by the question. 'No, we are not certain. This information has been extracted from a number of different sources and we have pieced it together, coming to the only obvious conclusion. It explains why no one at the Foreign Office knows anything about it. Brandenburg is playing this close to his chest. But, whether we are right or not about the Polish issue, is not the point. We are absolutely certain Brandenburg is set to name his heir. We have had it confirmed by several different sources. That in itself would be enough to have von Hessel doing whatever is necessary to win favour.'

Anna nodded. 'And so you think von Hessel is not looking to destroy papers to his detriment, but rather discover some that will discredit his cousin?'

'Precisely.' Clarence shook his head. 'Fools that we are, we have been looking in the wrong place.'

Frankie, who had said nothing during the entire exchange, finally spoke. She looked pale and her hands were not steady. 'The name Wahlstadt sounded familiar the moment you mentioned it, Clarence, but I could not think at first where I had heard it. But, I am absolutely certain Gerald was looking into his activities immediately before he died,' she said slowly. 'That must be why I recognised it.'

18

'Are you all right, Frankie?' Clarence asked, concerned by her pallor.

'Yes, fine. Don't fuss, please.'

'Pardon me, but you don't look fine,' Winchester said, clearly concerned also.

'Thank you, Your Grace. That is just what a lady wishes to hear.'

Winchester sent her a teasing smile. 'That is not what I meant.'

Frankie encompassed both Clarence and Winchester with her gaze. 'If this man Wahlstadt knew of Gerald's assignment, and if he has something to hide . . . oh no!'

Winchester got up, poured brandy for Frankie and crouched beside her chair, encouraging her to take a sip. 'Calm yourself, Lady St. John. I can imagine what you are thinking. Your husband died under questionable circumstances, generally believed to be an unfortunate accident, but you are now wondering if Wahlstadt had a hand in his demise.'

'It is hard not to think that way, given subsequent events.'

'The thought had occurred to me as well,

Frankie,' Clarence said. 'And I will do what I can to get to the truth, never doubt it.'

'I know you will,' Frankie replied, sitting back and waving the duke away. 'I feel much better now, thank you.'

'It must be a terrible secret for someone to go to such extremes,' Anna said thoughtfully.

'The Brandenburg family lost a great deal of land when Napoleon took their territories, but they are now well on the way to restoring their wealth and consequence. Brandenburg's heir will be set for life. He would consider it well worth a little collateral damage to secure that position.' Clarence stood. 'And so, if you will excuse me, I must get back to study St. John's documents.'

'Is there nothing to help you in the Foreign Office's archives?' Winchester asked. 'After all, you said yourself you had not been looking for anything other than proof of von Hessel's guilt.'

'I have someone looking now, but am not optimistic. Von Hessel is intimate with the Prince Regent. If there was something there to show his cousin in a bad light, I imagine the prince would have found a way to get his hands on it, just to oblige his friend. It would also explain why von Hessel was so anxious to have a private conversation with you, Frankie, and why he sent people down to Winchester

288

to try and get inside your house.'

'Yes, I suppose it does. But if Gerald found something important, surely he would have passed it on to the Foreign Office, rather than keeping it himself?'

'I am sure he would have, but . . . '

'Of course.' Frankie's eyes dulled. 'He died before he could do so, and no one from the government has come to me asking if he left anything important behind. He had a secretary who handled all his sensitive papers, so perhaps they spoke to him. It did not occur to me that any might have slipped through the net.'

'Precisely.' Clarence sighed. 'The whole business is a muddle. You must excuse me from our engagement this afternoon, my dear,' he said, turning to Annalise. 'Under the circumstances, I must give priority to these papers.'

'Yes, of course,' she replied, a hint of sarcasm shaping the delicate arch of her brow as she looked away from him. 'Your duty must always come first.'

Damnation, he had upset her, but surely she could see how important this was? He didn't wish to frighten the ladies by pointing out the obvious, but none of them would be safe until this business was resolved.

'I'm sorry,' he said softly, touching

Annalise's shoulder. 'I will try to call this evening.'

'Do not put yourself out for my sake.'

Annalise concentrated her attention upon the dogs sprawled at her feet, and still wouldn't look at him. He was a little disgruntled by her attitude. How could she not know he would much rather spend his time with her? And he would so much rather, he realised with a start. Normally a conundrum such as the one created by von Hessel would claim all of his attention, but duty paled into insignificance when compared to the prospect of Annalise's enticing company. And yet his damned duty was still . . . well, his duty, and he couldn't relax until he had assured himself of Annalise's safety.

Had he just seen a glimpse of the real Annalise? The indulged daughter of a wealthy duchy, used to always having her way? It seemed unlikely and hardly fitted with his enduring image of Annalise fighting her way out of a warehouse and finding her way home on a borrowed horse in the middle of a snowstorm. Nor did it jibe with her reaction to the poverty she saw on the streets that night. It was impossible to fake that degree of empathy.

Clarence was a good judge of character, and he was seldom wrong in his assessment of his adversaries. He didn't want to think he was wrong about Annalise either, because he *would* marry her. He would marry her regardless of her frequent hints implying a change of heart on her part, and his own niggling doubts about rushing into a lifelong commitment when they barely knew one another. Then he recalled his reaction to having her in his arms the previous evening as they waltzed together. It had satisfied a need in him he hadn't previously recognised, and such recollections effectively eradicated his momentary doubts. Nothing that felt so sublimely right could possibly be wrong.

His life, up until that point, had been meticulously arranged, and he had no time to dwell upon occasional fits of loneliness, or the feeling that something was missing from his life. That feeling had intensified now he was back in England, living in the huge barn of a house he had grown up in. A house that had never felt like a home and held no happy memories for him. Since meeting Annalise, he had imagined the place filled with laughter, children running about and bringing it to life. In his imagination, Annalise was in the centre of everything, always laughing, behaving recklessly; pretending she was not at least as clever as her sister. That was what he wanted, he realised with a jolt. He wanted it so much he could taste it. He had supposed Annalise wanted the same thing.

But perhaps she did not.

'I don't mean to tell you your business, Winchester,' Clarence said, speaking in an undertone as his old friend accompanied him to the door, where Faraday awaited them with Clarence's outer garments. 'But it might be better if you all remained at home this evening, especially Annalise and Frankie. I don't want anyone using them to get to me.'

'I understand.' Winchester slapped his back. 'Anna is getting . . . well, to be honest, I'm not sure what afflicts her. I have never seen her so out of sorts before.' He shrugged. 'Delayed reaction to her ordeal, I shouldn't wonder.'

'Try and persuade her to rest. She looks worn out.'

Winchester rolled his eyes. 'I shall certainly try.'

'I won't keep you in the dark. That I promise. This business is reaching its zenith and will be resolved very soon. I can sense it.' Clarence donned his hat. 'Just keep them safe, Winchester, and let me handle the rest.'

'I will do my humble best.'

They shook hands and Clarence walked through the door that Faraday opened for him.

* * *

Anna regretted the manner in which she had responded to Clarence almost before he left the room. She had been most ungracious, and wanted to call him back and apologise. She probably would have done so, had not Frankie and Zach been there. But if they had not been there, she could have expressed her views freely to Clarence, and would not have been so out of charity with him. She could see perfectly well that the situation was serious and significant, not just for them personally, but for the fragile peace that reigned across Europe.

She had never seen Frankie so discomposed before. Clearly, she believed Wahlstadt might actually have murdered her husband in order to protect his secret. How shocking! Frankie's marriage was a puzzle. Anna thought from a few unguarded remarks her friend had made during their earlier conversation that it had not been an especially happy union, but the possibility of her husband having being murdered had affected Frankie profoundly. Well of course it had! Even if Frankie had not loved her husband, she had lived with him for eight years, shining as a political hostess and doing all she could to enhance his career.

Frankie and Zach were now engaged in quiet conversation. Anna felt as though she was intruding and wandered from the room, deep in thought. A political hostess. Is that what Anna would become if she married Clarence? Heavens, she would be more of a hindrance than a help to him. She never had learned to keep her opinions to herself and her spontaneity would most likely undo all Clarence's diligent work in one fell swoop. She shook her head. It was no good. The more she thought about it, the more convinced she became that a marriage would make them both miserable.

Anna entered her bedchamber, restless, on edge, feeling as though something momentous was about to happen. Thinking about her engagement to Clarence, and the possibility of seeing it through to marriage. She loved her intelligent, handsome, dedicated diplomat with a passion that stirred her soul. But, leaving aside her suitability as a political hostess, she also knew if she did marry him, situations like the one that had developed today would become the norm. His duty would always come first, their plans would be cancelled at the last minute because of some emergency or other, and she would never get to enjoy more than a fraction of his company. Worse yet, she could never claim that special place in the centre of his heart, because it was already occupied by his *duty*. His cold-hearted father, who had so much to answer for in the manner he had shaped Clarence's character, had seen to that.

Annalise had no wish to live her life on those terms, and if that made her seem overindulged and selfish, then so be it.

The luncheon gong sounded. Anna made her way to the dining room, plastering a smile on her face because Mama had returned from her shopping spree and would notice at once if she seemed disgruntled. She listened with half an ear to the chatter about their purchases and their plans for the rest of the week.

'Did you manage to find the new bonnet you intended to look for, Portia?' Anna asked, just to contribute to the conversation.

Portia laughed. 'You should have been there to see what the woman in the shop tried to sell me. I looked like a walking fruit bowl.'

'It wasn't *that* bad,' Crista said, stifling a laugh.

'It was bad enough,' Portia insisted.

'You look tired, Anna,' Mama said at one point. 'Are you feeling quite well?'

'Yes, Mama.' Anna managed a reassuring smile. 'I am fine.'

'Well, I have decided we all ought to

remain at home tonight. Even if you are equal to the demands of the *ton*, my dear, they have quite exhausted me. We shall have a quiet family dinner and celebrate Amos and Crista's news in style.'

Anna nodded her agreement. 'Good idea,' she said, sounding listless in spite of her best efforts to appear enthusiastic for the scheme.

'We shall not be at home to visitors this afternoon, Faraday,' Mama said over her shoulder.

'Very good, Your Grace.'

Ah, Anna thought, glancing at Zach and understanding. Zach had advised Mama to keep them all safely at home until Clarence had resolved the matter of von Hessel.

That was all very well, she thought, escaping back to her chamber as soon as luncheon was over on the pretence of needing a rest, but she was in no mood to sit about and wait for Clarence to call with more news. She needed to speak with him, and she needed to do so now. Anna was not blessed with a patient nature, which was another reason why she and Clarence would not suit. She had good reason to know his patience was endless. Otherwise, he would not have lasted five minutes in his chosen profession.

She needed to apologise for the way she had behaved that morning, and then tell him she could not marry him. Goodness only knew, she had dropped enough hints — hints which he had chosen to ignore. Well, she would confront him now in his Moon Street apartment. They would be alone, and he would have to face the unpalatable truth. A small sob slipped past her lips, but she swallowed down her anguish, determined to do the right thing, albeit by rather unconventional means. Calling alone at his premises was a little unorthodox, but they *were* engaged to be married. Besides, no one would ever know.

Her heart lurched at the prospect of what she must do. Knowing they could not marry was one thing. Explaining that to the man she loved, the man who could make her insides melt just by smiling at her in a particular manner, the man whose kisses sent tingles cascading down her spine, was entirely another. But it was for his own good as much as hers. He did not love her and would soon come to see she was in the right of it. One of them had to have the courage to face the truth, and one thing Anna had never lacked was courage.

Having told Fanny she would not need her for several hours, Anna was assured of privacy. Her only problem was escaping the house undetected. She took an old cloak from the back of her wardrobe and wrapped it around her, pulling the hood low over her curls. The garment was a dark, dreary colour and completely enveloped her. She would not be recognised. She felt a moment's anxiety about going out alone for the first time since her abduction. It was something ladies of quality simply did not do when they were in London. But when had Anna ever allowed such considerations to deter her from a particular purpose?

'You are looking for excuses to delay what you know must be done,' she told her reflection severely. 'Stop feeling sorry for yourself and get the pain over with.'

She was no longer in any danger. Only Frankie was, she reminded herself, and Zach had ensured the entire family would remain safely at home with Frankie forming part of it. Anna straightened her shoulders, reminding herself she could do anything she set her mind to. This was nothing compared to escaping from that warehouse.

No, it was ten times worse, because she was about to tell the man she adored she could not marry him.

A debilitating pain ripped through Anna, momentarily halting her in her tracks. As soon as it passed, she opened her door and glanced cautiously along the corridor. It was empty. At this hour, the rest of her family would be going about their various activities or, as she was supposed to be doing, they would be resting. No visitors would be admitted, so she was fairly sure of a clean getaway. But not down the main stairs. Faraday always seemed to know when a member of the family was about and materialised in case he was needed.

Anna went to the door that led to the servants' staircase and pushed it open. To her considerable relief, no one was using it at that moment. It would be difficult to explain why she was doing so if anyone saw her. She tripped lightly down the stairs, expecting at any moment to be challenged, but she saw no one. Presumably, the servants had a little time to themselves at this hour also. Certainly, she heard voices and laughter coming from the direction of the kitchen. Taking advantage of the staff's preoccupation, she slipped through the boot room and out into the mews. Harry, the lad who cared for Betty, saw her and looked surprised. She held a finger to her lips to silence him and, keeping to the edge of the building so as not to be observed from an upstairs window, she made her way cautiously to the street.

Moon Street was not far away and Anna walked briskly, keeping her eyes focused directly ahead of her. The weather had turned bitterly cold again and heavy clouds threatened more snow. Thoughts of her snowball fight with Clarence temporarily robbed her of her resolve. Perhaps there was a way she could make this work after all.

No, she told herself, there most definitely was not. She refused to settle for half measures, and that was all there was to be said on the subject.

Anna reached the building in which Clarence's apartment was housed. The door to the street was not locked, and she pushed her way through it, into a refined entrance lobby with a chequered floor. There was a desk for a porter, which was unattended. Good. She had not stopped to think how she would explain her presence to anyone other than Clarence. Before the porter could return, she slipped up the stairs to the first floor. Clarence lived in apartment 2c, which appeared to be at the back of the building, facing the gardens. She stood outside his door, took a deep breath, and then knocked.

Her knock was answered by a manservant, who looked at her closely, his expression giving nothing away.

'I am here to see Lord Romsey,' she said, tilting her chin, defying him to send her on her way again.

Her upper class accent must have persuaded the man, because he stood back and allowed her into the hall.

'Whom shall I say requires to see him?'

Before Anna could answer him, Clarence stepped into the hall. He saw her, stopped dead in his tracks, and then blinked as though his eyes deceived him.

'Annalise? What on earth brings you here?'

19

Annalise looked up at him warily, probably taken aback by the anger he was making no effort to keep from his expression. The reckless nature he had briefly found so refreshing no longer seemed quite so enticing. He had changed his mind about her being intelligent, too. She clearly did precisely as she pleased, without sparing a thought for the consequences. Sampson was standing impassively to one side, reminding Clarence of the awkwardness of the situation, if any reminder was necessary. There was a remote possibility Annalise had a legitimate reason for calling, he supposed. Best discover if that was the case before sending her packing.

'Allow me to take your cloak,' he said, his crisp tone formal, rigid.

Annalise removed her hood slowly, a flash of wariness passing through her expression, as though she suddenly realised just how angry Clarence was with her. With a careless shrug that was more in character, she then removed the cloak itself and sent him a challenging look as she handed it to him. She wasn't wearing a bonnet, and her curls were in tumbled disarray. Clarence refused to be diverted from his justifiable annoyance by thoughts of just how glorious those curls would look, spread out beneath her on a pillow.

'Go with Pierce to the Foreign Office,' Clarence said to Sampson in an undertone. 'Take the carriage and keep a sharp lookout. Defend those papers with your life. Do not show them to anyone until I get there. I am unsure whom to trust. If Castlereagh should happen to see you before I arrive, tell him I shall be there in an hour to explain everything.'

Clarence took Anna's elbow in a grip tight enough to bring tears to her eyes. He noticed them and relaxed his hand, just fractionally.

'Please tell me you did not come alone,' he said, his voice tight with controlled anger.

'Well of course I did. I wished to speak with you.'

They were now in his drawing room, which doubled as his library. It was a room he had never imagined Annalise would see, but was too irate to wonder what she made of it. He shook his head and invited her, with an exaggerated bow, to take a seat beside the fire. He reached for his discarded coat, and then thought better of it. Annalise would have to become accustomed to the sight of him in waistcoat and shirtsleeves, which was the way he preferred to work.

'I don't know why you are so cross with me.' She tilted her chin in a defiant gesture he was starting to recognise. 'The walk was short, and no one could have recognised me beneath my cloak. Even if they did, it is not me they wish to speak with. I was perfectly safe.'

'Even allowing for the fact that ladies of quality *never* venture out alone in London — '

'Don't think to lecture me, Clarence. I came because it was necessary. I have three things I most urgently need to talk with you about.'

Ye gods! 'So urgent that it could not wait until I call at Berkeley Square again this evening, as I said I would? What could possibly be that urgent, especially when you knew I had more pressing matters to occupy my mind?'

'Unless your duties prevented you from calling. Besides, we are never completely alone at Sheridan House, and what I have to say ought not to be heard by others.'

Clarence shook his head, astonished by her naiveté, or was it more a case of selfish determination? 'Frankie is the person von Hessel wishes to speak with, it's true. But he will also know by now that I have her husband's papers. The people he sent to Winchester will have discovered that much. He also knows you and I are engaged. If he found you wandering the streets alone, what do you suppose he would have done?'

'Oh lud, I did not think.' She raised a hand to cover her mouth, contrite but still not seeming especially concerned by the problems she could have created. 'Still, no one *did* see me, so it does not signify.'

There was no reasoning with her. 'You will be missed at Sheridan House sooner rather than later. Think how distressed your family will become if you cannot be found. Again.'

She lifted her shoulders. 'I will be back before they know it.'

'Once you are missed, this is the first place your brothers will look for you. Do you really imagine they will believe I did not invite you here?'

'I will not allow that.'

Clarence sighed. Vince and Nate, possibly Winchester also, would not give her the opportunity to explain before they resorted to violence. Her younger brothers still bore him a grudge, even though he and Annalise were now engaged. 'What did you wish to talk to me about so urgently?'

'Well, firstly an apology.' She looked him

unflinchingly in the eye. 'I did not behave well this morning, and was quite ashamed of myself afterwards. I know how important your duty is to you, and I should not have shown how upset I was at your eagerness to return to it.'

'Thank you,' he replied, his temper cooling fractionally. Her apology was hardly necessary and could most certainly have waited. But the fact that it weighed so heavily on her conscience that she felt compelled to call upon him and make it immediately said much for her character. 'Your apology is accepted, but you ought not to have taken such a risk to make it.'

'I also wanted to offer my help reading Lord St. John's papers,' she said. 'I thought that way we could resolve the problem more quickly. I may not know much about diplomacy . . . ' She bit her lip, as though attempting to quell a giggle. The gesture was so typical of her, so uncontrived, that the remnants of Clarence's anger fell away. He would have the devil's own job keeping control of her when they were married, but it was a task he relished. 'All right, I know nothing about diplomacy, but I *can* read.'

'Thank you, but we have found the documents already. I was about to take them to the Foreign Office when you arrived.'

'You know what was behind it all?' She bounced on her seat and sat forward, full of energy and excitement. 'Do tell. Oh, but I am keeping you from the Foreign Secretary. No wonder you don't want me here.'

Oh, I want you. Rather desperately.

'Don't worry. Castlereagh keeps all his visitors waiting a mandatory hour, no matter how urgent their business. I think it makes him feel more important. Pierce and Sampson are there now with the documents. I will join them when I have seen you safely home.'

'Then please tell me what this was all about. I must know.'

'It is very simple actually. It transpires that Wahlstadt, the favoured nephew, is not quite as brave in battle as von Hessel. Someone, somewhere must have got wind of that fact, which is why St. John was detailed to quiz some of the soldiers in his regiment.'

'What happened?'

'The Prussian cavalry was in the throes of reorganisation at the time of the battle of Waterloo. To say it was a shambles would be an understatement. Guns and equipment continued to arrive during and after the battle, but these handicaps were offset by the Prussian army. It had professional leadership and acquitted itself well, concentrating for battle at twenty-four hours' notice.' Clarence paused.

'All except Wahlstadt's regiment. Orders were sent down the line to attack at a vital time, but Wahlstadt claims not to have received them. The enemy broke through the area he was supposed to hold, and many lives were unnecessarily lost as a consequence.'

Annalise gasped. 'He was a coward?'

'Absolutely. It's evident from St. John's personal diaries that he spoke to a number of men in Wahlstadt's regiment, who all said the same thing. All but two of those statements have disappeared.'

Anna gasped. 'So, you *do* think Lord St. John was killed for them?'

'It is looking increasingly likely. Fortunately, they failed to find two of the most damning ones. They were the oldest ones and St. John kept them with his personal journals, presumably because he didn't know who to trust with them.' Clarence shook his head. 'I know just how he feels.'

'But you have them now?'

'Oh yes, I have them now, and because of it we might well be able to prevent Prussia and the Russians going to war.'

'How?' She looked up at him with adoring faith in his abilities shining from her eyes.

'Brandenburg makes no secret of the fact he puts military valour ahead of all other considerations. He is a patriot and expects all able-bodied men to fight for their country, especially his nephews. When he hears of Wahlstadt's cowardice, which we shall ensure he does, Wahlstadt will not become his heir. Naturally, we shall also ensure he hears of von Hessel's despicable attempts to accrue evidence against his cousin.' Clarence rubbed his jaw. 'In his position, I would have tried to find that evidence, too. I can certainly understand how ill-used he must have felt, knowing his cousin was a coward and seeing his uncle heap accolades on him. It is the way he went about it that I take exception to. Besides, he would be no better at keeping peace than his cousin.'

'Could he not have spoken to the same soldiers as Lord St. John did?'

'They were too scared of Wahlstadt to speak publicly. I understand from St. John's diaries he had to use stealth, cunning and bribery to get them to talk to him. Von Hessel wouldn't know how to act diplomatically. If he did, he would not have had the ludicrous idea of kidnapping Frankie, or rather, you.'

'What a terrible farrago.' She canted her head and smiled at him. 'If this is the sort of international muddle you have to juggle with the entire time, you must be exhausted.'

Clarence returned her smile. He was powerless to help himself. 'Your name will not be mentioned, of course, but Branden-burg will learn of von Hessel's heavy-handed tactics through diplomatic channels. He is not stupid and will know he'll make an enemy out of Britain if he favours von Hessel. He cannot take that risk.'

'Which leaves the remaining nephew. The one with the twisted leg.'

'And by far the best man to succeed Brandenburg. He is a thinker, not a fighter, and knows what is best for both his country and Europe generally.' Clarence smiled. 'We will have no problems with Brandenburg if Heinrich takes control.'

'He is like you, then. You prefer cerebral solutions.'

'I have seen more than my fair share of wars. They resolve nothing.'

'But men *like* fighting.'

'Not all men.'

'Well, I am very glad we have got to the bottom of it all. Frankie will be able to leave Sheridan House now, if she wishes to.'

Clarence lifted one brow. 'What makes you think she will not?'

Annalise shook her head. 'A thinker and an observer, but you do not see everything.'

'Very likely not.' He smiled at her. 'What else did you wish to speak to me about, Annalise? You said there were three things.'

* * *

Anna inhaled sharply, her stomach fluttering with nerves. Now that the time had come, she hardly knew how to start, or if she even wanted to. She was so very proud of Clarence, of the way he had reasoned it all out and already thought of a diplomatic way to avoid another European war that might well have seen England dragged into it in defence of her allies. But she could tell she commanded less than half of his attention, and suspected his thoughts were already on his forthcoming meeting with the Foreign Secretary. That realisation strengthened her resolve.

'It's about our engagement. I thought it best, before Mama gets carried away with the arrangements, that we agreed between ourselves we would not suit.'

He had been lounging in an elegant sprawl in the chair across from her. She could see at once that her words had taken him by surprise. He sat up straight and looked at her askance.

'Why ever not?'

'Oh, Clarence, don't be so obtuse! You only offered for me to save my reputation, which you have done most adequately, just as you do most things. After another few weeks, it will be perfectly safe to break the engagement, and no one will remember our silly snowball fight, or the fact that . . . well, I think it would be for the best.'

'I disagree.'

'I beg your pardon?'

'I am perfectly satisfied with the arrangement.'

'Perfectly satisfied?' She stood up, arms akimbo, compelling him to stand also. 'Is that all you have to say on the matter? Do you realise just how cold and unfeeling that sounds?'

'What is it that you want from me, Annalise?' he asked in a velvety smooth tone that made her feel weak at the knees, as did the darkly intense, slightly bewildered gaze searing into her profile. He really didn't understand.

'I want a husband who has time for me. If that sounds selfish then I make no apology, but I have no wish to live my life in seclusion while you gallivant around solving the world's problems. Let someone else do it.'

'I have all the time in the world for you.'

'You do not. You are married to your career, and it will always take precedence.'

'Ah, so that is what this is about.' Hair cascaded over his brow as he slowly inclined his head. 'I should have anticipated.'

'Then we are agreed? We should break our engagement at a suitable juncture?'

'I don't recall agreeing to that.'

'But you just said — '

'What other objections do you have to the union?'

You don't love me. But she couldn't say that. If she did, he might very well say the words, just to placate her. That would be worse than not hearing them at all. 'We barely know one another.'

'Then we shall become better acquainted before the ceremony.'

'You make it all sound so reasonable,' she said sullenly.

'You do not wish to marry me?'

Now was the time to engage in an untruth. If she did, she was sure he would release her. She glanced at his face, noticed a hint of vulnerability in his normally resolute expression, and found she could not lie to the man she adored. He was watching her closely, and she was the first to look away. She said nothing at all.

'I thought as much,' he said softly, now looking infuriatingly pleased with himself. 'Then what else can it possibly be?' He paced in front of the fire, no doubt thinking it through in his usual rational manner. Anna wanted to scream that not everything could be rationalised. Sometimes one simply had to listen to one's heart. 'I have it. My kisses do not excite your passions.'

'Be serious!'

'Oh, kissing is a pursuit I take exceedingly seriously. If that *is* the case, then I agree that a union between us would not work. One cannot live a lifetime with a person who does not excite one's passions. That is simply too much to ask.'

'That is it,' Anna said, sounding a little desperate. 'You have identified the problem precisely.'

'Liar!' He chuckled as he took a step towards her, a predatory gleam resident in his eye. Anna had never seen this side of Clarence before, didn't know what to do to counter his very obvious intentions, and instinctively took a step backwards. If he laid so much as one finger on her, she would melt and all her protestations would have been a waste of breath. 'If that is true, why are you afraid to let me touch you? Why did you come here alone, for that matter, knowing that I would?'

'I knew no such thing.' She took another backward step. 'I thought you would be poring over your stuffy papers.'

'I had an incentive to deal with them quickly. I was most anxious to call upon my intended, you see.'

'Oh.'

Another step backwards and her legs hit the side of a chair. She was trapped. There was nowhere else for her to go. Clarence pounced, swept her from the floor and into his arms.

'Put me down!'

'Certainly.'

He sat on the nearest settee and settled her on his lap. She opened her mouth to give him a piece of her mind, but before she could do so, his lips covered hers in a firm, searing kiss that made all objections flee from her mind. To her mortification, her arms wound themselves around his neck with lightning speed, and a needy little moan slipped past their fused lips. She wanted to think it had come from him, but knew it had not. Clarence would *never* lose control to that extent, whereas she had no self-control to speak of whenever she was with him.

His large, capable hands swept down her back, coming to rest on her bottom for a moment or two, before moving upwards again. His thumbs gently brushed the outsides of her breasts, setting a fire lancing through her and making her truly yearn for him. The small part of her brain still capable of rational thought told her that by coming here, by allowing him to kiss her and more, and showing such enthusiasm for the occupation, she had made her position ten times worse. It was all his fault. He was the one with all the experience, and he knew precisely what he was doing to her.

But nothing had changed. She still could not marry him.

He broke the kiss and she felt a deep, masculine chuckle echo through his chest. He had proven his point most effectively and was enjoying his moment of triumph. Exasperating man! She tried to wriggle out of his arms and regain a modicum of dignity, but his chuckle merely turned into a rumbling laugh, and her efforts made no discernible difference. His arms tightened around her like steel bands. She would never get away until he was ready to let her go.

'No more talk of breaking our engagement, Annalise. I have already told you once, if you don't behave yourself, I shall have to spank you.'

She tossed her head. 'And I have told you that you wouldn't dare.'

'Don't provoke me, and we shall never find out.'

'Oh!'

His hands caressed one of her breasts through the fabric of her gown. Her nipple became hard and sensitive to his touch, sending more fiery sensations streaking through her. When he tweaked it, she felt as though she would explode with desire.

'Shush, sit still and take your punishment,' he said, bending his head to trail a line of damp kisses down the column of her throat. At the same time, his hand increased the pressure on her breast. 'Tell me if you like that.'

Like it? She was perfectly sure her reactions told him all he needed to know, but that did not mean her words should stoke his already overinflated ego. 'It is . . . er, acceptable.'

'Acceptable!' His eyes gleamed with amusement. 'We shall have to see if we can do better than that.'

'You have an appointment with the Foreign Secretary.'

'He can wait. This is more important.'

Anna blinked. 'You think I am more important than the Foreign Secretary?'

'I believe I just said as much.'

'Oh,' Anna said for a second time, startled when she felt her bodice slide away. He had found the ties and loosened it, and was now gazing at her breasts covered just by the thin fabric of her chemise. Acutely embarrassed, and yet dizzy with passion, Anna glanced down and noticed her nipples pressing like raised pebbles against the cambric. Clarence bent his head and sucked one into his mouth through the thin material. Anna's world exploded in a starburst of pleasure beyond her wildest imaginings. She wriggled about on Clarence's lap as he continued to feast upon her breast, conscious of the hard length beneath her bottom.

'Sit still, my love, or I shall disgrace myself.' His voice was gravelly. 'How could you ever imagine I would let you go?'

'I don't know, but — '

'Shush, what was that?'

'A door closing.' Anna sat bolt upright, passion replaced by embarrassment at the prospect of being caught half-dressed on Clarence's knee. 'Pierce must be back.'

'Wait in there,' Clarence said urgently, all but pushing Anna into what proved to be his bedchamber.

He had only just closed the door when she heard voices and froze with fear. The stranger's voice was not that of Clarence's secretary.

It was von Hessel's.

20

'Count von Hessel,' Clarence strolled into the hallway, the epitome of calm. 'My apologies. I did not hear you knock.'

'Romsey.'

Von Hessel strutted the length of the hall, clearly discomposed by Clarence's unruffled and courteous greeting. They both knew he had not knocked, but Clarence would never make such an obvious . . . well, observation. How the count had got past the porter — how Annalise had managed it for that matter — was not a subject Clarence intended to address at that juncture. He had learned long since not to ask questions he did not already know the answer to, or to which he would prefer not to hear the answer. It had been foolhardy to leave himself open to this unannounced visit by not even bolting his door after Sampson left. There had always been a possibility of von Hessel calling on him once he learned of the removal of Frankie's papers from her country estate. He blamed Annalise for his laxity. She made him forget who he was supposed to be, and he never seemed to act with rationality when she was anywhere near him.

'To what do I owe the pleasure?' Clarence asked.

'You have something that belongs to me.'

Without waiting for a response, von Hessel pushed rudely past Clarence into the drawing room. That was precisely what Clarence had been hoping to avoid. He was confident of being able to get rid of von Hessel, but if Annalise made so much as a sound, or if von Hessel somehow detected her presence, it would leave Clarence in an impossible position.

'You have the advantage of me, von Hessel.'

'Let us not play games,' Von Hessel snapped. 'You know what I want, and I know you have it.'

Clarence merely flexed a brow. 'Would you care to be more specific?'

The Prussian sighed. 'I have no quarrel with you, sir. I merely wish to see St. John's papers. I know you are keeping Lady St. John out of my reach at Sheridan House, and I know you sent to Winchester for those papers.'

He folded his arms across his chest in a pose that was probably supposed to intimidate. Clarence was merely a diplomat and von Hessel a war hero, used to getting his own way. Unfortunately, von Hessel couldn't know Clarence was not easily intimidated ... unless — no he must not think about Annalise, his weakness, hiding on the other side of his bedroom door. He had imagined her visiting that room many times, but never under such circumstances.

'I know you are here alone,' he added when Clarence didn't reply. 'I saw your manservant and secretary leave together a short time ago, and you retain no other servants. It seemed like a good opportunity to pay you a visit.'

Thank God, he had not seen Annalise arrive. The man might be brave on a battlefield, but he didn't know the first thing about negotiating. If he was aware of Annalise's presence, he would have said so at once, and Clarence would have given him everything he wanted without equivocation. Except he could not, of course, because what he wanted was on its way to Whitehall. God alone knew how this unbalanced individual would react when he realised the game was up.

'I am sorry to disappoint you, but there is nothing amongst St. John's papers that will serve your purpose.'

'And you suppose you know what that purpose is?'

Clarence inclined his head, but said

nothing more to confirm it. 'St. John's papers are there, on the side of my desk,' he said instead. 'You are perfectly welcome to look through them if you don't believe me.'

'If something was there, you would not invite me to look.'

Clarence affected confusion. 'I would not?'

'I mistakenly abducted your future wife, for which I apologise. The fools I hired could not follow simple orders, but I do understand you have every reason to bear me a grudge.'

'Then it is fortunate she escaped, since you would not have let her go.'

Von Hessel gaped, looking unsure of himself for the first time. 'You think I would kill a woman?'

'You thought nothing of abducting one.'

'There is a very great difference between abduction and murder.'

'Oh, you would not have carried out the murder personally, but your orders were to *get rid of her.*' Clarence fixed him with a death glare. 'Fortunately for you, Lady Annalise is very good at climbing trees.'

'I meant for those idiots to take her somewhere closer to her home and release her.' He strode about, clearly agitated. 'I am not the ogre you appear to think I am.'

Clarence fixed him with a hard look. 'Really?'

'Tell me what you found and where you have put it. I don't have time to waste, and am not a patient man at the best of times.'

He exuded an air of desperation, which made him unpredictable and dangerous. Clarence wasn't afraid for himself. Despite what his visitor thought, what most people thought, Clarence could defend himself if the need arose. The problem was he didn't trust Annalise to remain hidden, should it come to that. She was far too reckless to allow Clarence to resolve the matter and would assume there was something she could do to help him.

There most emphatically was not — other than to remain safe and undetected behind his bedroom door.

'I have nothing that will help you, von Hessel.' Clarence sighed and ran a hand through his hair. 'Just go home and think of another way to appease your uncle.'

'You don't seem to understand the significance of St. John's damned papers,' von Hessel thundered, shaking his head. 'And they tell me you are quick-witted. My cousin is a miserable coward, but he knows how to intimidate. He is an expert at covering his tracks and at making himself indispensable to my uncle. It would be grossly unfair if he became his heir.'

'I know you served with distinction.'

'That I did. I know what people say about me, but unlike your fat prince, I earned the right to wear my uniform and do so with pride.'

Clarence nodded, conceding von Hessel had a point.

'I regret I cannot help you.'

'Oh, but you can, and one way or another, you will. You have not gone to all this trouble only to find nothing. You also fail to make allowance for the fact that if my cousin becomes my uncle's heir, then I have nothing left to lose, and every reason in the world to seek revenge against those who have stood in my way.'

Von Hessel walked up to Clarence and slapped his face with considerable force. The sound was like a gunshot echoing through the room. Clarence's head reeled, but he barely felt the pain.

'Let us deal with this like gentlemen,' von Hessel said in a reasonable tone. 'Don't make me hurt you, Romsey.'

A muffled sound came from the bedroom — precisely the reaction Clarence had been dreading.

'What was that?' Von Hessel's head jerked in the direction of the sound.

'Pardon me?'

'I heard something. A noise.'

Von Hessel threw his head back and sniffed the air. Perdition, Annalise's fragrance lingered in the air. More to the point, her reticule was still on the settee. Von Hessel's gaze landed on it at the same time as Clarence's.

'Well, well, Romsey,' he said, grinning. 'It seems I underestimated you.'

So saying, he wrenched open the door to the bedroom and Annalise, dishevelled, her gown not properly retied, tumbled into the drawing room.

*   *   *

Clarence had thrust Annalise into his bed-chamber and warned her to remain absolutely silent. Breathless with nerves, she had done what she could to refasten her gown. It was awkward because the ties were at the back, and she couldn't manage it properly, but that was the least of her worries. She listened to von Hessel's peeved voice — a voice she had hoped never to hear at close quarters again. It sent shivers down her spine when she recalled the last time she had heard it, and became furious when her hands started to shake.

She absolutely would not be afraid of the man!

She listened intently, attempting not to

make any noise. She suppressed a snort when von Hessel asserted he had not intended to kill her. She knew better. She had heard the cold finality in his tone, and knew he was a ruthless man who cared only for his own welfare. Dear God, what would he do to Clarence when he did not hand over the papers? He could not. They were already at the Foreign Office. When von Hessel learned that, there was no telling how he would react. He would probably kill Clarence out of spite. Her beloved diplomat was not a violent man. He would not know how to retaliate if a trained soldier like von Hessel attacked him. The thought of losing him caused a gut-wrenching pain to rip through her, twisting and tearing at her insides. She swallowed against the ache in her throat, determined to do whatever she could to help the man she loved with single-minded passion.

Even though that love was not returned.

'Keep him talking,' she muttered beneath her breath.

Pierce and Clarence's manservant would come and look for him eventually, when he did not arrive at the Foreign Office. But Anna was not prepared to trust to luck and conducted a silent, methodical search of Clarence's bedchamber, looking for something, anything, she could use as a weapon. His room was meticulously neat, just like the rest of his life, but also dispiritingly sparse. His drawing room had struck her the same way. A single man's abode in which he clearly did no entertaining, it doubled as a library, books and papers neatly stacked everywhere. It was fitted with good quality furniture, but lacked soul — nothing to make it homely. Poor Clarence. His practical living arrangements had to be a direct reflection upon his upbringing. They evidenced a man trained not to show emotion, and displayed no hints about his character or aspirations. Anna was perfectly sure there was a warm, deeply sensitive, caring gentleman beneath all those layers of discipline and control. She wondered if she would ever get to unravel them and finally meet him.

Adjuring herself not to daydream, she concentrated upon her search for a weapon. She fully intended to intercede, but could hardly walk into the room clutching something with which to thump von Hessel's head. He would relieve her of it and laugh while doing so. No, she needed something small — something small and sharp that she could conceal about her person. She opened and closed drawers and cupboards as quietly as she could, counting upon the men's voices to drown out any sound she might make. At the same time, she strained to listen to their conversation — or rather to von Hessel's diatribe.

She was on the point of giving up her hunt when she happened upon the sapphire pin Clarence sometimes wore to secure his neckcloth, neatly placed in a box in the drawer that housed those neckcloths. Just the very thing! It fitted comfortably in her hand, and she closed her fingers around its stem at precisely the moment when von Hessel struck Clarence. Anna cried out in alarm. She simply couldn't help herself.

The door flew open, and von Hessel leered at her as he grabbed her arm and dragged her into the drawing room.

'Good afternoon, Lady Annalise,' he said courteously. 'Romsey was remiss in not advising me of your presence. I suppose he was trying to protect your reputation, but it seems a little late for that.' He smirked as his glance settled upon her inadequately fastened gown. 'I really did underestimate you, Romsey. Not that I can blame you, of course. I had her in my sights, being in need of an heiress, you understand. She would have been a much better proposition than Miss Outwood, but I knew Winchester would never give his approval.' He shook his head. 'Pity that.'

'And I would die before I gave you the time

of day,' Anna said dismissively.

'I think I could change your mind on that score.'

'And I am equally sure you could not.'

Von Hessel chuckled. 'She is a real little wildcat, Romsey. I envy you.'

'Are you all right?' Clarence asked her, his expression cloudy with concern.

'I might ask the same thing of you.'

'Touching as this reunion is,' von Hessel said, 'I don't have time to waste.' He kept a firm grasp of Anna's arm. 'I will ask you one more time, Romsey. Where are the papers I need?'

'On their way to — '

'No, Clarence! Don't say anything.'

'On their way where, Romsey?' Von Hessel pulled Anna so close his breath peppered her face. She was sorely tempted to stamp on his foot, or bite him — something, anything to distract him and give Clarence an opportunity to overpower him. She hated inactivity, but forced herself to bide her time.

'My secretary has taken them to the Foreign Office. You are too late.'

'I don't believe you. You would not let such documents out of your sight for any consideration.'

Clarence raised an indolent brow. 'Would I not?'

Anna sensed the moment when realisation dawned on von Hessel. 'Ah, of course. Lady Annalise is distraction enough to make even you forget your duty.'

'There is nothing for you here,' Clarence said quietly. 'Just leave.'

'I disagree.' That was what Anna had feared. 'This is what will happen. Lady Annalise and I will remain here and enjoy one another's company while you scamper off to the Foreign Office and retrieve those papers.'

'The Foreign Secretary will have them by now,' Anna said. 'You are too late.'

'I doubt that, but even if he does, Romsey is a skilled diplomat. He will think of a very good reason to take them back again.' He paused, sending Anna a salacious grin. 'I very much hope for your sake that he does.'

'I will go at once,' Clarence said reaching for his coat.

Anna couldn't allow that to happen. His willingness to act unhesitatingly against his conscience for her sake increased her determination. She knew when this episode was all over he would never be able to reconcile himself with his actions, driving yet another wedge between them. If she had not come here this afternoon, Clarence would already be at the Foreign Office and von Hessel would have been bested. It was all her fault.

Again.

She had to do something to make it right. She still clutched her pin, but that would only slow von Hessel momentarily. She glanced around frantically. Her eyes fell upon a Chinese bowl sitting on a table directly behind her; one of the few ornaments in the room. It would have to do.

She pretended to wilt against von Hessel's grasp. The action took him unawares, and while he was off balance, she thrust the pin into his thigh with all the force she could muster. He cried out, in surprise more than pain, she suspected. With him thus distracted, she picked up the bowl and crashed it against the side of his head. Blood poured from his ear; curses spilled from his lips. He pushed Anna violently, and she fell to the floor.

About to grasp von Hessel's ankle and attempt to tug him to the floor, a roaring sound distracted her. Unsure at first where it came from, she was not left in ignorance for long. Clarence, her gentle, intelligent, non-violent Clarence, bellowed like a wild bull as he lunged at von Hessel.

'No!' she screamed.

Von Hessel sent her an amused grin, simultaneously blocking Clarence's blow, which glanced off the side of his head, doing no real damage.

'You really are full of surprises, Romsey,' von Hessel said in a hectoring tone. 'I never would have thought anything could rouse you to violence. Although, I suppose, Lady Annalise is enough to bring out the hero in any man.'

Annalise couldn't stand it. She had to do something, anything, to even up this contest. Clarence would be killed, or badly injured, if she did not. Desperately, she did lunge for von Hessel's ankle this time. He merely glanced down at her, shaking off her hold as though she was an irritating fly. But the distraction gave Clarence the opening he needed. He pulled back one clenched fist and planted it in the centre of his adversary's face. Anna heard the sound of breaking bone and, from her position on the ground, saw blood spurt from von Hessel's nose. Clarence had clearly put considerable force behind that blow, but he wasn't finished yet. He used his other fist with even greater force, knocking von Hessel clean off his feet. He crashed his head hard against the fireplace as he fell, and lay there unconscious.

21

Clarence reached for Annalise and pulled her gently to her feet.

'Are you all right?' he asked anxiously.

'Clarence,' she replied, eyes wide and slack jawed. 'You used violence.'

Clarence glanced at von Hessel's sprawled form with murder in his eyes. 'The cove threatened you.'

'Yes, but even so, violence settles nothing. You said so yourself.'

He touched the curve of her face tenderly. 'Sometimes it is the only way. And,' he added, smiling, 'it can be very satisfying. Von Hessel won't be quite so pretty now. Broken noses never settle back quite the way they were before. However, he will have greater concerns than his appearance to occupy him when he recovers his senses, such as they are.'

His arms closed around her as his lips brushed against hers.

'Your poor face,' she said, reaching up to touch it where von Hessel had struck him.

'His is much worse.' He looked smugly satisfied, showing he was not so very different from her brothers when it came to his enjoyment of pugilistic pursuits after all.

'That's true. What shall you do now?'

'Much as I would like to remain here and continue what we started before we were so rudely interrupted, I cannot.'

'I understand.' She lowered her head. 'I'm sorry, Clarence. I made things difficult for you again, just by being here.' She sighed. 'Had I not been, you could not have given von Hessel what he wanted, you would have made him see that because you are so clever with words, and he would have left you eventually. That is another reason why we would not suit. I never could do as I was told.'

He chuckled. 'You are not yet familiar with my persuasive methods.'

She shook her head against his chest. 'Even so . . .'

'Now is not the time.'

He kissed her again and released her with reluctance. Annalise immediately crouched beside the unconscious von Hessel. Dear God, don't say she was concerned about his welfare after everything he had done to her? He was breathing, and that was all Clarence cared about.

'He's alive,' she said indifferently, her actions echoing his thoughts.

Clarence's relief was extreme when she

extracted his pin from the unconscious man's thigh and gave it back to him. He thanked her and placed it on a side table.

'That was very quick thinking on your part. I was beside myself, trying to think of a way out of this farrago that would not see you get hurt, and all the time you had the answer clutched in your hand.'

'It was the only thing I could find that he would not immediately notice.' She glanced at the broken Chinese bowl. 'I'm sorry about that. I hope it wasn't valuable.'

'It was a gift from someone I met in the line of duty. I never did like it much.'

'What happens now?' she asked, hugging her torso to ward off the shakes that beset her, presumably a delayed reaction after the fright she had received. It was nothing to the way Clarence had felt when von Hessel so arrogantly manhandled her. Every bone in his body had itched to go to her rescue, but he could not do it without further endangering her. When he was finally able to strike the man, his satisfaction and the relief he felt had been immense.

'Now, I tie this individual up, throw him in the windowless store at the end of the corridor and let him see how he likes being alone in a cold room, without light.' Annalise nodded, apparently satisfied with that arrangement.

'Then I shall escort you home before going on to the Foreign Office. I dare say I shall be delayed there for a while. Then I shall come back here with the sergeant-at-arms and have our mutual friend taken into custody. What happens to him after that is for the Foreign Secretary to decide.' Clarence sent her a smouldering smile. 'When I have done all of that, I shall come to Sheridan House and hopefully receive an invitation to dine.'

'I dare say that can be arranged,' she replied with a sweet smile that did not reach her eyes. His beloved girl was in shock, or denial. Clarence was unsure which.

'I ought by then to be in a position to put everyone's minds at rest regarding this entire sordid affair. Obviously, you cannot say anything in advance of my arrival, or they will want to know how you obtained that information.'

'I do realise that.'

'I know you do. Please don't think I underestimate your intelligence, but you have had a shock. Another shock. And it might make you speak without thinking.'

Von Hessel had started to regain consciousness by the time Clarence finished binding him hand and foot. He started making a God-almighty racket, so Clarence gagged him before throwing him into the store. He bolted and locked the door, pocketing the key.

'Right,' he said, wiping his hands. 'That has dealt with him. Let me settle your gown properly and take you home.'

They walked the short distance to Berkeley Square in taut silence. Clarence would give much to know what she was thinking. He certainly hoped she did not still plan to object to their marriage. He would release her from her obligation if she could persuade him that was what she really wanted. But he knew from the passionate manner in which she returned his kisses that it was not. How to convince her, though? That was the question. What was it she wanted from him that he had not already offered her?

'I shall go in through the mews,' she said. 'I can abandon my cloak in the boot room, and if anyone sees me they will simply assume I have been to see Betty.'

'Very well.' They halted at the side door, and Clarence kissed her hand, a plan taking root in his brain to win her around. Something he would not even have considered up until today, but which now seemed not only timely, but exactly the right thing to do. 'Try to stay out of trouble until I return later,' he said with a rueful grin.

Anna was able to reach her chamber without encountering any members of her family. She felt buoyed up after the events of the afternoon, yet also desperately tired. She fell asleep in a chair beside the fire and woke when Fanny brought her tea.

That afternoon's demonstration of the pitfalls of Clarence's occupation ought to have solidified her determination not to marry him. Unfortunately, it had exactly the opposite effect. His willingness to do whatever was necessary to keep her safe had affected her profoundly, because it spoke volumes about how much he cared for her, even if he didn't actually realise it. The longing that flowed between them when he embraced her affected her more profoundly still. How could she give this man up?

How could she not when his occupation would always come first?

Another woman she could compete against, and fight for the right to call herself Lady Romsey. Against the full might of the Foreign Office, she did not stand a chance.

With a heavy heart, she dressed for dinner in an evening gown of pale lemon Swiss mull, edged with cream Flemish lace. She had not long been in the drawing room when Clarence was announced. His eyes sought her out immediately, and she died a little more inside as she absorbed the warmth of his lopsided smile.

Her family listened with great interest as he related the results of his activities, leaving out all mention of her presence at his apartment.

'So, it is all over,' Zach said.

'I can return to Hampshire,' Frankie added. 'Which I had always intended to do at the end of this week. I have had quite enough of society for the time being.'

'We shall be returning, too,' Amos said. 'And will be happy to take you with us.'

'Thank you, Lord Amos. That is most obliging of you.'

'Von Hessel is now in custody,' Clarence explained. 'He will be released without charge, eventually. We cannot risk dragging Annalise's good name through the mud by having him stand trial for her abduction.'

'Thank you for that,' Mama said.

'He will be held for a while, until we have destroyed his cousin's reputation and made Brandenburg understand Britain would not look kindly upon von Hessel becoming his heir. Once we are satisfied that will not happen, we will let von Hessel go back to Prussia and face his uncle's wrath.' Clarence chuckled. 'I fancy he would prefer to remain here and try to mend fences with Miss

Outwood, but I am equally sure her family will not permit her to give him the time of day once it becomes known he has acted against this country's interests.'

'He hasn't,' Vince pointed out. 'Well, not directly.'

'Oh, I think you can leave it to my friends at the Foreign Office to start enough rumours to make him *persona non grata* in the best circles.' Clarence executed an elegant shrug. 'You know how these things are done.'

'Not precisely,' Nate said grinning. 'But you obviously do, which is all that signifies.'

Dinner was announced, and Clarence escorted Anna in. She tried to be her usual lively self and join in the conversation as she always would, but her heart wasn't in it, and she suspected it showed. She was conscious of Clarence sending her frequent concerned glances, but there was no opportunity for him to speak with her alone, which in her present unsettled state of mind, she considered to be just as well.

He left her at the end of the evening, promising to call the following afternoon. Anna trailed up the stairs, knowing that would be the time when they must settle matters between them once and for all.

★ ★ ★

It snowed heavily again overnight, but that was insufficient to deter Clarence from keeping his engagement to call upon Annalise. Her preoccupation the previous evening had concerned him almost as much as her continued determination not to marry him. He walked through the snow-covered streets to Berkeley Square, rehearsing in his head all the things he planned to say to her, nervous in a way he never was in even the most delicate of diplomatic situations.

The weather had kept the entire family at home, but Anna made no objection when he suggested a walk in the park. A hint of a smile graced her lips, presumably because she recalled their last venture into that open space and the havoc it had wrought. She returned quickly wearing the same velvet pelisse as previously, and they set off together with Annalise's hand firmly grasping his arm.

'Be careful,' he cautioned, just as he had once before. 'It is very slippery.'

'But you will not allow me to fall.'

He regarded her with absorption. 'Never,' he replied softly.

'Where are we going?' she asked a few minutes later. 'This is not the way to the park.'

'No, it is not.'

By that point, they had reached Moon

Street, and she didn't protest when they walked into the lobby of his apartment building. Clarence nodded to the porter and led her straight out again through the back door. They were now in the large garden. Annalise blinked as though she was seeing things, and it took her a moment to react to the surprise he had prepared for her. Chimes of her spontaneous laughter echoed around the open space when she eventually did so.

'Your work?' she asked, pointing to the rather lumpy snowman sitting in solitary splendour in the centre of the lawn.

'My reckless side that you have awakened,' he said softly. 'I apologise if he is not very lifelike, but it is my first attempt at a snow sculpture.'

'You never made one as a child?' Annalise shook her head. 'No, of course you did not. That was a foolish question.' She stared at his creation, and then at Clarence for a prolonged moment, a smile flirting with her lips. 'And yet you did this for me?'

He nodded. 'I thought you would approve.'

'Oh, I do, but the question is, did you enjoy yourself, or did you consider it a waste of time because you were not doing something more worthwhile?'

'Please don't insult my snowman's feelings. He's a very sensitive chap and considers himself to be very worthwhile.'

'Certainly he is. I know that, but I was unsure if you did.'

'Come on, it's freezing out here, and there is more.'

'More surprises?' She sent him an inquisitive look. 'Goodness, you spoil me.'

Without responding, he took her hand and led her back inside, up the stairs to his apartment. He used his key to let her in, locking the door carefully behind him, and adding the precaution of shooting the bolt across, even though he did not envisage any uninvited callers on this occasion.

'Pierce is at the Foreign Office,' he told her in answer to her unasked question. 'And I have given Sampson the afternoon off. We are quite alone.'

'I see.'

She seemed nervous as she removed her pelisse and handed it to him without looking at him. She wandered into the drawing room, from which all signs of the altercation with von Hessel had been removed, and took a seat beside the fire.

'Would you like something to drink?' he asked.

'No, thank you.'

They were being assiduously polite, yet distant with one another, like strangers meeting for the first time. An unspecified something hovered in the atmosphere, keeping them apart. Clarence was ill qualified to put a name to its interfering presence.

'I appreciate the snowman, Clarence,' she said at last, 'but it doesn't change anything.'

'I know.'

Finally, she looked up at him, her expression reflecting surprise. 'You know?'

'Certainly. I am not a complete numbskull. My duties at the Foreign Office will prevent me from devoting as much time to you and your interests as you would like. As you deserve to expect.'

Far from seeming relieved, Annalise appeared aggrieved.

'Then we are agreed we would not suit.' She returned her gaze to the flames dancing up the chimney. 'There is no more to be said on the subject.'

Clarence leaned forward, took one of her hands in his, and caressed her palm with the pad of his thumb. 'There is a very great deal to be said. You see, I am no longer in the employ of the Foreign Office.'

'Don't joke about such things,' she replied, snatching her hand from his grasp.

'I am not joking.'

Her head shot up again. 'You're not?'

'I had too many responsibilities before I

contemplated matrimony. I am now determined to make you my wife, and so something must go.'

'But you like what you do, and are very good at it.' She blinked, her eyes suspiciously moist. 'You would give it up for my sake?'

'Absolutely. I have grown tired of it all anyway.'

'But what would you do instead?'

'I have an estate I have neglected for too long. Your brother and I have plans afoot to recruit constables to keep law and order in the stretch of Hampshire between Southampton and Winchester.' His lips twitched. 'I will also have a wife who will lead me a merry dance.'

She shook her head. 'I don't know what to say.'

Clarence considered that unusual enough not to make a joke of it. 'As for you, Romsey House requires a complete overhaul. It has been shamelessly neglected also. And, of course, you will have duties as my wife to undertake.'

'I understand all of that.' She shot him an apologetic glance. 'You must excuse me. I am in shock. Never, not for one moment, did I expect you to resign your position. I would never have asked it of you.'

'You are not asking. It is already done. I

shall have to be on hand to see the von Hessel business through, but after that, I shall have nothing more to do with diplomacy. Now that I think about it, it was never my chosen career. My father chose it for me, and it never occurred to me to mind. I had just always assumed it was what I would do, I suppose.'

'Your father sounds like a tyrant.'

Clarence flashed a mirthless smile. 'A very apt description.' He shook off the melancholy, the feelings of inadequacy that always gripped him when his father's name was mentioned and sent her another, more genuine, smile. 'But I have not yet told you the best part of my plans for us.'

She widened her remarkable eyes. 'There is more?'

He stood up, took her hand, and pulled her to her feet. 'Come and look at this.' He led her to his desk where plans for a building had been laid out for her inspection. 'This is to be the Lady Annalise Romsey Academy for Orphans.'

'The what?'

'You said you wanted to help the disadvantaged.'

'And so I do, but I did not imagine anything on this scale.'

'The house is a derelict one on the edge of the Romsey estate. I plan to extend and renovate it. Then we, or rather you, will set up a school for the most deserving orphans from Southampton and Winchester. But not just that.' Clarence felt himself growing more enthusiastic by the moment as a kaleidoscope of other emotions filtered across her lovely face. 'We will apprentice them to appropriate trades, find positions for them, and . . . oh, so much more.'

'Clarence, this will cost a fortune.'

'I am not paying for it.' He grinned at her. 'You are.'

'Me?' She shook her head. 'You are not making any sense.'

'Your dowry, my sweet. I have no need of it, but I can hardly give it back, so we might as well put it to good use. Now, what do you say?'

*   *   *

What indeed? Anna was momentarily too stunned to speak. His generosity, the sacrifices he was prepared to make for her sake said so much more about him than he probably realised.

'I am overwhelmed,' she said simply, opting for the truth.

'But you approve of my ideas?'

He looked so anxious, so keen for her approbation, she burst out laughing and threw herself into his arms.

'How could I not? You are so thoughtful. I don't deserve you.'

His arms closed around her waist, and he held her in a tight embrace. 'It is I who is the fortunate one. But, in all fairness, I should warn you the idea of matrimony petrifies me. What if I turn out to be like my father? What if, when we have children, I am as strict with them as he was with me?' He shook his head, looking so lost, so unsure of himself that Anna's tender heart melted. 'I could not bear it. That is why I vowed never to marry, until I met you and you turned my well-organised life on its head.'

'Shush, that will not happen.' She stroked his hair, treating him as though he was one of the children he anticipated siring. 'You are nothing like your father, and if you showed the slightest tendency to be so, I would have something to say on the subject.'

'Good.' He kissed the end of her nose, almost chastely, but the expression in his eyes as he looked down at her was anything but innocent.

'For my part, I ought to warn you, I shall not be an easy wife.'

Clarence rolled his eyes. 'There, at least, we are in agreement.'

'I am so very opinionated, you see, and I

never would have made a good diplomat's wife. That was what concerned me.'

'I adore your forthright nature.'

'I hope you still feel that way after we are married,' Anna replied, unable to stop smiling.

'Then there is nothing left to be said or done. I should like to arrange for the wedding to take place sooner rather than later.'

'There is one thing left to do,' she said, biting her lower lip to prevent a devilish grin from giving her away.

'What, my love? What have I overlooked?'

She dragged him by the hand, back into the hallway and picked up her pelisse.

'We need to be outside.'

'We do? Why? It's freezing out there.'

'Precisely! We need to be out there for no other reason than the joy of being alive.'

'Then what are we waiting for?'

A short time later, they were back in the garden, hurling snowballs at one another. Anna rejoiced at the sound of Clarence's uninhibited laughter, a rare and precious sound she had never heard before. She managed a brief wave for the astonished porter whom she noticed watching them from a window, probably thinking the world had run completely mad. Clarence sneaked up on her from behind and circled an arm around her waist. She screamed with laughter as they tumbled to the snowy ground together. Then he was kissing her with enough heat and passion to ward off the cold.

Clarence had not actually admitted to loving her. It was obvious he did not know how to say the words, but he had shown her in so many different ways through his actions that it hardly seemed to matter anymore. Besides, Anna had a lifetime ahead of her in which to teach him how to express his feelings.

We do hope that you have enjoyed reading this large print book.

Did you know that all of our titles are available for purchase?

We publish a wide range of high quality large print books including:
Romances, Mysteries, Classics
General Fiction
Non Fiction and Westerns

Special interest titles available in large print are:
The Little Oxford Dictionary
Music Book
Song Book
Hymn Book
Service Book

Also available from us courtesy of Oxford University Press:
Young Readers' Dictionary
(large print edition)
Young Readers' Thesaurus
(large print edition)

For further information or a free brochure, please contact us at:
Ulverscroft Large Print Books Ltd.,
The Green, Bradgate Road, Anstey,
Leicester, LE7 7FU, England.
Tel: (00 44) 0116 236 4325
Fax: (00 44) 0116 234 0205

AT THE DUKE'S DISCRETION

Wendy Soliman

When Cristobel Brooke's father, jeweller to the rich and famous, is brutally murdered, Crista flees to her uncle's small village close to Winchester. But the criminals pursue her, forcing her to fall in with their plans. Lord Amos Sheridan, brother to the Duke of Winchester, is intrigued by Crista. Astounded when she becomes implicated in treasonous acts, Amos is determined to vindicate her. With the duke's backing, Amos and Crista launch a daring scheme to expose the villains. Meanwhile, Crista finds herself falling slowly in love with Amos. But he is a duke's heir, and she a nobody with a criminal past . . .

MISS DARCY'S PASSION

Wendy Soliman

When Dominic Sanford's parents die in a carriage accident, he is packed off to Scotland to be brought up in his uncle's household. Years later, he returns to his dilapidated estate that borders Pemberley. His father's journals have recently come into his possession, raising questions about his parents' deaths . . . Upon seeing Dominic for the first time at Colonel Fitzwilliam's wedding, Georgiana Darcy feels an immediate attraction. As she assists him in delving deeper into his family's history, they uncover a fiendish web of organised criminality. But Georgiana unwittingly plays a major role in the miscreants' plans — by involving her, Dominic has placed her directly in danger's path . . .

COLONEL FITZWILLIAM'S DILEMMA

Wendy Soliman

Lady Catherine de Bourgh has invited herself to Pemberley, intent upon bringing about an engagement between her daughter Anne and Colonel Fitzwilliam. But her ladyship has failed to take into account the remarkable improvement in her daughter's health and spirits since the arrival of her new tutor, the charismatic Mr. Asquith. Meanwhile, enchanted by the widowed Celia Sheffield, Colonel Fitzwilliam is perturbed to learn that her fortune is being contested by an individual in Jamaica — from whence Mr. Asquith also hails. And when the obsequious Mr. Collins shares grave rumours concerning the tutor's character, further suspicions are raised . . .